# THE
# THIN WALL

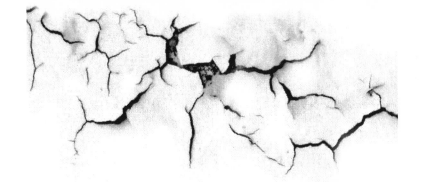

# E.M. PARKER

SECOND
SIGHT
PUBLISHING

ISBN-13: 978-0692875889
ISBN-10: 0692875883

This is a work of fiction. All of the organizations, characters, and events portrayed in this novel are either products of the author's imagination or are used fictitiously.

For more, visit www.authoremparker.com

*For Jackie*

"With what price we pay for the glory of motherhood."
~*ISADORA DUNCAN*

## Chapter One

Despite the highly embellished *Denver Post* review that called it the *"crown jewel of downtown urban living,"* the only thing that Fiona Graves found even remotely appealing about the Corona Heights apartment complex was the price. The fact that the one-hundred-unit high-rise had more than twenty available rentals didn't hurt either, though if she'd had the luxury of considering other options, this may have raised enough of a red flag to keep her looking.

As it stood, Fiona was the building's newest resident as of yesterday afternoon, a mere seventy-two hours after a spontaneous drive due east brought her thirteen hundred long, lonely miles from the rim of the Pacific Northwest to the base of the Rocky Mountains.

The irresistible combination of cheap rent and a building manager desperate for tenants likely contributed to the quick turnaround. But Fiona also believed that something else was at work, feverishly aligning the stars to ensure that her long voyage into the turbulent unknown began in the smoothest waters possible.

She didn't quite know what to call this something. She stopped short of calling it a guardian angel (if such a being existed, why had it been so conspicuously absent for such a large chunk of her life?). But she did consider it to be an intelligence capable of reconciling the desire to right the wrongs of her life with the disease that up until now had prevented her from doing so.

The apartment itself was a five-hundred square foot one-bedroom, complete with outdated appliances, dingy carpets, a bedroom window that didn't quite close all the way, and walls that were about as insulated as wet toilet paper.

With a monthly rent obligation of less than a thousand dollars, a paltry savings, terrible credit score, and no job prospects on the immediate horizon, Fiona didn't have any room to complain. She was lucky to be here, and she knew it.

But that didn't mean the torrent of loud music coming from the apartment next door would be tolerated for much longer than the five hours she had already endured it.

It began late last night, just as Fiona had begun unpacking the last of six boxes that contained the entirety of her life.

She couldn't pinpoint the genre of music other than to call it a soulless mishmash of techno synthesizers, computer-generated vocals, and a thick, distorted bass line that rattled the pictures she had hung on the wall.

She'd considered calling the manager—a man who less than twenty-four hours earlier had assured her that the building was as solidly constructed as a World War II bunker—but decided to let it go. It was Saturday night after all, and she couldn't begrudge anyone's need to blow off a little weekend steam.

*Let the youngsters have their fun,* Fiona thought with a smile, as if her impending thirty-fourth birthday had somehow relegated her to a life of smooth jazz records on the phonograph and *Golden Girls* reruns on television.

Exhaustion from the move brought on a deep sleep that night, so if the party had continued beyond her eleven p.m. bedtime, she was oblivious to it.

Unfortunately, she was fully aware of the noise that woke her early this morning and kept intruding on her as the day wore on.

The music was back, same electro-fusion garbage as before. But this time, something else accompanied it. What began as a persistently heated conversation between a man and a woman quickly escalated into an all-out screaming match.

Fiona couldn't make out what was being said over the din of music. She only knew that neither participant was very happy. And as she heard the first door being slammed shut, then the second, followed by the explosion of shattered glass, she feared that someone was going to get hurt.

Fiona knew from personal experience that it was all too easy to get hurt in such a circumstance.

But she also had no desire to involve herself in someone else's domestic drama. The situation playing out behind those paper-thin walls was ultimately none of her business. Besides, she didn't know anyone here, and no one knew her.

*"Hi there. My name is Fiona Graves, and I just moved in next door. Pleasure to meet you. Now would you please be so kind as to shut the fuck up?"*

For as badly as she wanted to have that conversation,

Fiona conceded that it probably wouldn't make the best first impression, even as it had become clear that her neighbors weren't at all concerned with the impression they were making.

The vortex of sound was increasing, now becoming a thunderous blend of screeching guitar riffs, angry demands, and pounding on the walls.

Since the offending noise was coming from behind her bedroom wall, Fiona had hoped that closing the door would be enough to stem the tide.

Those hopes were quickly dashed. The doors around here were, unfortunately, just as well-built as the walls.

She had thought that another neighbor, or even the building's manager, would have intervened by now. But as the fifth hour rolled into the sixth, and it had become apparent that no other intervention was coming, Fiona decided that she needed to do something.

By the time she walked into her bedroom, her hand was already balled up in a tight fist. She knew she would have to pound like crazy to be heard and had the handle end of her hammer at the ready just in case her hand wasn't enough.

After summoning as much strength as she could, Fiona picked her spot on the wall, raised her fist, and brought her arm back as if she were winding up for a pitch.

She was inches away from impact when something stopped her cold: a sound that rendered the music, the yelling, and the pounding nearly inaudible.

*Someone is crying.*

If Fiona hadn't still heard the woman's frenzied voice, she would have assumed that her prediction about someone getting hurt had come true.

But this wasn't the tearful aftermath of an argument gone too far.

Fiona put her ear to the wall and listened.

*A little girl.*

Based on what she heard, she imagined the child curled up against the wall, her hand covering her mouth to stifle the sound of her sadness.

Fiona knelt to the floor where she could hear the girl more clearly.

After a few moments, the quiet sobbing subsided, replaced with sniffles and deep breaths. The girl was trying to compose herself, even as the chaos around her persisted.

There was a light thump followed by a long sliding sound. The girl was apparently now standing up, keeping her back pressed against the wall as she did.

Trapped. Afraid of being heard.

Fiona rose with her, keeping an ear tuned to the rhythm of the girl's heavy breathing.

"Hello?" The word came out before she had the chance to consider it. "Are you okay over there?"

The pace of the girl's breath quickened, but she was otherwise silent.

"I understand if you're afraid to talk," Fiona continued, speaking as softly as she could. "How about you let me know with a quick knock. Once if you're okay, twice if you're not."

*And if she does knock twice? What then?*

Before Fiona could contemplate an answer, she was rocked by a single rap against the wall, so intense it shook the hanging pictures beside her. She clutched her pounding chest in anticipation of a second knock, but it didn't come.

Just then, the music stopped. So did the arguing. The only noise that Fiona could hear now was the rapid drumming of her own pulse.

Her ear perked at the sound of a door opening. Floor-boards buckled under the weight of heavy footfalls.

Fiona heard labored breathing again but couldn't tell if it was the girl's or her own.

The footsteps drew closer. They were slow and deliberate.

"Get out of there, Noah! We're not finished yet!"

The woman's voice tore through the air like a sonic boom, forcing Fiona to pull her ear away from the wall. By the time she put it back, the footsteps had stopped.

"Noah, get back in here!"

"Shut up," the man replied in a voice that was only slightly above a whisper. "I heard something."

"You've got no business in there." The woman wasn't screaming anymore, but her tone was no less cutting.

"In case you forgot, *I* pay the rent here, so everything is my business."

The man's voice was close, like he'd been standing in the exact spot where Fiona had heard the girl.

"I said, get out!"

The woman was now in the room too. A quick scuffle ensued as the man uttered something that sounded like "*bitch.*" Fading footsteps then led to the sound of a door being slammed shut.

Fiona kept her breath in her chest and her ear against the wall, searching for some hint of the young girl's pres-ence. But she heard nothing.

Perplexed, Fiona knelt to the spot where she had first heard her.

"Hey," she whispered. "Are you still there?"

The only sound she heard was her own voice bouncing off the wall and back into her ear.

Just as she had prepared to call out again, the music returned, this time louder than before.

Fiona slapped the wall with an open hand, but it registered as little more than a tap against the chaotic symphony of noise.

She turned away from the wall and out of the bedroom, her anger mounting with each brisk step.

To hell with first impressions. These idiots were going to feel every ounce of a wrath that had been brewing for the last six hours—a wrath that had indeed been brewing for the previous six months, long before she had ever set foot in Corona Heights or been subjected to the hellions who would become her next-door neighbors.

Fiona opened the front door and had taken her first step into the hallway when she realized that her cell phone was ringing.

If it were any other circumstance at any other time, she would have ignored the call and continued out the door. But her current circumstances dictated that she answer that phone, no matter where she was, no matter what she was doing.

She made it to the kitchen counter an instant before the fifth ring that would have sent the call to voicemail.

"This is Fiona," she answered, feigning composure as best she could.

"Good afternoon, Fiona. This is Paul Riley."

Fiona knew exactly who it was, but she still couldn't prevent the exhale of relief that came with the sound of his voice. "Mr. Riley. How are you?"

"What did I tell you about that Mr. Riley business? I work for you, remember? Paul will suffice."

Fiona could sense his smile over the phone.

"Right. I'll try to remember that."

"I appreciate it. So how are things? Have you settled into the new digs yet?"

"Settled isn't the word I would use."

"What do you mean?"

Fiona held the phone in the air. After a few seconds, she spoke again. "That's what I mean."

"Sounds like you've got one heck of a housewarming going on over there. Better be careful the neighbors don't complain."

"Not funny."

Paul snickered. "Sorry. I've been told my humor is an acquired taste, and considering we've only just met, it's probably best if I save myself the embarrassment, for now at least."

Even though Fiona couldn't remember the last time she found the humor in anything, she appreciated the gesture. "It's okay."

"I feel bad that you've gotten off to a shaky start there. Hopefully, the situation takes care of itself. In the meantime, I have some news."

"I'm listening."

"I spoke with Kirk's lawyer this morning, and they've agreed to a meeting."

Fiona gripped her chest to stall the emotion that was threatening to overwhelm her. "Wow. That's great."

"I realize it's Sunday, but I'd like to devise a game plan. Do you think we could meet at my office sometime this—"

Fiona cut him off. "Name the time, and I'll be there."

"I'm here now, so why don't you stop by as soon as you can."

"Twenty minutes."

Fiona already had on her shoes and coat, gathered her

purse, and made her way out the door by the time the call was finished.

It wasn't until she was in the hallway that she realized the music was still playing.

It was twice as loud out here, and she was stunned that no one else had put a stop to it.

She hadn't seen any of the other tenants milling about during her move-in—no one curiously peeking out of their doors to check out the new neighbor, no one offering to help.

Come to think of it, she hadn't noticed anyone else in the building at all. Not that she was paying attention.

She had more important things on her mind then, as she did now. She could investigate the building's occupancy rate later.

Right now, she had a meeting with a lawyer that held the promise of changing her entire life, a meeting that could help her finally right all of those wrongs.

Still, she struggled against the temptation to pound on the door.

In the ideal scenario, she would march inside—forgoing pleasantries and formal introductions—find something very heavy, and smash that stereo into microscopic pieces.

It was this image that caused her to linger in front of the apartment much longer than she had intended to.

"Let it go," she said aloud, even though she had trouble hearing the words. "Bigger fish to fry."

With that, she allowed herself to move down the hallway and into the waiting elevator.

Before she could press the first floor button, she heard a door opening.

Her new vantage point didn't allow for a view of the

apartment, but based on the loud music now filling the elevator's cabin, she knew exactly which apartment it was.

Fiona tensed. Despite the vigilante story line that played out in her mind, the thought of coming face to face with whoever was in there made her nervous.

What if they saw her standing in front of their door?

What if they came out to confront her?

In her mind, she'd done nothing wrong. If anything, she was the victim here. And if a confrontation were in the cards, she wouldn't hesitate to let them know that.

Fiona held the elevator door open, anxiously waiting. What she heard next caused her blood to run cold and made her wish that she'd closed the doors the moment she got in.

"You can't do anything now, Natalie. She's gone. Close the door."

It was the same angry male voice she'd heard on the other side of her bedroom wall.

Fiona immediately pushed the button and watched the elevator doors slowly close. But before they could close all the way, the apartment door slammed shut, dampening the music, along with her vigilante spirit.

And suddenly, Corona Heights' dirt-cheap rent wasn't all that appealing anymore.

## Chapter Two

"How do you know they were talking about you, Fiona?"

Dressed in a warm-up fleece and faded blue jeans, Paul Riley looked out of place in the high back leather chair behind his mahogany executive desk. The only hints of warmth in his minimalist office space were the pictures on the wall behind him of his wife and three adolescent sons.

The placement was odd, and Fiona couldn't escape the feeling that it was strategic. His family was beautiful—the perfect depiction of love and stability—and it was all she could do not to stare at them as Paul spoke.

Perhaps that was the strategy.

"If they knew you were standing outside their door, wouldn't they have come out when they first saw you?"

"I don't know what they were thinking. But I do know they were talking about me. I was the only one in the hallway."

"It could've been something else entirely. From the

sound of it, they were probably on a bender, taking God knows what, and they were completely paranoid. For all they know, you could've been the Blessed Virgin Mary herself."

His broad smile revealed a set of the whitest, straightest teeth Fiona had ever seen. But his sharp good looks did little to quell her irritation at his second failed attempt at humor.

Paul, to his credit, picked up on the cue immediately. "Looks like I'm 0 for 2 on the jokes."

Fiona nodded, hopeful that he would spare himself the indignity of a third awkward exchange.

"The remainder of this meeting will be joyless and humor free," he mused. "Scout's honor."

The irony of that statement bringing a smile to Fiona's face wasn't lost on her.

"And what was it you were saying about the little girl?" he continued.

"It sounded like she was crying."

"Did she say anything when the parents came into her room?"

"No."

"Did they say anything to her?"

"No."

"That's odd."

*Odd* was a major understatement. "Honestly, I'm just glad it's over."

"I hear you. Let's hope they got it out of their system."

Fiona found herself staring at Paul's perfect family again. "Let's hope so."

After a long silence, Paul reached into his desk drawer and pulled out a thin manila envelope. "I suppose we should get down to business."

Fiona straightened up in her chair.

"First off, I want to thank you for coming in on such short notice," he continued. "I realize it's a bit unusual meeting like this, especially on a Sunday, but we have to be as prepared as possible for what's coming."

"I understand."

"And part of that preparedness is letting you know just how difficult this fight is going to be. If I'm being honest, difficult may not be a strong enough word to describe what we're actually up against."

Fiona had trouble swallowing the large knot that suddenly formed in her throat. "Fortunately, I've never been under the illusion that it was going to be easy."

"Good. As I mentioned during our initial consultation, my job is to represent your interests to the best of my ability, and I plan to do just that. But I'm not here to sugarcoat the situation in any way. The fact of the matter is that you're one of the handful of female clients I've ever represented who were on the wrong end of a child custody decision."

Fiona shifted uncomfortably in her chair.

"It's quite rare in divorce proceedings that mothers end up losing parental rights to the extent that you have," Paul continued. "The Washington state courts were firm in their ruling, and the stipulations for amending that ruling were explicit. The burden of proof to show that those stipulations have been met is squarely on you, and regardless of the outcome of this meeting with your ex, the court's decision is binding. I just don't want you going into this with any false hopes."

"I'm aware of that. And I've done everything they've asked to prove that I'm a fit mother. I've completed treatment, stayed active in a program, took all their classes and weekly UAs. I've been a walking public service announcement for what *not* to do if you ever have designs on being a good parent. I've met their stipulations and then some, so I don't think I'm coming into this with any false hopes. I'm coming here knowing that I'm finally ready to be a full-time presence in my son's life again."

It was a speech that Fiona had been prepared to give ever since she made the decision to pack up what remained of her existence and follow her ex-husband, Kirk, and eight-year-old son, Jacob, to a new state, and what Kirk had undoubtedly hoped would be a new life.

Being the primary guardian, he was fully within his rights to move Jacob wherever he wanted, without so much as a whisper to Fiona of his intentions.

As it turned out, Kirk did inform her of his intentions—through a letter sent to the facility where she was carrying out her second stint of court-ordered alcohol rehabilitation. By the time she completed the sixty days, Jacob and Kirk were gone.

This meeting would mark the first time that she'd seen her ex-husband in over ten months. Nothing in their recent history suggested that Fiona should feel optimistic about the outcome, but optimism was the only thing she had to hold on to. Paul had referred to it as false hope.

"May I play devil's advocate for a moment?" he asked in a somber voice

Fiona didn't like the sound of that. "I suppose."

"What if I told you that this may not be the best course of action right now?"

Her eyes grew wide with surprise. "What do you mean?"

"I'm sure you probably heard the same thing from your lawyer in Seattle."

The knot in her throat expanded. "She said I shouldn't come here yet."

"Did you at least consider taking her advice?"

"Not even for a second."

"Okay. But try to understand this from the court's perspective. It's been nearly eleven months since Kirk was awarded custody. Before that, the two of you were tied up in divorce proceedings for the better part of a year. The mandate was clear-cut about visitation and the level of contact you were to have with your son."

Paul glanced at the summary judgment he'd pulled from the manila envelope. "You are to have no unsupervised contact with Jacob unless and until you receive written approval and have shown sufficient progress in your sobriety. Not contacting the court at any point prior to your arrival here could be seen as circumventing their order. You took a major risk."

Fiona didn't need a mirror to know that her cheeks were turning bright red. It happened every time she got angry or embarrassed. Right now, she was both.

"Why not initiate proceedings from Seattle?" Paul continued. "Why come here? Your son has only been in Denver for a short time, and he's most likely still adjusting. Granted, I don't know the entire situation, but I can imagine that the move was difficult for him. Regardless, he's finally adapting to his new normal, and your sudden appearance could bring the unintended consequence of thrusting him back into another battle between you and your ex-husband. I'm assuming you didn't inform Kirk before you decided to come."

"That's right."

"I'm sure he wasn't happy about that."

"Who cares if he's happy?" Fiona snapped in an involuntary outburst that surprised her.

A long silence.

"I'm sorry. I didn't mean that."

"It's all right," Paul offered with a thin smile.

"I'm just frustrated. Everything has been about him. He's *the* Fit Parent. *I'm the* Alcoholic Degenerate. *How wonderful it is that* he's *willing to step up*. I screwed up in the past. I get that. But I'm still Jacob's mother. He needs me just as much as he needs Kirk." Fiona reached for the box of tissue on Paul's desk. "I've thought about this for a long time, and I wouldn't be pursuing it if I weren't 100 percent committed. I am 100 percent committed."

"I know that, Fiona. And trust me when I say that I'm on your side. I had to ask those questions because they are the same ones that Kirk and his lawyer are likely to ask. The meeting will be informal. It's not a deposition, so you won't be cross-examined, but in some ways, it may feel like it. I wanted to see how you would hold up under that kind of pressure."

Fiona's nerves began to settle, and the burning in her cheeks subsided. "So, did I pass?"

"We still need to smooth out the edges a bit, but it's a good start. I appreciate your passion, and in the long run, it will serve you well. But the name of the game here is diplomacy. I have no doubt that you and Kirk want the same thing. The question is, how can you both best achieve that goal?"

"We have to work as a team," Fiona declared, not sure if such a thing were even possible.

"Now you're getting it."

"It's a two-way street, though. I can't be the only one willing to play ball."

"Exactly, and we'll work on that. But as I said, my only focus right now is getting you prepared."

Fiona gripped her knees to stop them from shaking. "Okay. Where do we start?"

"Well, you've already gotten things rolling by finding an apartment. I'm still not sure how you scored such a great deal in this crazy rental market, but hats off."

Based on what she'd experienced in her first few hours there, Fiona would be hard-pressed to call Corona Heights a great deal. "Sure beats sleeping in my car."

"Indeed. Any movement on the job front?"

"No. I'd hoped to get something in place before I moved out here, but so far, the pickings have been pretty slim."

"What are you doing for money?"

"The trust from my mother is providing enough of a cushion for six months' rent and your fee. I've got a little savings beyond that, but nothing that will sustain me long-term."

"Even more reason to get moving on that job search. Six months will go by much faster than you realize."

"I know," Fiona answered, bracing for the inevitable lecture that was to follow.

"And what about a program?"

"I haven't found one yet."

"That should be your top priority. Your ability to commit to a twelve-step support group, especially when you do so under your own initiative, will speak volumes to the court and your ex-husband."

"I'll work on it."

"Let's try and get something lined up before we meet with him. Will that be possible?"

The burning in Fiona's cheeks returned. This time it

was fueled more by embarrassment than anger. "I'll do my best."

"Good. And one more thing."

"What?"

"No contact with Kirk or Jacob before the meeting."

Fiona feigned outrage at the suggestion. "I'm not that stupid."

"It's not about being stupid. It's about taming an instinct that has fueled your every action for the past year. It's about being patient in a situation where patience seems like the most absurd practice imaginable. It's about not sabotaging your progress by letting guilt cloud your judgment."

"I've engaged in enough self-sabotage to last a lifetime. I'm ready to try a different approach."

"Do you promise? No Kirk and most especially no Jacob?"

Fiona leaned forward in her chair, looking Paul square in his eye. "Scout's honor."

It was the first time in their brief relationship that she had lied to him.

As her eyes refocused on his perfect family, she waited patiently for at least a twinge of guilt to rise in her chest.

It never came.

## Chapter Three

Thanks to some rudimentary online detective work, Fiona had Kirk's address before she ever set foot in Denver. And despite her pledge to Paul, she had the directions to Kirk's house plugged in to her cell phone before she left his office.

Confident that he hadn't yet changed his phone number (Kirk was a creature of habit much like she was), Fiona had considered calling him ahead of her visit, a whimsical notion that she thought better of almost immediately.

She then considered the more direct approach of ringing his doorbell and hoping for the best. She dismissed that idea even faster than the phone call.

That left her with only one viable option: good, old-fashioned stalking.

For the duration of her thirty-minute drive from Paul Riley's downtown office to Kirk's Northeast Denver address, Fiona had considered the range of scenarios that she could encounter and the outcomes inherent in each.

Aside from the heartfelt, tear-filled reunion that was the stuff of her fantasies, not one of those outcomes was good.

Yet she made the drive anyway, increasingly aware that a reunion with Jacob wasn't the only thing she yearned for.

Despite everything that happened, she still loved Kirk.

She loved him for the man she met twelve years ago when she was a happy, idealistic journalism school graduate in awe of his prodigious success as a Seattle Seahawks beat reporter.

She loved him for being the man who stuck by her through those early years when denial of her drinking problem gave way to eventual acceptance and naïve confidence that she would beat it.

She loved him for being the man who stepped up as the singular pillar of stability in Jacob's life when she could no longer do her part.

The ticket on their marriage had been stamped long ago, but some small part of her was still hopeful enough to believe that civility could exist between them.

However, showing up on his doorstep out of the blue was not going to aid in that cause.

*I'm smart enough to know that. So why in the hell am I still here?*

Fearful that her old self-destructive tendencies were beginning to take hold, Fiona parked at what she considered to be a safe distance from his house and waited. For what, she wasn't sure.

Perhaps it was for a glimpse of what their new life looked like or a sign that Jacob wasn't happy with that new life, or confirmation that her coming here was the absolute right thing to do, despite everyone else's opinion to the contrary. Perhaps it was a combination of everything.

What she wanted most was to see her son.

Most of the scenarios that Fiona imagined during the drive here involved him.

What would the first words spoken between them sound like? Would Jacob even recognize her? Things change so quickly in a child's life. He could have already adjusted to an existence without a mother, his mind able—out of will or necessity—to push away all memories of the previous eight years.

Fiona couldn't blame him for that. The graveyard of her subconscious was littered with those memories, their decayed remains buried deep enough to be absorbed by the brittle, uncultivated soil.

But the thought of her own son not remembering her was a wretched one, sending shockwaves of pain and nausea throughout her body.

*Stop being ridiculous, Fiona. You're his mother. You gave birth to him. Of course, he remembers you.*

She kept her eye trained on the front door for more than an hour before resigning herself to the fact that the glimpse she was hoping for wasn't in the cards.

With her emotions teetering between disappointment and shame, Fiona started her car and pulled away from the curb, frustrated more in herself than the result of the trip. She drove slowly as she passed Kirk's townhouse, looking for any signs of activity. There were none.

She let out a deep sigh of relief that no one was there to see her making such a desperate fool of herself.

*Dodged your first bullet, Fiona. Now go home, get your mind right, and do this thing the right way.*

She was prepared to do just that when something in the rearview mirror caught her attention.

Though it was still some distance away, Fiona recognized Kirk's candy-apple-red Jeep Cherokee the instant she saw it. A glance at the front Washington State license plate confirmed it.

*Shit.*

Resisting the urge to speed away, Fiona idled at the end of the block, watching through the rearview mirror as Kirk pulled into a spot in front of his house.

He emerged from the driver's side and walked around to retrieve something out of the back.

Her vision momentarily obscured, Fiona reversed her car a few feet. She ran the genuine risk of being spotted, but she didn't care.

From her new vantage point, she could see Kirk picking up bags of groceries, a deep smile on his face. He was engaged in an animated conversation with someone. Fiona assumed it was Jacob, and she held her breath as she waited for him to appear.

She let out an audible gasp when he emerged from the passenger's-side door, a smile equal in depth to his father's on his bright, handsome face.

He'd grown an inch or two in the time since Fiona had last seen him, tall for his age, much as she imagined Kirk had been.

His sandy-brown hair was longer than she remembered. It framed a thin, freckled face and deep, cavernous dimples— the same dimples that had made her fall in love with Kirk. His frame was sturdy. Had he put on weight? It was perfectly normal at his age, but she noticed it, nonetheless.

Fiona noticed everything about him, most notably how happy he looked.

The thought stirred something unexpected in her. For the first time, she wondered if she were truly doing the right thing by coming here.

Despite her self-reassurance, maybe Jacob had moved on and forgotten her completely. Children could be incredibly resilient, their defense mechanisms much more powerful than those of adults.

Maybe Jacob had grown to accept that his mother was a worthless drunk, incapable of taking care of herself, much less him, and he had made peace with that.

Then Fiona reminded herself that he was only eight, and most likely incapable of drawing such nihilistic conclusions about his world or anyone in it. Time was still on her side.

But she was positive that Jacob had asked difficult questions, and she was equally positive that Kirk had few satisfactory answers. Coming back now, as Paul had warned, might only upset the balance in Jacob's life that had presumably been restored.

Fiona felt no hesitation as she packed away her life in Washington to make the two-day drive here, bringing nothing with her except pictures of Jacob, a few pieces of furniture, a ten-day wardrobe, and a ton of hope. But now, her doubts were bubbling to the surface.

*There's no room for second-guessing, Fiona. Remember the promise you made to yourself. It's all about him, despite what some judge, or even his father, says about it. Jacob needs you in his life. And you need him in yours. Desperately.*

As Kirk and Jacob approached the front door, Fiona made a move to get out of her car.

She wanted nothing more than to grab her son, squeeze him, and never let go.

She wanted to imagine the excitement on his face when she told him that instead of going inside to put away groceries with his father, the two of them would spend the day together, drinking hot chocolate and eating sausage-and-mushroom pizza.

He would fill Fiona in on his new school and the scores of friends he had already made; they would talk about soccer or baseball or whatever newfound interest he had picked up, and all would instantly be right in both of their worlds.

Like the last year and a half had never happened.

But Fiona knew that was nothing more than the fantasy plot she'd concocted on the ride over here. The reality, she knew in her heart of hearts, would be much different.

She drew a quick, deep breath, bit her lip to keep from crying, and looked away.

Her attention fell on a group of teenagers crossing the street in front of her. One of them, a long-legged boy with equally long dreadlocks, looked at Fiona with a hint of concern.

Despite her best efforts, she was sobbing uncontrollably.

By the time she'd gathered herself enough to look back in the rearview mirror, Jacob and Kirk were gone.

## Chapter Four

Fiona was met with silence as she exited the elevator and stepped into the sixth-floor hallway that led to her apartment.

Her pace slowed as she approached unit 607, the one next to hers.

She crept past the door on the balls of her feet, not admitting to the fear that her normally heavy gait would be enough to alert the people inside. She opted for the more acceptable reasoning that the light footsteps would allow her to hear any noise that she would need to bring to the manager's attention before she had been lulled into her apartment.

Thankfully, she heard nothing.

*Party's over. Drugs have worn off. Enough offending the world for one day.*

Fiona glanced at her watch. Three twenty-six p.m. She could only pray that the hellions weren't resting up for a fresh round tonight.

The quiet would be necessary if she were going to plot

out a successful course for her continued sobriety, find gainful employment, and acquire the thus-far elusive skill of diplomacy, all in the eighteen hours before her scheduled meeting with Kirk.

If her ill-advised detour to his house were any indication, she would need to address her chronic lack of judgment, as well.

Fiona was under no illusion that this was going to be easy. At least that was her line to Paul Riley. But for the first time, she was beginning to feel the weight of the work that lay ahead.

The road to redemption, she had already come to realize, was full of twists and turns, red lights, potholes, and traffic jams. Now came the truly difficult part. After what felt like millions of miles logged, the destination was finally in sight.

This was the homestretch, the last leg of the race. If she didn't get this part right, all the work done up to now would amount to nothing.

There could be no more impromptu trips to Kirk's house. She had to operate with precision. Cool and calm. Stability personified. Just the way a mother is supposed to be.

With her marching orders in place and her plan thoroughly diagrammed, Fiona felt a surge of adrenaline as she reached for her keys.

Before she could put them in the door, they fell out of her hand and onto the floor, hitting with a clang that reverberated through the tight hallway. Just as she bent over to pick them up, she heard the slow creak of a door opening.

*Obviously, they've been waiting for me.*

Fiona closed her eyes, bracing for the worst.

"Oh, hello there."

Not the voice she was expecting.

"I've been wondering about my new neighbor."

The voice was calm, comforting, motherly.

She opened her eyes and looked up. The woman staring down at her was smiling. Warm. Welcoming.

Fiona hadn't felt genuinely welcomed anywhere in a long time. "Sorry, I'm a bit of a klutz," she said as she stood up. "I hope I didn't startle you."

"Not at all, sweetheart. I suffer from an overactive hearing problem, an unfortunate side effect of being a single old woman in modern America. You have to know what's going on around you at all times. And there's usually a lot going on around here."

Fiona nodded. "It's certainly been active the past few hours."

"Entirely too active if you ask me. That racket last night was getting ridiculous. I was going to have my son march over there to tell them to turn it down. Fortunately, it stopped."

"They must have sensed he was coming."

The woman's gentle smile grew wider. "Perhaps. Anyway, I'm Iris. Iris Matheson." She extended her hand.

"Fiona Graves. Nice to meet you."

"Likewise. You just moved in, right?"

"Yes, a couple of days ago."

"I've been meaning to stop by and officially welcome you. Most people don't have the manners to do that kind of thing anymore."

Fiona looked around the empty hallway in what felt like an empty building. Iris had been the first tenant she'd seen here, let alone met. "I've noticed."

"Don't get me wrong. There are some very nice people here. You just have to strain a bit to find them."

Fiona smiled. Iris seemed nice enough. She was a slightly chubby woman with a round face and long gray hair that she wore in a ponytail. Her ocean-blue eyes were fixed on Fiona as if she were doing her best to get a read.

"Well, speaking of manners, would you like to come in for a cup of coffee? I just brewed a fresh pot."

The offer was tempting, but Fiona had marching orders to carry out. "No, thank you. Another time, though."

"Okay, well, feel free to stop by whenever you'd like. My thirty-seven-year teaching career came to a long-overdue end recently, and I suddenly have lots of time on my hands. The company is always nice. Besides, I have the lowdown on everyone in the building. I'd be more than happy to get you up to speed."

Iris had the twinkle in her eye of someone sitting on juicy gossip that she desperately wanted to dish out, and Fiona couldn't deny that the possibility of learning more about the people here was intriguing.

"I'll most certainly take you up on that."

Iris placed a gentle hand on her shoulder. "Oh, good. Well, I guess I'll get back and straighten up the mess that my wonderful son left behind. He was helping me get rid of some things. Not much, just a small bureau, some old clothes, and a footlocker. But it apparently entitled him to every morsel of food in my refrigerator. All he left for me was a stick of butter and a sink full of dirty dishes. He damn near killed himself trying to drag that footlocker to the elevator, so I guess allowing him to eat me out of house and home was the least I could do."

Iris smiled again, the thought of her son clearly warming her. "Anyhoo, it was certainly nice meeting you, Fiona. Sorry it didn't happen sooner."

"Nice meeting you too, Iris. I look forward to that

coffee."

With one last smile, Iris walked into her apartment and closed the door. Three lock clicks later, she was securely inside, leaving Fiona alone in the hallway.

The sudden quiet was unsettling.

She turned to unlock her door, but as she did, she noticed something on the floor in front of unit 607: two red splotches that clearly stood out against the light gray carpet. She bent down for a closer inspection.

The splotches were dry-soaked into the fiber, but she was almost positive they weren't there before. She immediately looked around for more but couldn't find any.

*That's odd,* Fiona thought. *Why hadn't I noticed that?*

Her mind spit out endless possibilities, none of which she wanted to give voice to.

The longer she looked, the more the dark red stains resembled blood.

*Blood?*

There had to be a reasonable explanation for its existence aside from the one in her mind. Iris's son must have cut his finger carrying that footlocker.

*That's it. Freak accident.*

It felt like a suitable answer. Perfectly logical.

And Fiona desperately wanted to believe it.

---

Her unease intensified as she entered her apartment.

The space suddenly felt foreign, just as it had when she first toured it two days ago.

Her furnishings were sparse—a futon, two nightstands, and a folding card table that doubled as a dinette—but they were hers, and as such, should have provided at least the illusion of familiarity. Instead, she felt like an intruder commandeering a space that didn't belong to her with the misguided notion of claiming it.

She sat her coat and purse on the kitchen counter and made her way to the refrigerator. The water bottle that she had opened the night before was still on the shelf exactly where she'd left it.

"See, Fiona? You do live here."

She opened the bottle and took a drink. The cold soothed her warm throat. A familiar thirst had settled in since she left Kirk's, and it felt good to quench it with something so benign.

It hadn't always been this easy.

After finishing her water, Fiona walked over to the card table—which, in addition to the dinette, had also functioned as her work desk—turned on her laptop, and opened a blank Word document. She titled it *Operation Jacob*.

She would begin by creating a to-do list, which would undoubtedly be extensive, followed by a brainstorming session that would include potential job avenues, twelve-step meeting sites, and a script of what she would say when she first saw Kirk. The script would be especially important. She couldn't afford any spontaneous outbursts.

Before she sat down, she thought it best to change out of her blouse and jeans and into the yoga pants and over-sized T-shirt that she favored on weekends.

Fiona knew something was wrong the instant she walked into her bedroom.

The picture was of Jacob dressed in a Darth Vader costume, holding court during the celebration of his fifth birthday. It was Fiona's favorite, the one she made sure to protect with extra bubble wrap for the move, the very first one she hung on the wall.

Now it was facedown on the floor, next to the nail that she thought she had secured it to. A tiny hole in the wall was the only thing left where the picture had once been.

As Fiona moved closer, she noticed something else: the paint around the nail hole was chipped, as if an adhesive had been carelessly ripped away from the wall.

But there was no adhesive, not that Fiona had seen, anyway. And if she recalled correctly, the paint wasn't chipped when she hung the picture. At least, she didn't think it was. Prone to a chronic lack of focus on everything unrelated to Jacob, Fiona had stopped trusting her memory long ago.

It stood to reason that the wall blemish could have been there all along. But what about the picture? The two-inch nail she'd hammered into the wall was secure; that much she knew. Whenever she had decided on a new spot to hang a picture that she had previously put up, she needed the hammer to pull the nail out, and on a few occasions, there was some major effort involved in extracting it, so it shouldn't have simply come out on its own.

But apparently, that was exactly what happened.

Fiona's mind suddenly fixated on the condition of the picture.

A close inspection revealed no damage. Jacob had handpicked the black wood frame, the words *Best Mom Ever* inscribed on the front. Much like the photo, it held extraordinary sentimental value, and she was relieved that it was still intact.

*Who's to say that the laws of physics can't be broken from time to time*, she thought as she put the picture on the end table next to her bed. *Accidents happen.*

If it were merely an accident, why did she feel so nervous?

The question would haunt her for the rest of the day and into the night.

There would be no work on *Operation Jacob*, no marching orders carried out. There were only thoughts of the falling picture and the bloodstains and the apartment that suddenly felt less hospitable than the jail cell that had once been home for the longest night of her life.

After a light dinner and a couple of fruitless hours staring at her computer, she re-hung the picture (making sure it was extra secure this time), settled onto the uncomfortable air mattress that she hoped would be temporary, and fell into a restless, agitated sleep.

Her dreams were scattered, dark. A car accident. Jacob in the back with no seatbelt. No survivors. Iris Matheson in a hospital gown serving her coffee. Kirk in the shower with a woman she didn't recognize.

Mostly, there was crying. Distant, pleading crying. Jacob in pain. Upon seeing him, Fiona reached out, hugged him, and the pain on his face went away, replaced with that patented dimple-filled smile.

But the crying persisted, so close now that Fiona could feel it.

She woke up with a start, clutching her chest, realizing that the emotion had been hers. Tears clouded her vision as she sat up.

After allowing her eyes to adjust to the darkness of her bedroom, she made her way off the air mattress and into the bathroom, where she splashed cold water on her face.

The dark circles that she took great care to conceal during the day were on full display, the result of a year's worth of stress and worry and lack of sleep. A tousled mess of dark brown hair fell over a pair of even darker brown eyes that were stained red with the lingering emotion of her dream. She tugged at her cheeks, stretching the taut skin as far as it would go. It snapped back into place with barely a thought. "No wrinkles at least," she said aloud, though that fact offered little solace.

Having seen enough of her two a.m. self, Fiona turned off the bathroom light and made her way back into the bedroom. The air mattress was just as uncomfortable as when she left it, but her eyes were heavy, and she felt sleep coming on quickly.

The first thud of something hitting the floor caused her eyes to snap open.

The second caused her to sit up.

The third caused her to leap out of bed.

Through the dim filter of moonlight from her bedroom window, Fiona could clearly see the objects on the floor, but she still hoped that the late hour was somehow playing tricks on her mind.

When she turned on the lamp beside her bed, she realized that what she was seeing was no trick.

Jacob's birthday picture had fallen to the floor again, in nearly the same spot as it had before. The two pictures hanging on either side of it had also fallen. Just like before, the nails used to hang them had come out of the wall and were resting next to the frames.

As Fiona inched toward the wall, she saw another familiar sight: chipped paint where the other two pictures had been.

Unconcerned with the laws of physics or logical explanations or the condition of the pictures, Fiona scurried out of the bedroom, slammed the door behind her, and spent the rest of that endlessly long night on the futon.

She didn't sleep a wink.

## Chapter Five

The next morning, Fiona showered, got dressed, left her apartment, and drove to her lawyer's office without giving a single thought to the previous night's events. She ignored the fallen pictures on her bedroom floor, the blemishes on the wall, the red stains on the carpet outside of 607, and the complete emotional and physical exhaustion that now permeated every cell in her body.

Denial was the most potent defense mechanism in Fiona's arsenal, and more times than not, the most destructive. In this case, she didn't have a choice but to employ it.

She had to be 100 percent present for her meeting with Kirk. Anything short of that could have end-of-the-world consequences.

Despite her better judgment, Fiona had extremely high hopes for this meeting. She had spent hours in front of the mirror, testing different hairstyles, applying, and reapplying makeup, all with the purpose of presenting the best version of herself possible.

Without much of a wardrobe to choose from, or time to buy anything new, she chose her favorite yellow sundress—the one that clung to her slender body in the perfect way—pairing it with a black cashmere cardigan to cover her shoulders. It was a comfortable look that wasn't too informal. It didn't hurt that the dress had always been Kirk's favorite.

*False hope.* Paul's words of warning echoed in her mind for the entire drive to his office.

Upon arriving, she was met in the parking lot by a young man in an exquisitely tailored pinstriped suit.

"Hi, Ms. Graves. My name is Jason Guzman, Mr. Riley's assistant. Mr. Lawson and his attorney have arrived, and they're waiting for you in the conference room."

From the short tone in Jason's voice, Fiona guessed she was running late. She had been hyperaware of the clock all morning and was sure that she had left herself plenty of time to get here before the 9:30 start time.

Why she hadn't noticed until now that the clock in her car read 9:43 was a question she couldn't answer.

"I'm so sorry," she said, her eyes cast down in embarrassment. If she couldn't look this kid in the eye, how was she going to react to Kirk?

She barely had time to think about it as Jason quickly led her through the spacious office and into the conference room.

The look of exasperation on Paul's face was palpable as he stood to greet her. He attempted to mask it with a forced smile.

"Good morning, Fiona. So glad you made it. We were getting worried."

Based on the looks she received from the other two men in the room, Paul's was the minority opinion.

Kirk and his ridiculously stoic lawyer sat at the conference table. Neither had stood to greet her. Kirk, for his part, hadn't even shifted in his seat, choosing instead to keep his hands tightly folded on the table.

Kirk was barely a year older than Fiona's thirty-three, but as she studied him up close, the signs of aging were apparent. Patches of gray lined the edges of his thinning black hair. Lean and athletic during all the time Fiona knew him, he'd put on weight. Cheeks that were once defined by a chiseled, square jaw now looked puffy.

But what she noticed most were his eyes. They looked tired. Perhaps it was more wariness than exhaustion. Wariness of her presence. She felt an unexpected pang of sympathy for him.

It wouldn't last.

"Hi, Kirk," she said, her voice cracking with nervousness.

"Fiona." His tone was flat.

She took the seat directly across from him. Face to face. As she had feared, she was unable to meet his stare.

"Fiona, this is Michael Stanley," Paul said, motioning to Kirk's lawyer. "And of course, you know the gentleman to his right."

An awkward hush filled the room. After what felt like an hour, Michael spoke.

"I'm sure Paul has already briefed you, Ms. Graves, but just to reiterate, this is an informal meeting. Nothing said here will have an impact on your custody status or the court's ruling. My client was kind enough to take time out of his schedule to accommodate your wishes to meet, but legally, he wasn't obligated to do so."

"We're aware of that," Paul said. "And given the

circumstances and short notice, we appreciate Mr. Lawson's time."

Kirk sat rigidly in his chair. Fiona could feel the weight of his glare.

Michael continued. "We have to admit that your request came as a bit of a surprise."

"That's putting it mildly," Kirk chided.

Still unable to look him in the eye, Fiona focused on Kirk's hands, specifically the left one. Bare. She let out a quiet sigh of relief.

"I get that it was unexpected," Fiona said, finally able to make eye contact. "But I was hoping that by meeting like this, we could—"

"Could what, Fiona?" It was the first time that Kirk's expression revealed any kind of emotion. It wasn't the emotion Fiona was hoping for. "What the hell are you doing here?"

His reaction caught her off guard. She scrambled for a response from the script that she had mentally prepared during the drive here. "I think it's obvious, Kirk."

"Are you really thinking about Jacob? Or are you thinking about yourself? Because if you were truly thinking about him, about his well-being, you wouldn't be here right now."

"I can't believe what you're saying." Fiona's voice was rising and faltering at the same time. "What do you expect me to do? Pretend that he doesn't exist? It's bad enough you move him halfway across the country without—"

"Like I had to get your permission," Kirk interrupted. "I'm sorry, but you lost that right."

"You had to know that I wasn't going to start some new and improved life in Seattle while my son was living a thousand miles away."

"Maybe I should have moved him two thousand miles away."

Kirk's words took the air out of the room. For a moment, the only audible sound was the squeaking of Paul's chair as he shifted uncomfortably in it.

"Why do you hate me so much?"

Kirk's stare was suddenly distant, traces of regret in his downcast eyes. "I don't hate you, Fiona."

"Then why do you say the things you do?" She was determined not to cry, but that determination was wavering with each passing second.

"Because I don't understand what this is."

"This is me trying to see our son, Kirk. *Our* son."

"Ms. Graves," Michael jumped in, "the judge's order was clear."

No matter how many times she heard her maiden name, she still hadn't gotten used to it. "Why does everyone think they have to remind me of what the judge's order was?"

Michael continued as if he hadn't heard her. "If you're interested in visitation, you need to petition the court, demonstrate your sobriety and that you're otherwise not a risk, either to yourself or to Jacob."

"What part of that isn't clear?" Kirk barked.

"I'm better now."

"Until you can prove that, how do you expect me to trust you?"

"You know I would never do anything to intentionally hurt him."

"And you know that I would never allow him to be in a situation where he could be hurt."

"Are you saying I would—"

"It's not about what I'm saying, Fiona. It's about the

fact that you got behind the wheel of a car, totally shit-faced, with our son inside, and proceeded to wrap yourself around a goddamned telephone pole."

"Okay, everyone, let's do our best to remain civil," Paul interjected. "No good can come from this bickering. Not for either of you and certainly not for Jacob."

"It's obvious he doesn't have the first clue about what's good for Jacob!" Fiona finally allowed her simmering anger to boil over. She welcomed the release.

Kirk stood up. "You're right. No good can come from this," he said to Paul. "I was out of my mind to agree to this." He quickly made his way to the door, his lawyer close behind.

"Mr. Lawson, please wait."

Kirk stopped before he left the room, this time turning his attention to Fiona. "I don't know what you hoped to accomplish by coming here, but you aren't doing anyone any good. Not Jacob, not me, not even yourself. His life is just fine, Fiona. He's happy for the first time in a long time. You know how difficult this ordeal was for him. He took it twice as hard as either of us. And just when he's finally come to terms with it, you show up out of the blue. Do you really want to put him through that hurt all over again?"

"Kirk, I don't..." Fiona suddenly couldn't find the words. Nothing in the script had prepared her for this scene.

"Because that's exactly what will happen. And God help me if I don't do everything in my power to prevent it."

Fiona trembled as Kirk walked out of the room.

Michael turned to her before he exited. "I'm sorry you wasted your time coming here, Ms. Graves." One last nail in the coffin. "Goodbye, Paul."

"Michael."

Looking just as shell-shocked as his client, Paul put a hand on Fiona's shoulder. "I'm sorry that didn't go better."

"I thought you were here to defend me," Fiona said bitterly. "Why did you let him talk like that?"

"Unfortunately, he had the right to say whatever he wanted. We weren't in court. I couldn't object."

"He treated me like I was some kind of monster. Like I tried to hurt Jacob. Like I would hurt him now."

"I hate to say this, but I warned you this could happen. Legally, the power rests with him."

"You heard him. He doesn't want me to see my son at all."

"He can't prevent you from seeing Jacob altogether. It's the court's responsibility to ensure that you have proper visitation per what has already been mandated. And they will do that. Trust me. You still have options."

"Options? Even if the court grants me shared custody, by the time Kirk is finished, Jacob will want nothing to do with me. I wouldn't be surprised if he hasn't already turned him against me."

"You don't know that."

Fiona began pacing the room. "Kirk didn't agree to meet because he wanted to see how I was or because he wanted to hear what I had to say. It didn't matter how I looked or what I said. I didn't have a chance. He wanted nothing more than to make me feel like shit. And guess what? He totally succeeded."

Fiona abruptly stopped pacing and sat on the windowsill, her face buried in her hands. "I'm such an idiot for thinking it could be any different."

"Please tell me you're not giving up," Paul said as he sat down beside her. "This is the time to dig your heels in and fight. You've come entirely too far to turn back now. I know how much you want this, how much you've been through to get here. This battle is just beginning, and I absolutely believe it's one we can win. I need you to believe that too."

Fiona wished that she could have summoned a defiant response; some *hell no, I'm not giving up* rah-rah speech, some hint that she still had the strength to persevere.

Instead, she could only walk out the door, all the while dwelling on the warning she had tried so hard to deny.

*False hope.*

## Chapter Six

Not yet familiar enough with the city to have a favorite spot where she could go to clear her head, Fiona retreated to the only place she could. But in the harsh glare of daylight, her apartment felt even more cold and soulless than it had the night before.

She had tried to pass the time by creating work for herself: scrubbing countertops that were already spotless, sweeping floors that didn't have a crumb in sight, wrestling with the faulty bedroom window that was beyond repair. She even re-hung the pictures that had mysteriously fallen the night before.

None of it provided an adequate distraction.

The image of Kirk hovered like a dark cloud over her entire being, as did the humiliation of his seething judgment, judgment that bordered on disgust. As much as Fiona resented him for it, she also understood.

On more than one occasion, she'd imagined how it would feel if the roles were reversed, if it were Kirk who had picked up their only child from school after an afternoon of heavy drinking, dozed off behind the wheel, took a corner too wide and too fast, and crashed head-on into a utility pole, injuring Jacob and nearly killing himself.

From where would she summon the strength to forgive or the empathy to understand? How long would it take for Kirk to fully regain her trust? If he regained it at all. How easy would it be to dismiss any promises made after that as the empty platitudes that they likely were?

Each time she considered the last question, the answer was always the same: *Frighteningly easy.*

"Why should Kirk see me differently? Why would my moral ground be any higher than his?"

Fiona asked the questions aloud with the hope that someone would answer them. But aside from Paul, there was no one to talk to, no one to provide a comforting word of encouragement. No one to tell her it would be okay.

It didn't matter. It would have all been a lie anyway.

She paced her apartment for hours, afraid of being still. Something terrible was chasing her, and Fiona worried that if it caught her, the outcome would be dire beyond any worst-case scenario she could have ever constructed.

Despite her best efforts, it eventually did catch up to her.

It began with the screaming in her head, followed by the red-hot burning in her throat. This time, water did nothing to quench it.

Even though she had fought tooth-and-nail to keep it at bay for the last 310 days, the craving for a drink enveloped her like a warm, familiar blanket. Succumbing to that warmth meant no longer having to distract herself. It meant no more humiliation or regret. It meant feeling nothing. And right now, nothing was good.

But time and experience told her that it was all a

mirage. The familiarity, the warmth, the numbness. It was simply there to mask a truth that threatened to expose both her self-delusion and the façade of stability that she tried to hide behind.

Tonight, she would have to face that truth again. Tonight, the veil would be lifted, and it wouldn't reveal a changed woman ready to make her world right again. The woman revealed tonight would be the one that she had always feared: the hopeless alcoholic who never learned how to cope with her father's death, her mother's neglect, her own inability to connect, or her propensity to sabotage herself and anything good that found its way into her life.

The cravings told her that she had no business coming here, and if she truly wanted what was best for Jacob, she would have stayed right where she was. The cravings told her that the last year of AA meetings, the self-righteous chest-beating, and the feeble promises of a different outcome now meant nothing.

*You're a fraud, Fiona. Jacob is better off now, and you know it. This is all you've ever been and all you'll ever be. Stop conning yourself. You're just better at controlling it now. You know how to stop at one. That's right, just one. And then you can throw away the rest of the bottle. Just one. Aren't you tired of hurting? Aren't you just sick to death of the pain and the tears and the fear? Come on, just one.*

Sinking deep into the nylon fabric of her air mattress, Fiona wept. It was the only thing she could do to quiet the frantic whispering in her head.

As she wiped away tears, she recalled an incident with her father that occurred just days before his car drifted across a highway median and into the path of an oncoming semi truck.

No matter how late it was, no matter how long the shift, he would always peek inside her room before shuffling off to bed. Most nights, she awoke to the sound of his heavy footfalls. On this night, she stayed up in anticipation of his appearance.

But something different happened this time. This time he passed her bedroom without peeking inside, continuing instead down the hallway toward his own bedroom. The first sound Fiona heard was her mother's strained voice.

*"Nathan, what's the matter?"*

The second sound she heard was one that she has never forgotten in the twenty-six years since it happened.

Her father was crying.

Alarmed, Fiona ran out of bed and into the hallway, where she saw her mother and father embracing. He had nearly collapsed in her arms.

*"I can't stop, Maggie. I've tried. I swear to God, I have."*

*"I know, honey. I know. That's why you have to let someone help you."*

The image shook Fiona to her tiny core. Without saying a word, she ran up to her father and wrapped herself around his waist. By then, she was crying, too.

*"Daddy, are you okay? Please don't cry. Please don't."* She said the words repeatedly, words that were now replaying in her mind just as clearly as when she'd first spoken them.

With the fog of sadness casting an ever-widening net around her, Fiona kept hearing that seven-year-old voice. *"Don't be sad anymore. You'll be okay."* As if prompted by the words, she sat up in bed. After a few deep breaths, her nerves settled.

Calm quickly gave way to the blunt-force trauma of guilt.

"Christ, what am I doing?"

Through the haze of damp eyes, she looked at the unopened bottle of Bushmills whiskey resting on her nightstand. The instant she picked it up, the frantic whispering returned.

*Open the bottle. Take one sip, then toss out the rest.*

*Throw it against the wall and watch it shatter into pieces.*

*Calmly walk into the bathroom and pour it down the sink.*

*Who in the hell are you fooling? Drink the whole fucking thing!*

Fiona slowly unscrewed the gold cap. The thick, peppery aroma filled her nostrils with warmth.

*One sip, then down the sink.*

The rim of the bottle was touching her lips before she realized that she had raised her arm. Her grip tightened as she tipped the bottle up.

*Just one.*

But before the first taste could cross her mouth, Fiona heard something.

*"Are you better now?"*

She froze. The voice sounded like the seven-year-old from her memories, but unlike a memory, this voice did not exist in her mind.

*"Did someone hurt you?"*

It was in her room.

*"Can you hear me?"*

Knocking on the wall caused her to jump out of bed.

She held her breath as silence fell over the room. With the bottle suddenly feeling heavy in her hand, she put it back on the nightstand, screwing the cap on as tightly as she could. "Not one drop, and I'm still losing my mind."

*"So, you are still there."*

Fiona jumped again, this time covering her mouth to stifle the involuntary yelp that had escaped her chest.

The young voice was coming from the same spot where she had heard the knocking. The same spot where she had heard the crying a day earlier.

"I'm sorry. I didn't mean to scare you."

Fiona approached with cautious steps. She placed an ear to the wall and stood there for what felt like an eternity before mustering the courage to speak. "Are you talking to me?"

"You're not crying anymore. Does that mean everything is okay now?"

Against her already failing judgment, Fiona answered. "Yes, I'm okay. How long have you been listening to me?"

"Long enough to get worried. You sounded really sad."

Fiona suddenly felt awkward. Not only did she have to deal with the fact that she had become a blubbering fool who nearly fell off the wagon, but now this little girl, and possibly the rest of the building, had to deal with it too. "You don't have to worry anymore. I'm sorry if I woke you."

"You didn't wake me."

Fiona glanced at her clock: 9:43 p.m. "You're up awfully late. Isn't it a school night?"

Silence, then: "Why were you sad?"

Fiona still felt tears in her eyes as she looked at the bottle that would soon find its way into the garbage. "I guess I just had a bad night."

"I have those sometimes."

Fiona thought back to yesterday and the sounds she heard coming from the girl's apartment. "I bet you do," she whispered under her breath.

"What did you say?"

*Mind your own business, Fiona.* "Nothing."

"I'm glad someone is living there now," the girl continued. "The apartment was empty for a long time."

With each passing moment, Fiona was wishing that someone wasn't her. "How long have you lived here?"

"Since I can remember."

"How do you like it?" She regretted the question the instant it came out.

"I wish we could live someplace else, but my mom says we can't move."

"Why not?"

"She says we belong here. I don't agree, but I'm just a kid, so my vote doesn't really count."

Fiona smiled. "Not until you're eighteen."

"Only eight more years to go. Lucky me."

At least she now knew how old the girl was. That left one other question. "What's your name?"

"Olivia. What's yours?"

"Fiona."

"Nice to meet you, Fiona, even though we're in separate rooms and can't actually see each other."

"Nice to meet you too, Olivia. And yes, talking from different rooms is a bit strange."

"How do you like it here?" Olivia asked.

Fiona took a moment to consider her answer. "Let's just say it's a little more active than what I'm used to."

"You're talking about my mom and her boyfriend fighting, right?"

Fiona felt bad about broaching the subject and suddenly felt compelled to lie. "No, not at all."

"It's okay. I know you think they're bad people."

"I swear that wasn't what I was thinking."

"I heard you talking to me the other night, when Noah and my mom were fighting. I'm sorry I couldn't answer. I wanted to."

"It's okay. I could tell you were upset, and I wanted to know that you were okay. Are you okay there?"

A long silence passed before Olivia answered. "You're

right to think that Noah is a bad person. My mom is always sticking up for him, no matter what he does, so I guess that makes her just as bad."

"Do they ever hurt you?"

"No." The hesitation in Olivia's voice said otherwise. "My mom does try to be a good mom whenever she can."

"I'm sure she does," Fiona declared, not believing it.

"I want to talk about you, Fiona. How do you like living here?" Olivia asked again.

"I moved in only a few days ago, so it's hard to say. Sometimes the only thing that matters is having a roof over your head."

"Even if you aren't safe?"

"What do you mean?"

"I mean having a roof isn't everything. You also have to feel safe, right?"

"I suppose so."

"Do you feel safe here?"

"Why would you ask that?"

Olivia hesitated before answering. "Things happen here that make me feel not so safe sometimes. I wondered if they happened to you too."

Fiona briefly lost her breath. "What things?"

"This."

Three heavy knocks on the wall broke the silence in the room.

"I hear it all the time," Olivia continued. "Not so much since you moved in, but before that, when your apartment was empty, it happened almost every night. Sometimes, it was a light scratching. Sometimes, it sounded like someone was trying to break down the wall. Have you heard anything like that?"

"No," Fiona answered, fully aware that she was lying. "I

heard you knock on the wall before we started talking, but that's it."

"Have you put any pictures on the wall since you moved in?"

"Yes."

"And have they fallen down without you touching them?"

Fiona couldn't lie this time, even as she felt the tension building in her chest. "Yes."

"It happens here, too. My mom says the pipes in the wall vibrate, and that causes the knocking and the falling pictures. But I don't believe that."

"What do you think it—"

"Shh."

"What's wrong?"

"Someone's coming. I have to go."

"Olivia, wait. I want to ask you about—"

"Quiet."

The next voice that Fiona heard wasn't Olivia's, but it was familiar nonetheless.

"First, it's the talking, then it's the pounding on the walls. I have to be at work in five hours! How do you expect me to be productive if I can't sleep?"

The anger in the man's voice hadn't lost an ounce of its edge in the nearly twenty-four hours since Fiona had last heard it. ˈ

"Leave it alone and come back to bed. Please."

The tone in the woman's voice, on the other hand, had lost all its previous bite. Now she sounded weak.

"Find a way to deal with it, Natalie. Or I promise I will."

"I'll deal with it, okay? Just don't go in there."

The sound of a door slamming shut gave way to silence. Fiona pressed her ear against the wall.

"Olivia?"

No response.

"Are you still there?"

A light shuffling of feet. "I don't think I should talk right now."

"It's okay, honey. You can talk to me anytime you want."

"I hope that things don't get worse in your apartment. I hope you stay safe."

"What does that mean?"

"Don't ignore the knocking. It's not the pipes in the walls."

"Olivia—"

"Bye, Fiona. I'm glad you're not sad anymore."

"Olivia?"

Fiona kept her ear pressed to the wall, waiting for a response. She heard nothing.

It was as if the girl was never there.

## Chapter Seven

A heavy rapping on the front door stirred Fiona out of a rootless, dreamless sleep. She was on her feet and out of the room so quickly that she hadn't had time to check the clock, but it felt very late.

The knocking continued as she stumbled bleary-eyed into the living room.

"Who the fuck is it?" she blurted out before she could turn on the filter that ran from her brain to her mouth.

"Denver police. Could you please open the door?"

Fiona was suddenly wide awake.

She opened the door to the sight of a silver-and-blue badge inches from her face. Behind the badge stood a statuesque brunette who looked like she would have been more at home on the set of a superhero movie than in the hallway of Fiona's grungy apartment building.

She was tall, shapely, and despite her soft facial features, incredibly intimidating. Most police officers who showed up at your door in the middle of the night were.

"Hello, Miss. I'm Detective Chloe Sullivan, Denver PD. Apologies for the intrusion at such a late hour."

Her even voice and easy smile were enough to reassure Fiona that she wasn't here to arrest her.

"No problem," she answered, finally feeling safe enough to open her door all the way. "I'm sorry for the rude greeting."

"Thick skin is a necessity when you're knocking on doors at two in the morning. Do you have a moment?"

"Sure. What's going on?"

"There was a disturbance on this floor earlier in the evening, and we've been talking to your neighbors to see if anyone saw or heard anything out of the ordinary around 10:30."

"What kind of disturbance?"

"I can't divulge that."

Fiona's heart dropped as she thought about her conversation with Olivia. *Things happen here that make me feel not so safe sometimes.* She looked past the detective and into the hallway. There was no visible activity. "Can you at least tell me where the disturbance was?"

"Apartment 612."

That would explain why Fiona saw no activity. Apartment 612 was down the hall and to the right, near the elevator. Far away from her. Far away from Olivia. She breathed a quiet sigh of relief as she turned back to the detective.

"Did you know the tenant in that unit?" Sullivan continued.

"No. I just moved in a few days ago, so I don't know many people here."

"What about the neighbors on either side of you?"

"I've met the woman in 603. Iris. Very nice." Fiona didn't feel compelled to mention the hellions in 607.

"I'll stop by 603 next. In the meantime, I'll get back to my original question."

"Did I see or hear anything strange around 10:30."

"Right."

Fiona had seen and heard nothing but strange things since moving in, but Detective Sullivan wasn't asking about falling pictures or red stains on the carpet or odd conversations with ten-year-old girls. "I can't say that I did."

"You just moved in, so I guess it wouldn't help to ask if you've noticed anyone in the building or on the grounds who looked like they didn't belong."

"Sorry. I can't really help you with that, either."

"I understand. It must be hard in a place this size to keep up with all of the comings and goings, regardless of how long you've been here."

"I moved in three days ago, and I still can't remember where the laundry room is. They should give you a map with your keys."

The detective smiled politely. "Well, if anything does come to mind, I would love for you to give me a call." She pulled a card out of her jacket pocket.

"Of course," Fiona answered as she eyed the card. *Detective Chloe Sullivan. Major Crimes Unit.*

Her heart skipped. Something serious had happened here, a reality reinforced by the sudden appearance of two uniformed officers in the hallway. They had just exited an apartment a few doors down and were now making their way toward Fiona and Detective Sullivan.

"Excuse me," Sullivan said as she broke away to greet the pair. They huddled in a tight circle as they spoke. After a quiet exchange, the officers continued down the hall while Sullivan returned to Fiona.

"Did something happen?"

"No, we're simply coordinating our canvassing effort. There are a lot of doors to knock on, and we've only just started."

Fiona nodded despite feeling uneasy.

"Again, sorry for the intrusion. I appreciate your time. We're keeping the building manager updated, and if anything develops, I'm sure he'll let you know."

"Okay."

"By the way, I didn't catch your name."

"Fiona Graves."

"Thank you again, Ms. Graves. Remember, if you have any questions, don't hesitate to call."

Detective Sullivan was preparing to walk away when Fiona stopped her. "Actually, I have a question now."

"Yes?"

"I understand that you can't talk about the specifics of what happened here, but can you at least assure me that I shouldn't be worried for my safety or anyone else's in the building?"

"We haven't determined that there is an immediate threat. It appears that the incident was isolated to 612. But there is still a lot we don't know, so I can't say anything with certainty. As far as your safety is concerned, we'll have officers stationed in the building for the remainder of the night and into tomorrow while we determine the full scope of what happened. We're here investigating a possible crime, but we also want to make sure that everyone feels safe."

"I know that should make me feel better."

"But it doesn't."

"Given the fact that you're with the Major Crimes Unit,

and the fact that you don't seem to have a suspect in custody yet, no, it doesn't make me feel better."

"Just know that we're doing everything we can to resolve the situation, and I feel confident that we will. The first few hours are always the toughest, but something always breaks."

"Have you gotten much help from the other tenants?"

"Honestly, no. But we still have a lot more of them to talk to, so hopefully, that will change."

"What about the people in 607?" The question came out before Fiona had the chance to consider it.

"There was no answer when I knocked. Story of the night so far. You're one of the few tenants to actually open the door. That's why I wasn't upset at your less-than-hospitable greeting. At least it was a greeting."

"Note to self: Don't drop the F-bomb until you've confirmed that the person on the other end of your door isn't a homicide detective," Fiona said with a rueful smile. "If you knew the day I had, you would understand."

The detective returned her smile. "No need to explain, Ms. Graves. After the day I had, I probably wouldn't have stopped at the F-bomb. Take care and try to get some sleep."

"Easier said than done, but I'll try."

Sullivan had begun to walk away again when Iris Matheson's door opened.

"What's all the commotion out here?" she muttered as she stepped into the hallway.

"Hello, ma'am. Detective Chloe Sullivan. Denver PD."

"I can see that," Iris answered as she looked the tall woman up and down. "Is the air up there the same as it is for the rest of us down here?"

Sullivan smiled, clearly accustomed to such comments.

"The air up here is just fine. Do you mind if I ask a few questions?"

"Ask away, Detective."

Sullivan laid out the situation the same as she had for Fiona, followed by the same series of questions. Iris could provide only slightly better answers than Fiona, offering up Donald Tisdale as the name of the tenant in 612, that his occupation was as a janitor at a local high school, and his status as a certified hermit with no callers, male or female, that Iris had ever seen. He was quiet and didn't cause trouble, so to her, he was a good neighbor. But she couldn't recall any instance of their having a conversation that lasted longer than five minutes.

"Are you aware if Mr. Tisdale ever had issues with other tenants in the building?" Detective Sullivan asked as she eagerly scribbled in her notepad.

"Donald was never a bother to anyone. Now, do I think it's weird that he hardly ever came out of his apartment except to go to work or that he could barely look you in the eye when he spoke to you? Yes, I do. But I have unnaturally high expectations of people. No one that I knew had an issue with the way he conducted himself."

*Not even the drug-addicted freakazoids who live next door to me?* Fiona thought, wisely deciding not to give it voice.

"This is all very helpful, ma'am."

"Iris Matheson. You woke me at this ungodly hour. The least you can do is call me by my proper name."

Fiona fought to contain her smile.

"This is all very helpful, Ms. Matheson." a contrite Sullivan answered.

"It's Mrs."

"*Mrs.* Matheson. I really appreciate it."

Iris nodded. "Can you tell us anything else about what may have happened?"

"Not really. As I was discussing with Ms. Graves, we're still in the early stages here, so there isn't much to report. It seems that Mr. Tisdale was a bit of a mystery to everyone, so aside from the basic information you provided, we don't have anything else to go on. Part of making sense of a crime is attempting to understand at least something about who the victim was. So far, that's been our main obstacle."

"So, you're admitting that some kind of crime occurred here?" a wide-eyed Fiona asked.

"Sweetheart, she wouldn't be here if there hadn't been one," Iris said gently.

"Ladies, I'm not admitting to anything," Sullivan insisted. "I was making a general statement."

"We understand, Detective Sullivan. You start admitting to the residents here that Donald was murdered, and you'd have a full-fledged panic on your hands. You're right in keeping that close to the vest. Not everyone here is as even-keeled as Fiona and I." Iris leaned in close. "But just so you know, your secret is safe with us."

Sullivan nodded uncomfortably. "Again, thank you for the information. If anything comes up that we may have missed, please call." The detective reached inside her jacket for another card, but Iris put her hand up before she could retrieve it.

"Save it. I can use Fiona's if I need to."

"Okay. I'll be floating around the building if you need me. In the meantime, you ladies get some sleep, okay?"

"We'll try. And thank you." Fiona liked Sullivan and offered her approval with an extended hand, which the detective promptly shook.

Iris said nothing as Sullivan walked away.

After a short conference with the two uniformed officers who were patrolling the floor, the three of them disappeared around a corner. It was only after they were gone that Iris spoke.

"Well, that's a real how-do-you-do, eh?"

"Yeah, that was really something."

Iris put a hand on her shoulder. "You poor thing."

"What?"

"First, it's the nonsense with the loud music, then this. You haven't even been here a week. What you must think of this place."

*You don't know the half of it.* "My mind is too shot right now to think about much of anything."

"I understand."

"Can you at least tell me that this is all an anomaly? That I'll wake up later, and this place will be normal, like any of the other half-dozen apartment buildings I could have moved into?"

"I would gladly tell you that," Iris said with a soft smile. "But I'm a horrible liar."

Fiona couldn't hide her disappointment. "Great, so what can you tell me?"

"A lot more than I told that detective. Interested in that coffee now?"

There was no hesitation on Fiona's part this time. "Absolutely."

## Chapter Eight

Walking into Iris Matheson's apartment felt like walking into an antique shop. Aside from the flat-screen television mounted conspicuously in the corner, nothing here looked like it could have been purchased after 1965.

From the fine china to the delicate lace throws that fell over her wood-trim velvet sofa to the American Old West art collection that looked like it should have been part of a museum display, Iris kept an immaculate home.

"I feel like I just stepped into some kind of time warp," Fiona said as she inhaled the warm scent of apple-and-spice potpourri. "What an amazing space you have here."

"Thank you. Every item is an original. No dollar-store knockoffs for me," Iris answered with a gleam of pride in her eye. "These things have followed me everywhere I've gone. You should have seen my collection before we were forced to sell the house. Drove my husband crazy. He tolerated it because he loved me, but he wasn't the least bit upset when we had to put it all in storage. I still have most of it locked away. Probably worth a fortune by now, but I'd never dream of selling it."

At the word *husband*, Fiona began scanning the apartment for photos. Almost as if she were reading her mind, Iris picked up a frame off the coffee table and gave it to her.

"That's my Sam. Handsome devil, isn't he?"

Fiona couldn't help but smile as she took the photo.

The grainy 8x10 appeared to be taken during a night out on the town for a much younger Iris and her sharply dressed husband. It was a candid photo of the pair sitting at a restaurant table. Sam gazed deeply into Iris's eyes as they engaged in intimate conversation. It was obvious from his gaze how much he adored her.

Fiona thought back to the time when Kirk adored her the same way. It seemed like two lifetimes ago.

"That was always my favorite shot of us," Iris said as she took the photo and set it back on the coffee table. "We were sitting there having dinner when a man suddenly walks up with a camera and takes our picture. Of course, he wanted to charge us for it, but he promised it would be worth every penny. Turns out he was right."

"How long were you married?"

"Forty-three wonderful years. We started dating in high school and never looked back. It's been nearly two years since he passed, and not a day goes by that I don't…" Her voice trailed off as she began straightening the other pictures on the coffee table.

Fiona used busy work to fight back her emotions in much the same way.

"Sounds like you two were really doing something right to last that long," she said, attempting to steer Iris's emotions back in a positive direction.

"Oh, yes. I mean, we certainly had our ups and downs, but what marriages don't? The bottom line is that we loved each other. I was meant for him, and he was meant for me. When you have that kind of foundation, all of the down-times are manageable."

Fiona could only nod.

"What about you, dear? Married?"

"Divorced."

"Oh, I'm so sorry."

"Don't be."

"May I ask what happened?"

Fiona was initially taken back by the intrusive question, but women of Iris's generation, mothers especially, had a tendency toward intrusive questions.

"We sucked at managing the downtimes."

Iris nodded her understanding. "Children?"

Fiona's legs suddenly felt unsteady. She pointed at the couch. "Do you mind?"

"Oh gosh, where are my manners? Of course not."

Fiona sat, thankful that she could do so before her legs gave out. After a few quiet breaths, she said, "We have an eight-year-old son, Jacob."

Iris beamed. "That's wonderful. Such a great age. I'd love to meet him. Where is he?"

"He…he lives with his father."

Iris's smile promptly went away. "I see."

"That's the reason I'm here. To be closer to him. There are some things that I need to change to have the relation-ship with him that I want." Fiona thought about her near-miss with the bottle. "I'm slowly getting there."

"Well, there isn't a more powerful force in the universe than a mother's love for her child. I feel that love from you, and I'm sure your son does, too. You'll do your work, and you'll be the mother that you want to be. I have no doubts about that."

Fiona hadn't heard words of encouragement like that in a long time, and she breathed them in like oxygen. "Thank you. I'm really trying."

"I know you are. And I know it's not easy. If you need any support or advice along the way, I've been around the block a few times. My Quinn is thirty-four, but in a lot of ways, he still acts like he's eight, so I can relate to what you're going through."

Fiona met the offer with a genuine smile. "Deal. But we should save that conversation for another day."

"You're right. Much more pressing business to attend to. How about that coffee I promised?"

"Sounds great," Fiona said as she rose to her feet. "Can I help?"

"Nope. I'll only be a minute. You just stay here and relax."

With that, Iris disappeared into the kitchen.

The life finally returning to her legs, Fiona walked around the living room.

The vast array of knickknacks and collectibles was rivaled in sheer number only by the family photographs. Though there were a few more of Sam, the majority featured Iris's son. From infant pictures to prom and graduation pictures, there was little doubt about who the true light of her life was.

The most recent pictures showed Iris and her adult son sitting in the stands during a Denver Broncos game. He was a handsome man, despite his flat, joyless expression.

As she looked closer, Fiona realized that Quinn had barely smiled in any of the pictures.

*Ah yes, the strong, brooding type,* Fiona thought. She fell for them every time. Exciting at first, but they always broke your heart in the end. She'd wondered how many hearts Quinn had broken. From the looks of it, certainly not his mother's.

Almost on cue, Iris emerged from the kitchen with two steaming mugs. "Told you I'd be quick. This Keurig machine is amazing. The coffee is done in thirty seconds, and it's perfect every time." She set the tray down on the table. "Not sure how you take it, but I have milk and Stevia."

"Black is fine," Fiona said as she took a mug.

"I'm with you on that. Cheers."

Fiona tapped Iris's raised mug. "Cheers. Thank you for having me over. I would've been entirely too nervous to go back to my apartment right now."

"I hear you. I had to laugh when that detective told us to get some sleep. Like that was even possible after what just happened."

"What do you think happened?"

"Maybe we should sit," Iris answered, promptly moving to one end of the couch.

Fiona sat at the other end. "Detective Sullivan's card said she was from the Major Crimes Unit. To me, that translates to homicide. She didn't exactly say that Donald Tisdale was murdered, but her presence here pretty much implies it. Don't you think?"

"He was murdered. There's no doubt about it." Iris didn't even blink as she said the words. "The 'why' and 'how' are different questions altogether."

Fiona took a long pull from her coffee mug. As the warm liquid touched her lips, an image of the empty whiskey bottle in the bottom of her trashcan flashed in her mind. She blinked, and it went away. "Do you think the detective knows more than she's saying?"

"I'm sure she *thinks* she knows what happened. And she might be right. Most likely, she's not. Either way, she would never tell us."

"So, what do you know that she doesn't?"

It was the question that had brought Fiona here, and now that she'd asked it, Iris seemed hesitant to answer. She took a slow sip from her coffee mug and gently put it down on the table. "Corona Heights is a very interesting place. Being here for the short time you have, you've probably come to realize that."

Fiona nodded. "Interesting is certainly one way to put it."

"Had you gotten a sneak preview before you signed the lease, you would have kept right on looking. Am I right?"

"One hundred percent."

Iris smiled. "I figured. I've only lived here for a few years, but I've heard plenty of stories from the old-timers, the ones who managed to stick around, anyway. They would tell you that it hasn't always been this way. This used to be a pleasant place to live. There was once a waiting list to get in, if you can believe that. Neighbors talked to each other. There were families on every floor. People cared. It was so different."

"What happened?"

"Most of the good people moved away."

"Why?"

Iris took another long drink from her coffee until it was gone. "That was delicious. Would you like another cup?"

"I'm fine, thanks." Iris was stalling, and Fiona wasn't taking the bait.

"I should probably stop too. I'd like to get to sleep at some point."

"Why did most of the good people leave?"

After another moment of hesitation, Iris finally dove in. "It apparently started some years ago with a family on the third floor. John and Lisa Coleman and their two daughters, Caitlyn and Anna. The four of them were found dead by Arthur, the maintenance supervisor, after other tenants kept complaining about strange smells. It was eventually reported on the news that they had been dead for a week and a half. No one knows for sure how or why, but each of them was found with arsenic in their systems. There were empty cups next to each body. Whether they were forced to drink it or each of them did so willingly was a question that the police couldn't answer."

Iris set her empty mug on the table and continued. "They seemed like such a good, loving family. No one could imagine them doing this to themselves. But there was no sign that anyone had broken into the apartment, and nothing was disturbed. If someone made them drink it, the Colemans didn't put up much of a fight."

"Was it some kind of murder-suicide?"

"A couple of the tenants who knew John and Lisa pretty well claimed that they'd had marital problems in the past. There was apparently infidelity on Lisa's part. They told their friends they were receiving marriage counseling, but John had changed. He became withdrawn, started drinking a lot. The arguments became constant. Lisa threatened to leave with the girls, but nothing ever came of it. Time had seemed to heal their wounds. They were getting better as a couple. John stopped drinking and eventually forgave her affair. Just when it looked like they were fully back on track as a family, they were all found dead."

"That's awful," Fiona said with a shudder.

"There's more," Iris replied. "After the Colemans were found, people started reporting unusual disturbances to the building manager."

"What kinds of disturbances?"

"The smells, for one. Even after the apartment had been cleared out and thoroughly cleaned, people on the floor said they could smell the stench of the Colemans' death for months afterward. It would be fine for days. Then out of the blue, it would hit them. Some said it was so strong that it came through their doors and vents." Iris paused. "The noises came next."

"Noises?"

"Footsteps in the hallway with no apparent source, the sound of children crying..."

Fiona raised her hand to stop Iris. "You're putting me on with all of this, right?"

"I know it sounds crazy, and I wasn't around to personally experience any of this. But apparently, a lot of people did, and they moved away because of it."

"So, you're telling me Corona Heights is haunted?"

"No, but what I am telling you is that a lot of strange things, unexplained things, have happened here. The knocking on the walls, for instance."

That stopped Fiona's skepticism cold. "The what?"

"The knocking on the walls late at night. That's the one thing I have experienced. It usually occurred in the same spot in my bedroom, normally around ten or eleven at night. I would have chalked it up to my neighbors having a little too much fun, except there was no one living in the apartment adjacent to mine at the time."

Fiona thought back to her conversation with Olivia. She had essentially said the same thing. Though she was afraid to confirm it, she knew that Iris would draw the same conclusion about where the knocking originated from. "You mean *my* apartment?"

"I can't say that with certainty. It's more likely that it was something inside the wall itself."

"That's not much better, is it?"

Iris put a gentle hand on Fiona's knee. "I can see that I'm starting to frighten you with this talk, and I'm sorry. Honestly, there was probably nothing more to it than bad plumbing."

The same thing that Olivia's mother said.

"Your apartment isn't haunted," Iris continued. "And neither is mine. I only brought it up to illustrate my point about the building."

"Which is?"

Iris looked as if she was beginning to regret that the conversation even came up. "Again, I'm not trying to scare you."

"Too late."

"I'm sorry."

"I'm sure you are. But the cat is already out of the bag, so you may as well tell me everything."

"I have told you everything."

"You told me about a family that died years ago, and unexplained knocking on your wall. How does any of that relate to what happened tonight?"

Iris took a deep breath of resignation. "You asked earlier if Donald's death was an anomaly."

"That's right. And you told me it wasn't. What you haven't told me is why."

"Donald Tisdale isn't an anomaly because there have been more mysterious deaths in this building per capita than anywhere else in the state that isn't a hospital or psychiatric institution. It's an absolute fact. Go online and search for yourself."

Fiona suddenly wished that she had just gone to bed. "So, you *are* telling me that Corona Heights is haunted."

"Cursed may be a more apt description."

"My God, what's the difference?"

"Haunted implies that a foreign energy, possibly malevolent in nature, is occupying a particular space and claiming it as its own. Corona Heights is cursed, in my opinion, because its dark energy doesn't come from an outside source but is instead embedded in its very foundation. The building is the source."

Fiona swallowed hard, her mind too numb to produce a suitable retort. "What are you basing this on aside from your opinion?"

"I've experienced a lot in my time here. I've seen young people move in bright-eyed, optimistic, and full of life. By the time they leave for good, many of those same people are cynical, unhappy, and even depressed. Some are in poor physical health. They probably couldn't tell you why this is any more than I could. But I've seen it happen too many times to think that it's some kind of fluke."

"So why are you still here? Why haven't you become one of those cynical, unhappy former residents that this place is apparently so good at producing?"

Iris glanced at the photos on her coffee table before answering. "This is my home. I have too much invested here to be run out by anyone or anything. And every now and then, my faith that good people can once again occupy this place is renewed. It was certainly renewed when I met you. Corona Heights won't get the better of you. I have no doubts about that. Your strength is undeniable. It's a strength forged out of hardship and struggle. You've been through a lot to get here, and you aren't going to let anything get in the way of your destiny with your son, least of all anything that happens here. You don't have a thing to worry about."

"Tell that to my hands." Fiona could barely control the shaking as she lifted them in the air.

Iris took Fiona's hands and held them in hers. "This news has been a bit traumatic for everyone, myself included. I don't like revisiting the history of this place, but events like Donald's death make it necessary. I'm telling you all this only to provide context. The last thing I want to do is to frighten you." She squeezed Fiona's hands tighter. "I know we've only just met, but I like having you here, and I hope you'll stick around. If you do, you'll be fine. Please trust me on that."

"I haven't been fine so far."

"What do you mean?"

"You're not my only next-door neighbor."

Iris's face flashed with understanding. "The Shelbys in 607."

"So now I know their last name. What else can you tell me about them?"

Iris sat back on the couch, clearly hesitant to broach the subject. "Not much. Natalie apparently moved in a few years before I did. Never been much for friendly conversation, that one. In two years, I can probably count on one hand the number times we've talked. Same with her boyfriend. What a royal piece of crap he is."

Fiona could certainly vouch for that.

"Honestly, they both could use a swift kick in the rear-end by someone willing to teach them some manners."

"What about their daughter?"

Iris was silent as if her question didn't fully register.

"Olivia," Fiona added.

"Yes, of course. Olivia. Sweet girl from what I've seen. Far cry from her mother. I would love to get to know her more, but she never seems to be around."

"You don't run into her in the hallways or outside?"

"I've seen her once or twice on the children's playground, but that was some time ago. I once baked a plate of cookies and brought them over, but Natalie told me that Olivia wasn't feeling well and couldn't come to the door. She wouldn't even accept the cookies, for crying out loud. How rude can you get?"

"When was the last time you actually saw her?"

Iris paused to search her memory. "Honestly, I can't even tell you. I know it's been a while." She paused again. "Wait, that's not true. I saw her with Noah walking down the hall to the elevators. Had to be a month ago. They were some distance away, and I only saw them from the back, but I'm pretty sure it was her."

"Don't you think it's strange that you rarely see her? It's the middle of the school year. She should be out and about all the time."

"If you really knew the people in 607, you wouldn't think it was strange at all. Natalie barely leaves her apartment. Such a waste too. She's entirely too young to be a shut-in. I don't know what they do for money, but as long as they don't bring trouble to my doorstep, it really isn't my business."

"I actually talked to Olivia."

Iris looked surprised. "You did? When?"

"Last night."

"But I thought you hadn't met them yet?"

"I haven't. Not Natalie or her boyfriend, anyway." Fiona paused as she considered how to word the next part. "I actually talked to Olivia through my bedroom wall."

"Come again?"

"I was in my bedroom when I suddenly heard this voice asking if I was okay. I'd been a little upset and she must have heard me. At first, I thought I was hearing things, but as she continued, I eventually concluded that it was real."

"What did she say?"

"She told me her name, how old she was, really basic stuff. I got the feeling she just wanted someone to talk to." Fiona was telling only half the story, but she had no desire to fall down Iris's cursed building rabbit hole again–even if Olivia had essentially echoed the sentiment.

"How long did you talk?" a now-riveted Iris asked.

"Just a couple of minutes. She heard her mother coming, and I think she was afraid of getting in trouble for being awake. It was pretty late."

"Well, that's one more conversation than I've had with her."

Fiona couldn't tell if the tone in Iris's voice was jealousy or irritation. Either way, she thought it best to abandon the discussion.

"I really appreciate the coffee and the great company, but I should get some sleep. Hopefully, the next time we do this, it'll be under much better circumstances."

Iris looked disappointed even as she nodded her understanding. "I'm the one who should be thanking you. I needed the company much more than you realize. I know the conversation was a bit dark at times, but I really do feel better about things now, especially knowing that you won't be moving out the moment the sun comes up."

"I promise I won't. For better or worse, I'll be here a while."

"I choose to think of it as for the better."

"Then I will, too," Fiona said with a tired smile.

When they stood, Iris held her arms out for a hug. Despite the tenor of their conversation, Fiona felt a genuine sense of comfort in her presence, and her embrace reflected that.

"Thank you, my dear," Iris said with a gentle sigh. "I needed that."

"Me too."

When they finally let go, Iris looked at her with a wide smile and said, "Let's say we end this on a wildly positive note."

"I'm all for that."

Iris picked up a small black box off the coffee table and handed it to Fiona. "For you."

"What is it?"

"Open it."

When she did, she saw a smooth, oval-shaped purple stone attached to a necklace. "It's beautiful."

"I've had it for a long time. It's an amulet designed to ward off bad energy while inviting in the good. I can't tell you with scientific certainty that it works, but I believe it does. I want you to have it."

"No, I can't."

"I insist. I have plenty more. I just happen to think this one works the best. Please."

Fiona took the stone out of the box and held it up to the light. It was unlike anything she had ever seen, its color deep and rich yet translucent. She never gave much thought to the energy of things, but she couldn't deny feeling something as she held it. It was probably nothing more than the power of Iris's suggestion, but that suggestion infused her with an instantaneous feeling of confidence that she didn't want to relinquish.

"Thank you," she said. "I promise to take good care of it."

"I know you will. Now, allow me." Iris took the amulet and walked behind Fiona. After clasping it, she said, "Looks perfect on you."

"If this helps to ward off all my personal demons, I'll wear it enthusiastically."

"Good."

After another embrace, Iris opened the door, and Fiona stepped into the hallway. "You make sure you get some rest, okay? And please take our conversation with a healthy grain of salt."

"I'll try. And I'll try," Fiona said, not sure if she would actually be able to accomplish either. "Goodnight, Iris."

"More like good morning. It'll be light in a few hours."

As she stood alone in the quiet hallway, Fiona couldn't help but wonder how long she would have to wait to truly experience that light.

## Chapter Nine

Detective Chloe Sullivan watched with a solemn gaze as two crime-scene technicians loaded Donald Tisdale onto a gurney for transport from his apartment to the Denver County morgue freezer that would keep his lifeless body preserved until an autopsy could be performed.

After more than a year in Major Crimes and dozens of homicides investigated, Sullivan figured that she would have become numb to it all by now. The frozen look of terror stamped on a victim's face. The dense, coppery smell of blood. The finality of death, and the realization that yet another person would never again see their loved ones, or eat their favorite meal, or fulfill the next day's to-do list.

The dull chest pain that she felt after Tisdale's final departure was just the latest reminder that she still had a long way to go.

Along with Sullivan, there were two uniformed officers, three CSI techs, and a medical examiner, all fighting for access to the same five feet of space where Tisdale's body was found.

The thick plaited rope that had served as his noose was being dusted for fingerprints, while the chair that he had apparently stood on was put under forensic lights in the search for any useful bits of trace evidence.

Detective Marcus Greer, Sullivan's partner, waded through the crowd to get to the kitchen where she was quietly sipping on a bottle of water.

"You wouldn't happen to have another one of those, would you, sport?" Greer asked with a hopeful glint.

"Always thinking of you," Sullivan replied as she handed him the unopened bottle that she brought in anticipation.

"You will be canonized one day, Chloe Louise Sullivan. Mark my words." Greer opened the bottle and downed its contents in less than four swallows. After he finished, he turned his attention to the crime-scene work. "What are they looking for exactly?"

"Anything in support of the prevailing wisdom that this was a suicide."

"You mean the rope and hanging body weren't enough?"

"Not for me," Sullivan answered emphatically.

"Okay. What about a note? Has one been found yet?"

"No. Not in the apartment, anyway."

"What about a social media post? That seems to be all the rage these days."

"Tisdale didn't have any social media accounts, at least not under his legal name. Given the fact that his driver's license says he was seventy-one, he did low-level work as a janitor and had no computer in his apartment, it's probably safe to assume that he wasn't very tech-savvy."

"Assumptions don't solve cases."

"Assumptions are all we have right now," Sullivan countered. "I mean, aren't we *assuming* he committed suicide?"

"Absent evidence to the contrary, yes."

"So, what does the current evidence tell you?"

Sullivan followed Greer as he made his way out of the kitchen toward the technicians in the living room. "The evidence tells me that Donald Tisdale, aged seventy-one, was working a dead-end job that barely paid above minimum wage when he should have by all rights been retired. The evidence also tells me that he was in debt up to his asshole, and there are piles of overdue notices on the kitchen counter to prove it. He was unmarried, alone, barely knew anyone here, he was tired of working, tired of struggling, and he wanted a way out."

Sullivan nodded. So far, his logic was holding up. "Go on."

Greer pointed to the rope tied to a utility hook that had been attached to a doorframe. "He put a lot of thought into this. He knew that the light fixture wouldn't be strong enough to support his weight, so he went to the trouble of screwing a hook into the frame, a big job that probably took some time. But he knew it would hold up. We know this was done recently because there's paint and fresh dust from the doorframe on the carpet. If this were a foul-play situation, taking the time required to create such a setup would be seriously inconvenient at best."

"And the absence of a suicide note?"

"He didn't need one. He had those overdue bills and a copy of his monthly check stub to tell the story for him. It's unfortunate that he couldn't find another way, but at the end of the day, he made his choice."

Sullivan patted him on the back. "I have to admit, that

was really well thought out, and to most anyone else in the world, it would make total sense."

"But you're not buying it."

"Call it my finely honed woman's intuition, call it your run-of-the-mill hunch, but no, I'm not buying it."

"All right, Detective. My turn to quiz you. Look at the evidence through those rose-colored lenses of yours, and tell me what you see."

"Everything you said about the dead-end, low-paying job and the mountains of debt makes sense. But according to the building manager, Tisdale was never late on his rent. Not once in seventeen years. In fact, he had just paid this month's rent in full two days ago. Why would he do that if he had even an inkling that he was going to kill himself the next day?"

Sullivan could see Greer's wheels turning in search of the not-so-clever comeback that had become his trademark. Thankfully, he couldn't summon one this time. "Continue."

"There were lots of bills, yes, but nothing that couldn't have been fixed. It's not like they were coming after the guy's house or car or retirement. He didn't have any of those things. Being into a credit card company for ten grand is no reason to end your life. I could understand if he had some underlying issue like depression or bipolar disorder, but the few people who knew him claimed that he was always in a good mood. Based on what we've seen, he wasn't on any kind of medication, not for his heart, not for his blood pressure, and not for any psychological issue. To me, there's no obvious reason why this man would want to commit suicide."

"Sometimes people don't need a reason, Chloe. Sometimes they're just tired."

Sullivan shrugged as she looked around the apartment.

Aside from the piles of mail in the kitchen and black dust on the walls and doors from the CSI techs, the space was orderly. Nothing to suggest an unwelcome guest. The door was intact, ruling out forced entry. And, as Greer rightly pointed out, the large hook in the doorframe indicated time and planning, neither of which supported the intruder theory.

There was also the matter of motive. If someone wanted Tisdale dead, why go to these extremes to do it? Based on the condition of the apartment, robbery didn't appear to be involved. If Sullivan were to look at the evidence objectively, Greer's argument beat her own hands-down. This was a suicide. Open and shut. All she had to do was take the evidence for what it was.

She could make Greer's week by admitting that he was right. They could go back to the precinct, hammer out the paperwork, grab a quick bite of breakfast, and she could retire to her bed for a much-needed ten-hour hibernation. Another case in the books. Easy-breezy.

Except it wasn't.

"What's that?" she suddenly asked Greer, pointing to a baseboard near the kitchen sink.

Greer walked into the kitchen, bending down in front of the sink for a closer inspection. Sullivan didn't need to get any closer to know what she was seeing.

"I can't believe I didn't notice that earlier," she said.

"I don't think anyone noticed it." Greer took a penlight out of his jacket and shined it on the tiny pool of red under the sink. "It's definitely blood, and it's definitely fresh."

"How in the hell did no one else see this?"

"Hey, Collins, I need you in here quick!" Greer yelled over his shoulder.

The crime-scene tech entered the kitchen immediately.

"We just found some in the bedroom, too. Come take a look."

Sullivan glanced at Greer in disbelief as they followed Collins.

She noticed it the second she walked in, plain as day, on the baseboard between the bed and nightstand.

"This pool is larger than the one in the kitchen," Collins said as he took out a glass vial to collect it. "And it appears to be just as fresh."

"What the entire fuck?" a wide-eyed Greer said.

"Tell your people to keep looking," Sullivan said to Collins. "Every nook and cranny, every square inch. If we missed something this obvious, God only knows what we'll find once we start digging."

Collins left the room to relay the message.

"So, what do you think now?" Sullivan asked.

Greer took a long look at the pool of blood and shook his head. "I'm starting to think you may be right."

For as good as it felt to hear those words, Sullivan couldn't take any satisfaction in them.

"How do eight highly trained, highly experienced crime-scene investigators miss something this obvious?"

The most immediate answer in Sullivan's mind was that the blood wasn't there before. But that would have been impossible.

"I couldn't begin to tell you, Marcus. What I can tell you is that there's a lot here that doesn't add up. I've been saying that from the beginning."

"That woman's intuition thing is no joke."

"Apparently not in this case."

Greer began walking around the bedroom, looking in corners, under the bed, inside the closet, for what, Sullivan wasn't sure. She suspected he didn't know, either. But he now knew, as she did, that there was more to be found.

"What else is your intuition telling you?"

The instant Greer asked that, Sullivan felt a chill so strong that it physically shook her. "It's telling me that this place is creepy as hell."

Greer blew out an audible sigh of relief. "Glad I'm not the only one who thought that."

"I felt it the minute we walked in."

"Same here. I didn't want to say anything, being the fearless badass that I am. But the air here is definitely strange."

Sullivan thought back to her canvassing of the building and the run-ins she had with various tenants.

Of the few who answered their doors, the only one who didn't set off her Spidey-senses in a major way was the woman in 605. Everyone else, including the older woman next door to her, seemed like they were cast right out of a David Lynch movie.

"What do you say we go help out the techs?" Sullivan suggested. "The sooner we can find what we're supposed to find, the sooner we can wrap this up and get the hell out of Dodge."

"Right behind you, sport."

As she rejoined the team in the living room, Sullivan's finely honed intuition communicated one last bit of unfortunate news: she wouldn't be finished with this place anytime soon.

# Chapter Ten

For the second time in three nights, Fiona had barely slept. No great shock, considering the harrowing events of the last twenty-four hours, but that didn't make her exhaustion any less debilitating.

She had spent much of the morning attempting to make sense of her bizarre conversation with Iris.

When that wasn't successful, she turned her attention to Olivia's bedroom. It had been quiet for the remainder of the night and into the morning. And only now, as she got dressed in the hope of making something useful out of the day, did she hear proof that someone was alive in the apartment: the muted sound of an expletive-filled reality television show.

*Why doesn't that surprise me?*

After getting dressed, Fiona consulted the Denver Central Committee of Alcoholics Anonymous directory for the nearest meeting location.

Having several options, she chose the *Sunrise Serenity* group. She had nothing to go on but the name in making her decision, but the idea of finding a bit of serenity some-where definitely had its appeal, even if that somewhere was a smoky room filled with fellow lost souls confessing their various sins.

Of all the awful things that happened last night, her near-miss with the bottle was the worst. She may have come a long way in her sobriety, but she still needed help maintaining it, and if last night were any indication, she always would. Attending a meeting would be her first step in admitting that.

Before Fiona left her bedroom, she put an ear to the wall and listened.

Aside from the television, the apartment was quiet.

Fueled by an unexplainable compulsion, she tapped on the wall and whispered. "Olivia? Are you there?"

It was 11:38 in the morning, which meant that the girl should have been in school. But that didn't stop Fiona from calling out again.

"Olivia? If you're there, can you say something?"

She heard nothing but the television, as the volume suddenly and inexplicably grew louder.

"That's it, time to get out of this psycho ward."

---

Fiona tiptoed past Olivia's apartment then made her way to the elevator. Once she rounded the corner, apartment 612 would be in sight.

Her mind shuddered at the idea that something as awful as a murder could have occurred so close to her, and she readied herself for the possible torrent of emotions that would hit her should there be any signs of it.

The only thing she saw as she came upon the apartment was a yellow strip of tape across the closed door. She had assumed that the words on it read *Crime Scene*, but she didn't want to look close enough to find out for sure.

Fiona kept her head down until the elevator arrived. The doors were barely opened when she pushed her way inside. She was in such a hurry that she hadn't noticed the man exiting the cab until her shoulder collided with his.

"Oh, my God, I'm so sorry," Fiona cried as she grabbed the small man by the arm to stop him from tumbling over. "I didn't see you. Are you okay?"

"Yes, I'm fine." The man's gruff voice betrayed his light, friendly face. "No one told me there was a fire on this floor."

Fiona's face turned red with embarrassment. "There isn't. I just need to watch where I'm going. Are you sure you're okay?"

"I'm fine. One hell of a hip-check you've got there, young lady. The Red Wings could use a bruiser like you." The man tugged at his thick gray beard as he smiled. "Not a whisker out of place."

"That's a relief."

His emerald-green eyes suddenly lit up with recognition. "You're the new tenant in 605, right?"

Fiona couldn't hide her surprise. She wasn't aware that anyone here even knew she existed. "Yes, I am. Fiona Graves."

"Ah, yes. Fiona. I've been meaning to stop by to introduce myself. I'm Arthur Finley, the facilities manager."

"So, you're the guy I need to call to fix that stubborn bedroom window that puts up a fight every time I try to close it."

"There's always something that needs fixing around

here, so I'm afraid you'll have to take a number. But I'm definitely your guy."

"Good to know." Fiona extended her hand. "Nice to meet you, Mr. Finley."

"Please, call me Art. And it's nice to meet you, too." His bright face took on a solemn expression as he looked over Fiona's shoulder. "I guess you heard about that business last night."

"A detective came by my apartment, asking questions. She didn't share much, but I got the feeling it was pretty bad."

Arthur nodded. "Yeah, pretty bad."

"What do you know about it?"

He took one more look at 612. "Were you headed down?"

"Yes."

"I was on my way to check on a faucet leak in 601, but if it's okay, I think I'll head down with you."

"Of course."

When Fiona stepped onto the elevator, Arthur followed. "First floor?" he asked before pressing the button.

"Please."

Arthur didn't speak until the elevator doors closed. "I've been talking to Phillip Barlow, the building superintendent. The police told him that Donald had been dead for at least twelve hours. Mr. Barlow was the one who found him, and the only reason he did was because another tenant complained that Donald's television was too loud. It probably would have been me who opened that door, but I stayed the night at my son's place. He's getting married in a couple of days, and his rehearsal dinner was last night."

"That's wonderful," Fiona offered with a smile, though it felt awkward under the circumstances.

"Thank you. I couldn't have been more relieved that I wasn't here, to be honest. I don't know how I would've reacted had I been the one to find him."

"Did you know Donald well?"

"I considered him a friend. He and I talked nearly every day. We'd go out for beers, catch an occasional Rockies game, sometimes a movie. He was a really good man, and I enjoyed spending time with him."

"I'm so sorry for your loss."

Arthur's face contorted as he struggled to fight back emotion. "It's just not right, what they're saying about him."

"What are they saying?"

"That he committed suicide."

A loud ding filled the elevator as it reached the first floor. The doors opened, but the two of them remained inside.

"I've known that man for well over fifteen years. He wasn't depressed, he wasn't upset, and he sure as hell wasn't suicidal. He had some financial trouble, but who doesn't in this economy? He wouldn't kill himself over that. He wouldn't kill himself period."

"But the police think he did?"

"I don't think they know anything."

Iris had told her the exact same thing. Fiona didn't want to believe it then, but it was more difficult to dismiss now.

"So, what do you think happened?"

Arthur met her question with silence. It was clear that he had an answer, he just didn't appear willing to share it.

After a few seconds, Fiona finally said, "I know it's a difficult time for you."

"It's a difficult time for everyone here. I'm just sorry this is your first Corona Heights experience. You seem like a sweet person."

Fiona's lips quivered as she attempted a smile. After a glance at her watch, she said, "I'd love to chat more, but I should probably get going. I have a meeting to attend, and it's not the kind you want to be late for."

Arthur's face softened. "Of course. I apologize for holding you up. Hopefully, you don't take this old man's babbling too seriously. The police are doing their job, and I need to have faith that they'll figure this out. For my own sanity, I need to believe that."

"They'll figure it out," Fiona offered as she put a hand on Arthur's shoulder. "I don't think your faith is misguided."

"Thank you."

Fiona stepped out of the elevator. "I'll see you around, Art."

"See you around. I'll let you know when I'm available to look at that window."

"Sounds good."

Fiona was near the front door when the sound of Arthur's voice stopped her.

"Hey, wait a second. You live next door to Iris Matheson, right?"

"That's right."

"Have you met her yet?"

"She and I had coffee early this morning, actually."

A look of quiet amusement came over Arthur's face as he approached her. "What a character she is, huh? I don't know what your experience has been so far, but just know that she's ultimately harmless. Iris's problem is that she lets her overactive imagination get in the way of her good sense. Spend enough time with her, and she'll have you believing that this building is crawling with witches and warlocks and every manner of supernatural evil that your nightmares can conjure up."

Fiona's hand instinctively went to the amulet hanging around her neck, ignoring the fact that the purple stone suddenly felt warm to the touch.

Arthur continued. "She's tried to spin her yarn on me a few times, even called me this morning to go on about what she thinks happened to Donald. When she gets like that, I deal with her the same way I suggest you deal with her should you find yourself in a similar situation: calmly, politely, and without an ounce of disbelief in your voice. As I said, she's harmless, but she's also passionate about her beliefs. And people who are passionate about that kind of stuff can never be underestimated. Piss her off enough, and she may think that you're one of those supernatural evils. God only knows what she's capable of then. Just a friendly word of caution."

"I'll keep that in mind." Fiona tried to move toward the door but her feet felt stuck to the floor.

"Sorry, I'm holding you up again," Arthur said with a wide smile. "You run along now. Don't be late for your meeting on account of me."

Only after Arthur said that did Fiona's legs come back to life. She practically galloped as she made her way out of the building.

The fresh air felt like new life.

All she wanted to focus on was the task that brought her here in the first place. But with each hour that she spent in the presence of this increasingly strange collection of people, the new life with her son that once held the promise of being a foregone conclusion now seemed further and further away.

## Chapter Eleven

The *Sunrise Serenity* group met in the back storeroom of what was once a shipping warehouse. The story of the building's origins was told for the benefit of the newcomers, as it probably was before every meeting. But beyond the tidbit that the space was once home to the country's largest manufacturer of number 2 pencils, Fiona didn't pay much attention to the presentation.

She was plenty attentive when it came time for testimonials. As had happened in every AA meeting the world over, attendees began with their first name, followed by those famous four words that some people spend a lifetime building up the courage to say in public.

When Fiona was called upon to say those words aloud for the first time eighteen months ago, she sat in the circle for well over an hour, listening to stories of triumph and tragedy, relapse and recovery, before finally summoning the will to speak up.

*My name is Fiona, and I'm an alcoholic.*

Today there was no hesitation in her announcement.

More than anything, she felt relief that she could finally rid herself of the unattainable perfection that came with telling the world that she was clean and sober and never looking back.

She had spent the last painfully long year trying to convince everyone—from Kirk to the courts to her lawyers to herself—that perfection through sobriety was not only attainable but sustainable. After last night, she knew it was neither.

"The biggest mistake I made," she told the attentive group of twelve, "was trying to convince myself that being perfect was the only available route back into my son's life. I'd had so many missteps in the past that I felt like I didn't have an ounce of room to screw up, and I white-knuckled my way through life for a long time believing that. Unfortunately, it caught up with me last night. I almost screwed up big time, and it could have cost me everything."

"What I got from that experience, aside from a hard kick in the ass, was the gift of total self-awareness. For better or worse, this is who I am. I've struggled with alcohol my entire adult life, and I'll struggle with it for the rest of my life. I'm not perfect because I haven't had a drink in 312 days. I'm perfect because no matter what happens, no matter how many times I slip up, I'm willing to fight. I'm perfect because I haven't had a drink today. But tomorrow, the battle starts all over again. Having the courage to face that battle day after day is all the perfection I'll ever need."

Fiona felt a rush of adrenaline at the sound of applause. The feeling stayed with her for the entire session, long after the last recovery story had been told, long after the last sobriety coin had been handed out.

The group had indeed lived up to its name. Fiona felt a

true sense of serenity for the first time that she could remember.

Just as the meeting was wrapping up, someone new walked in.

Aside from the overgrown beard that was so inexplicably popular with men these days, he was nondescript. His wardrobe was basic: white T-shirt, blue jeans, and black work boots. But his energy immediately changed the air in the room.

It wasn't a change for the better.

"Looks like I'm a tad bit late," he said as he surveyed the group. Fiona was quick to avert her eyes when he found her.

"You're never too late," Melinda, the group leader, said with a welcoming smile. "There's a seat right over there. Join us."

The man nodded and made his way to the empty chair across from Fiona. Based on the quiet acknowledgment from the others in the group, she'd guessed that he was a regular. Still, he didn't look the least bit comfortable being there.

He said nothing as he sat down. After it became apparent that he wasn't going to speak up on his own, Melinda intervened. "No need to be nervous. Just jump in whenever you're ready."

The man shifted in his seat, anxious hands clinging to his thighs. The haze in his eyes told Fiona that he'd been drinking, but she pushed the judgment aside.

"Okay, well, I guess I should know the drill by now, huh, guys?" He spoke in a slow, thick drawl that all but confirmed Fiona's suspicions. The smattering of nervous laughter from the group told her that others had suspected it too. "So here goes. My name is Noah, and I am…I am a certified alcoholic."

*"Hi, Noah,"* the group buzzed in unison.

But Fiona didn't say a word. Her body was frozen; her mind was screaming.

*It couldn't be. It couldn't possibly be.*

"Unfortunately, I've had a few rough turns since the last meeting," he continued. "The fights with my girlfriend, they've…Let's just say they've escalated." He paused to reflect. "They always do this time of year."

"What is it about this time of year specifically?" Melinda asked.

Noah hesitated. "Stuff with her daughter, but it's not worth getting into here. It's been wearing on me, though. I can tell you that for sure. I get so frustrated with her. My temper flares up–another thing I'm working on. Next thing you know, Natalie and I are in a shouting match, and my first instinct is to run out and find something to drink."

Fiona's heart sank. *My God, it is him.* She fought the urge to excuse herself from the group, fearing the attention it would bring. Yet the voice in her head wouldn't stop protesting. *Why in the hell are you still sitting here? Get up and leave before he recognizes you!*

"I hate that I haven't gotten this under control yet," Noah continued. "As many of these meetings as I've been to, you'd think I'd have a better grip on it by now."

"Don't beat yourself up, man," one of the group members offered. "None of us got this thing licked yet."

The group voiced its agreement while Fiona stayed silent, careful to conceal the horror that flooded her being.

Noah's face softened enough to allow a half smile. "I really appreciate the love. Seriously. I don't have much in the way of family, except for Natalie. You guys come pretty damn close. I've been meaning to say that for a while."

"I think I speak for all of us when I say that the feeling is mutual," Melinda replied.

The warm exchange, genuine as it may have been, did nothing to ease Fiona's anxiety.

As Noah continued a testimonial that highlighted the various ways in which he had failed to live up to the twelve steps since the last time Sunrise Serenity met, his eyes scanned each member of the group, searching for those who would most validate his struggle. Fiona knew this because she did the same thing when recounting hers.

She kept her stare focused on the floor in anticipation of the moment when he would look at her. When that moment finally came, she closed her eyes, hopeful that the darkness would quell the awful stirring in her chest. When she opened her eyes, the stirring was still there. When she glanced in Noah's direction, she knew why.

"As we've talked about in the past, having the ability to identify your triggers before you're set off will help keep them at bay once you do encounter them. What would you say are your most potent triggers, and how do you cope with them?"

Melinda's question was directed at Noah, but his eyes weren't on her as he pondered an answer.

"Judgment. Condescension. Those are the big ones. I also can't stand when people look at me with fear, like they're trying to make me out to be something that I'm not."

"Does that happen often?" Melinda asked.

"No. But when it does, it really pisses me off."

"Who looks at you with fear?"

Only when Melinda asked this question did Noah break eye contact with Fiona.

"My girlfriend, mostly."

"Is it ever warranted?"

Silence, as Noah considered his answer. The instant he looked up, Fiona's eyes fell to the floor again.

"Maybe when I drink. But I would never hurt her."

Fiona felt the weight of his glare again.

"I know the arguing sounds bad sometimes. We can get pretty loud, and I'm sure our neighbors think we're killing each other. But that's not the case. Natalie is the only good thing in my life, and I'm the only good thing in hers. We wouldn't hurt each other, not like that, anyway."

*The only good thing in her life? What about her daughter?* Fiona bit down on her tongue to prevent it from speaking her thoughts, but the anger on her face wasn't so easy to conceal. When she looked up, Noah looked away.

"So, what's more important to you, the conflicts that you have with your girlfriend or how you think others might perceive that conflict?" Melinda asked.

"They're both important. Yes, I know my actions matter, but when your neighbors look at you like you're some kind of walking disease every time you leave your apartment, when they complain to the manager every time you play your music above a whisper, or when they stand outside your door, listening, waiting to hear something that convinces them they need to call the cops, that shit matters, too, and I have to swallow it constantly. I'm over it."

"It sounds to me like much of your battle is internal, the same as it is for most of us," Melinda asserted. "Sometimes, our perceptions, whether they be of events, or people, or intentions, can completely cloud our judgment and adversely affect our reality. The key is to not project the feelings we have about ourselves onto other people. Doing so only exacerbates the negative self-image that we're convinced everyone else is responsible for creating. You're the only one responsible for that self-image."

At that last statement, Melinda looked directly at Fiona. "Don't judge other people as a means of deflecting judgment away from yourself."

Fiona allowed Melinda's words to settle in, and for a moment, she let herself believe that they had been properly directed at her. Then she thought about the music, and the constant yelling, and the frightened little girl whose well-being had seemingly never once been considered, and the guilt went away.

"Is there anything else you'd like to share before we end the meeting?" Melinda asked, turning her attention back to Noah.

He swallowed hard before answering; the first sign of vulnerability that Fiona had detected in him. "I guess I should address something that some of you may have been wondering about since I walked in. I did have a drink last night. Okay, I had a few. I feel like shit about it. I know I failed myself, and I failed you guys, too."

Murmurs of encouragement poured in from the group.

"You didn't fail, Noah. You showed up here, ready to start over. The way I see it, that's a victory."

Melinda's statement brought back Noah's half smile, though nothing about it felt genuine to Fiona.

The entire episode was little more than a sympathy grab, a way to ease the guilt over what he did and what he most likely planned to do once he left the meeting.

Fiona remembered Melinda's cautionary words about judgment, but she could also see right through Noah. She knew what kind of man he was before she ever laid eyes on him, and nothing that she witnessed from him now did anything to change that.

She only hoped that she could maintain the resolve to keep her mouth shut long enough to let the meeting end peacefully.

"I want you to take this with you," Melinda said to Noah as she reached into her pocket and pulled out a silver coin. "This one represents the new life that comes with your first full day of sobriety. It's the same one you received when you first came, but this one will have a brand-new date. Only you know when that date will come. When it does, bring the coin back, and I'll have it engraved for you." She held it out for him. "Deal?"

Noah hesitated before finally walking over to retrieve it, more theatrics that Fiona didn't buy for a second.

"Deal."

The sound of vigorous applause brought a merciful end to the meeting.

Before Noah's arrival, Fiona had envisioned the session concluding with grateful hugs and words of thanks to the other attendees, a few of whom she had seen as possible sponsor material.

But because of him, all she wanted to do now was leave the premises as quickly as she could, with the intention of finding a new AA group as far away from this one as possible.

Surely, the odds were not such that she could run into him in another group. Then again, she never would have imagined the odds being short enough to bring them together in this one.

So, Fiona made sure that she was the first one out of the building when the meeting ended, not allowing anyone the opportunity to corner her for conversation or even a thank-you.

She hadn't seen Noah as she scurried out, but she assumed that she'd had a healthy head start on him.

Fiona could hear the chatter of other group members behind her as she crossed the parking lot, but she had no desire to turn around long enough to identify them.

She felt relieved as she reached her car.

*Home free.*

Sure, it got a little bit hairy at the end with the unbelievably random appearance of the hellion that had helped make her stay at Corona Heights an unmitigated disaster, but she lived through it, and when she eventually looked back at the experience, there would be more positive than negative.

There was more chatter as she unlocked her car. Closer now. She again refused to look back.

As she reached out to grab the door handle, she heard her name. Ignoring it, Fiona opened the door. She had one foot inside the car when she heard her name again, this time directly behind her.

"Fiona, hold up a second."

It was Melinda.

"You've got to be kidding me." Fiona uttered the words quietly under her breath, but the irritation on her face as she turned around more than told the story.

"Oh, I'm sorry. Were you in a hurry?" Melinda said, clearly taken back by Fiona's expression. "If so, I understand. I just wanted to thank you for coming."

Irritation became anxiety as Fiona looked over Melinda's shoulder to see others from the group approaching cars that were parked near hers. "No, it's fine. I am in a bit of a rush, but I do appreciate what you did in there. It was really helpful."

A man waved to them as he got in the car parked next to Fiona's. "Have a good one, Melinda."

She answered with a warm smile. "You too, Darren. See you next Tuesday."

"I'll be here." Then he cast a glance at Fiona. "Your story was very inspiring. Thank you for sharing. Good luck with your son."

Fiona wanted to feel the gratitude that this moment should have brought, but she was preoccupied with what she saw as she looked over Melinda's shoulder a second time.

Noah stood outside his oversize truck, chatting idly with a woman from the group. The instant Fiona spotted him, he looked back, his face expressionless, his body completely still, as the woman beside him kept talking.

"Thank you for the kind words," Fiona said absently as the man parked beside her got into his car. "Good luck to you too."

He waved and drove away.

Melinda promptly reengaged Fiona. "We'll be meeting again at the same time next week. You're a wonderful addition to our group, and I would love to hear more of your story. I've gone through something very similar."

With that, she finally commanded Fiona's full attention. "You have?"

"Yes. Five years ago, my two children were taken from me by Child Welfare and put in a foster home. I'd been a heavy cocaine user for most of my adult life, getting clean just long enough to deliver healthy children. But once it truly got hold of me, nothing else mattered, not even my girls. I always say that it takes an act of God to get someone clean who's been using for a long time. My act of God came in the form of men with badges barging into my home and leaving with my children. I was never the same after that. It took a long time and a lot of work, but my girls are with me now. You'll never do anything more important than what you're doing right now. I know how hard the journey can be. But I also know it will end well for you and your son."

Tears were streaming down Fiona's cheeks before she had the chance to stop them. For a moment, her anxiety went away. Her desire to forget about Sunrise Serenity and everyone in it went away. For a moment, she felt strong, she felt whole, and she felt assurance that the fight would be won. Most of all, she felt gratitude.

"I appreciate your confidence, Melinda. I'm not a natural at this happy ending stuff."

"It's the truth."

The two women concluded their conversation with a tight embrace. To Fiona's surprise, it felt like the most natural ending in the world.

When she finally let go, she was certain of one thing: there would be no leaving Sunrise Serenity.

"See you next Tuesday," Fiona said, meaning it.

"See you then."

She watched as Melinda walked back to her car, not noticing until she got inside her own that Noah's truck was no longer in its parking spot.

She quickly scanned the rest of the street and the surrounding street. Much to her relief, there was no sign of him.

*Dodged your second bullet,* she thought as she blew out another deep sigh of relief, started her car, and drove away.

## Chapter Twelve

With most of the day still ahead of her, Fiona decided to capitalize on the success of her AA meeting by launching the next phase of *Operation Jacob*: the long-overdue job search.

Years ago, in what seemed like another existence entirely, Fiona had held a position on the editorial board of the *Seattle Times*. She was well respected in the city's journalism and media circles and was on the fast track to becoming the publication's youngest-ever managing editor.

From the beginning of her time at the paper, there were whispers about her issues with alcohol, but Fiona went out of her way to keep the depth of those issues hidden.

For the most part, she'd succeeded, until the day of her car accident and subsequent arrest. Then, in one terrifyingly dark moment, everything she had worked so hard for was gone.

Prior to her move here, she'd sent her résumé to a variety of local newspapers and online publications, including the *Denver Post*, the *Mile-High Dispatch*, and *5280 Magazine*.

When it became clear that none of them planned to respond, Fiona was saddled with the realization that finding gainful employment would require a broadening of her search to depths which she would have previously never considered.

And today, she planned to do just that, starting with the coffee shop three blocks from her apartment.

She'd first visited the City Perk Café the morning she signed her apartment lease. Coming from Seattle, she'd frequented more than her fair share of quaint, neighborhood coffee shops.

The City Perk certainly fit the bill, with its rustic bistro feel, homemade French pastries, and classical music soundtrack. The *Help Wanted* sign had caught her attention the moment she walked in, and she had considered asking for an application right then. But the prideful notion that the job was beneath her ultimately won out.

Today, she had a much different notion.

She was worried that the position had been filled in the four days since she'd seen the posting and braced for disappointment as she approached the café. She joyously exhaled when she saw that the posting was still there, taking it as a sign that her job search may have finally ended.

*Gotta start somewhere, kiddo.*

City Perk was largely empty of customers, save for the gruff-looking character in the back with a half-eaten Danish in one hand and a pencil in the other. The first time Fiona was in there, the man, who she assumed was a regular, grunted and groaned his way through a crossword puzzle for the entire time she sat next to him. Based on the gloomy bewilderment that flooded his face today, she'd guessed that he was undertaking the task again.

The girl behind the counter smiled brightly as Fiona approached.

"Hi there, welcome to City Perk."

The chipper redhead immediately walked up to the register, eager to help her new customer.

Chipper didn't come easy to Fiona, and she hoped that it wasn't a necessary function of the job. If so, her employment here would be brief.

"What sounds good today?" The girl's brightly lettered name tag said Norah.

Fiona dug deep but managed a smile equal to the barista's. "I'll take a large coffee, please."

"Sounds perfect. Anything else?"

"Yes, I noticed the job posting in your window. Is the position still available?"

"As a matter of fact, it is." She reached under the counter and pulled out an application. "Here you go. There's a pen right next to you."

"Thank you," Fiona said as she took the application. "When are you looking to hire?"

"Immediately. Do you have barista experience?"

"I was born and raised in Seattle, so…"

"Enough said," Norah replied with a knowing smile. "If you want to fill out the application now, go ahead and grab a seat and I'll bring over your coffee. It's on the house today."

Fiona nodded her thanks and took a seat at a nearby table.

She studied the application closely before filling it out, searching for *the* question. It was the sixth item down, right there in bold, black letters.

**HAVE YOU EVER BEEN CONVICTED OF A FELONY?**

She didn't have a choice but to answer the question truthfully, even though she knew it could be the deathblow to her chances of landing this, or any other position.

Yes.

**WHAT CRIME WERE YOU CONVICTED OF?**
Driving under the influence and child endangerment.

*Yeah, I'm sure Norah can't wait to have a coworker with that kind of stain on their record,* Fiona thought. *I bet the mere thought of it makes her want to turn cartwheels.*

Fiona hadn't worked steadily since the incident, choosing instead to go about the business of healing herself.

Absent a regular income, the only thing that kept her afloat was a once-sizable life insurance policy left behind after her mother's death, and a 401(k) that she was forced to cash out to help pay for her legal expenses.

She got nothing in the divorce settlement, aside from the assets she had acquired on her own. The house was in Kirk's name, so when he sold it, she received nothing. Not that Fiona cared anything about his money. She only wanted what she believed to be rightfully hers: the title of fit mother.

When she completed the application, she walked to the counter where Norah was standing by.

"All finished?"

"All finished," Fiona replied with forced enthusiasm. "Should I expect to hear something soon?"

Norah gave the application a once-over before answering. "I'll pass this on to Brian, the owner, when he comes in this evening. I'm sure he'll get in touch quickly."

"Thanks, Norah. I appreciate your help."

"You're more than welcome," Norah paused to look at

the top of the application. "Fiona. If you want to hang out a little longer, I can get you a refill on that coffee."

She looked around the café. Not another soul in sight. She certainly welcomed the quiet after everything that had transpired in the past couple of days. "I'd love that."

When Fiona received her refilled mug and sat back down at her table, she took a moment to breathe in as much of the calm, comforting atmosphere as her chest would allow.

She imagined being in a place far from here; someplace warm, perhaps tropical, with sand stretching as far as her eye could see, and a sky as royally blue as the ocean waves below it.

There was no stress in this faraway place, no pain, regret, or lost time. It wasn't cold and remote like her new apartment had become. This place felt like home.

Kirk was there, the Kirk who still admired her more than anything else on the planet. Jacob was also there, the happy child who never spent more than a day away from his mother, always looking forward to seeing her, laughing with her, and eating her less-than-perfect meals. And never, ever, did this Jacob have to wonder if his mother would be there for him. Because in this place, she always had been.

This place had joy. This place had laughter, the kind that she hadn't heard in a very long time.

She could hear it in her mind now. It called to her, pointing the way to that warm, sandy, happy home in the sun where life existed as it always should have–that place so dismally far from here.

Thankfully, she'd found a way to get there, even if *there* was only a momentary pit stop in her mind.

*Follow the laughter.*

It continued to point the way, beckoning her to close

her eyes and trust that it would take her where she needed to go.

Fiona trusted.

She believed.

She let go.

When she closed her eyes, the laughter drew closer.

She was almost there now. All she needed was the courage to go forward.

Fiona was finally prepared to take her first step onto that warm, sunbaked sand, when the gentle chime of a bell suddenly brought her back.

She opened her eyes to the sight of someone walking through the café door. Straining to adjust to the sunlight, she could make out only a silhouette.

The first thing she saw when her vision finally returned was the thick black sole of his work boots, then the blue jeans that were rolled up to the top of the boots, then the bright orange dragon tattoo that stood out against the crisp white of his T-shirt.

The bearded face was the last part of Noah that she saw, but she didn't need to see his face to know who he was. The chill that tore through her body had already announced it.

As she had done at Fiona's arrival, the barista perked up when he approached. If she was as put off by Noah's presence as Fiona was, she didn't show it.

"Welcome to City Perk. What sounds good today?"

"I'll get a large coffee to go, same as always." The smile on Noah's face belied his joyless tone.

"Sounds perfect. Anything else?"

"Nope."

As Noah reached for his wallet, Fiona thought about getting up from the table as quietly as she could and slipping out the door, but her proximity to the counter made such a move impossible.

Her only hope was that Noah would take his coffee and walk out the door without noticing anything else around him.

Those hopes were dashed with the next words that the barista spoke.

"If you need cream, it's right behind you." She pointed over Noah's shoulder to the condiment station right next to Fiona.

When Noah turned around, his flat smile went away. "No, thanks. I take it black."

Fiona looked down at her phone as Noah approached, hoping that he would take it as a sign to keep walking.

"I recognize you."

She closed her eyes at the sound of his voice, offering yet another cue that she prayed he would take. It didn't work.

"From Sunrise Serenity. You were there, right?"

Resigned to her fate of no escape, Fiona opened her eyes and looked up at him. "Yes."

"I thought so. I popped in a little late, so I didn't get the chance to hear your story. You a first-timer?"

"No."

"Me neither, as you probably gathered from my testimonial. I had four months sober before last night. Crazy how those urges can sneak up on you, isn't it? Always hits when you least expect it."

The churning inside Fiona's stomach caused her to clutch it.

Noah, seeming oblivious to her discomfort, took another step toward the table. "Nothing I haven't dealt with before. I'll get my shit together one of these days." His joyless smile returned. Fiona had seen that same smile in herself. It was always designed to hide something. In Fiona's case, it was her pain. She wasn't sure what Noah was hiding, but it certainly didn't look like pain. "How long have you been sober?"

He asked the question loud enough to attract Norah's attention. She looked embarrassed to have overheard it and promptly found something to do in another area of the café. But in Fiona's mind, the damage had already been done. When she looked back at Noah, the anxiety in her eyes had been replaced with ire.

"Not to be rude, but I don't know you."

He appeared slightly taken aback by Fiona's shift in tone but quickly recovered. "I'm Noah."

"I'm sorry, Noah, but this isn't a conversation I really want to have right now."

"You got it all out in the group. I totally get it. I guess next time I shouldn't be late if I want to hear your story, huh?"

Fiona shrugged and looked down at her phone, hoping that her cavalier response would help facilitate his exit. When it became clear that it wouldn't, she looked up.

Noah wasn't smiling anymore.

"I get that you don't want to talk about the AA stuff. I don't like talking about how much I still want to drink, either. But don't act like you don't know who I am."

Fiona sat stone-faced, even as she could feel everything else in her body breaking down.

Noah continued. "Even if I hadn't recognized you the moment I walked into the meeting, which I did, your nervous eyes would've told me that you were someone I should recognize. If that was your poker face, it definitely needs work."

"I have no idea what you're talking about," Fiona declared without an ounce of resolve in her voice.

"Yes, you do."

As Noah moved closer, Fiona slid back in her chair. Her worst fears about her second night in Corona Heights were coming true. Noah did see her lingering outside his apartment. He'd even referenced it in the meeting, though she wanted to dismiss it at the time.

There would be no dismissing it now.

Still, she tried. "What are you talking about?"

"We share the same struggle. It's unique to a handful of people, so when you see it in someone else, you connect with them right away. I saw it in you, and I think you saw it in me, too."

"I'm sorry, but I still have no idea what that mean–"

Noah interrupted her by helping himself to a seat at the table.

"You don't mind, right?" he asked after he sat down. Unfazed by her silent response, Noah continued. "I don't think it's an accident that we're sitting together at this table right now. Just like it wasn't an accident that we saw each other at Sunrise Serenity." He leaned in closer. "Just like it's not an accident that you moved in next door to me." He moved even closer. "I really think we can help each other, Fiona."

"How do you know my name?"

"The building always buzzes when somebody new moves in. People talk. More than they need to most times. Our little Corona Heights is nothing if not active."

"You still haven't answered my question. How do you know my name?"

"The same way you know mine."

"I didn't know your name before the meeting."

"Don't lie. The walls told you. Just like they told me."

Fiona began to gather her things. "I don't know what you're talking about, but you're seriously creeping me out. If you don't want to leave, I will."

"There isn't a single word spoken in Corona Heights that those walls will protect. It doesn't matter if you yell or if you whisper. That bitch can't keep a secret to save her dark, twisted life."

"Okay, it looks like I'm the one leaving."

Noah spoke again before she could walk away.

"You heard my name when Natalie yelled it for the millionth goddamned time. I heard yours when you whispered it to Olivia."

Fiona shuddered as a violent wave of fear washed over her.

"I heard you talking to her. So did Natalie. Just like we hear you knocking on the walls. Why do you do that?"

"Because your loud music disturbs me." The words were forceful and bold in her head but fell apart as they came out of her mouth.

"Is that why you stood in front of our door? To tell us that our loud music was too loud? Because if that really was your intention, it occurs to me that you would've made your presence known. Instead, you just stood there, listening. What were you trying to hear?"

"I didn't…" Words completely failed her this time.

"You can see how something like that might be taken the wrong way, can't you? I mean, if I was lingering outside your front door, you would probably call the cops."

Fiona edged away from the table, neither willing nor able to engage Noah any further. "This is really awkward and uncomfortable, so I'm going to end it by apologizing for standing outside your door. Okay? I apologize."

"What about Olivia?"

"What about her?"

"Do you apologize for that?"

"Olivia initiated the conversation with me. I don't have anything to apologize for, and neither does she."

"Your conversation caused a major incident in our home last night."

"The things that happen in your home have nothing to do with me."

"Tell that to Natalie."

"What is that supposed to mean? I haven't done anything to Natalie. I've never even *seen* Natalie."

"Yet you talk to her daughter like the two of you are the best of friends, asking questions, getting her to say things that she has no business saying. Natalie is very protective of her family, as any decent mother should be. This world isn't always the safest place, especially for kids, and she goes out of her way to make sure that hers is safe."

"She wasn't unsafe talking to me."

"Natalie doesn't know that. If you walked in her shoes even for a minute, you would understand why she feels the way she does." Noah paused, allowing his smile to return. "But wait, you do understand, don't you? You feel it with your own son."

"How in the hell do you know about my son?"

"Like I told you, that bitch we call home can't keep a secret to save her life."

"I'm not going to stand here listening to this. I don't care who you are, or who your girlfriend is, or what you've heard when you've eavesdropped on my conversations. Just make sure this is the last time you and I speak, okay? Whenever you see me, whenever I see you, we keep it moving. Same goes for Natalie."

"Same goes for Olivia. Don't talk to her anymore."

Fiona had walked away from the table, but Noah's words brought her back. "And what if I do?"

"That girl has been told explicitly that she's never to talk to strangers. Ever. She knows it's for her own good. Yet, she does it anyway. So, she was punished. Do you want that to happen again? Do you want Natalie to come down on her even more than she already has?"

Fiona stared at him in silence, afraid to contemplate what he meant by punished.

"I didn't think so." With that, Noah stood up from the table. "I have to go back to work now, but I would sincerely like to end this on a positive note."

All Fiona wanted was for this man to disappear from the face of the earth in the fastest, harshest way possible. "After what you just said to me, how could you think that we could conclude with anything approaching positivity?"

"Because, like I told you, it's not an accident that we've come together like this. The struggle we share, it's real."

"What struggle?"

"The struggle to maintain a sense of sanity in the insanity that defines our lives. The struggle to trust our eyes when the things they show us constantly defy explanation. The struggle to not give in and say 'fuck it' the moment the slightest thing goes wrong, which is almost impossible because shit goes wrong all the time. I was there when you walked inside that liquor store last night. I watched you hesitate before picking up that bottle of whiskey. I recognized the relief on your face when you finally made the decision to take it. I stood behind you while you paid for it, watching your hands shake like crazy as you signed the receipt. I completely understood you, and I understood why you couldn't bring yourself to knock on our door. You couldn't trust the words that would come out of your mouth. Most of us who share the struggle feel the same way, especially when we're on the edge of disaster like you were."

"Wait, you were *following* me?" Fiona's anger now brewed beyond the brim, her voice close to a shout, her arms locked straight at her sides, fists clenched.

The barista stopped her busywork in the corner and looked up at them, her eyes widening, her mouth slightly open as her own breathing quickened. She backed up as she reached behind her for her cell phone—just in case.

Noah appeared unfazed. "I had no business walking into that liquor store. But I felt sorry for you." He laughed at Fiona with dead eyes. "Look what it got me." He held up the silver AA chip that indicated his first day of sobriety.

"*You* felt sorry for me? Fuck you!"

A faraway look fell across Noah's face, and his eyes slightly lost focus as his voice fell an octave, down into a nearly dreamlike tone. "The significance of that encounter didn't truly dawn on me until I saw you this morning. Then I knew that you were here to help me; that we were here to help each other."

His bizarre turn unsettled Fiona even more. "I have no desire to help you. Nor do I need your help. What I need is for you to leave me the hell alone."

Something came over Noah that looked like profound disappointment. He quickly shook it off. "Whether you realize it now or not, you'll need my help at some point. I promise you that. When that time comes, sadly, I may not be so willing."

Having finally heard enough, Fiona walked to the door. "Have a wonderful day."

"Just so you know, I don't control anything that Natalie

says or thinks. Once she's made up her mind about some-thing, there's no changing it. She's already made up her mind about you. I'd like to be able to change it for her, but since you don't need my help, maybe you can do that yourself."

"I don't really care what Natalie thinks about me."

"But you care what Olivia thinks, right?"

Fiona's lingering silence answered the question.

"And therein lies the problem. You've made yourself perfectly clear in not wanting my help, but I'm going to offer it one last time in the form of a friendly warning. Don't talk to Olivia anymore. For your sake, for her sake, hell, for my sake. I'm the one who has to feel that woman's wrath. If you don't want to be in the same boat, I suggest you focus on your own goddamned child."

Without saying another word, Fiona walked out the door and to her car, barely making it before the dam of pent-up emotion burst wide open.

Through the haze of angry tears, she saw Noah walk out of the café. He briefly paused to scan the street, presumably in search of her, before climbing into his truck and peeling off.

All she could think about as she made her way home was Olivia. What was once a passing curiosity about the girl's life had suddenly morphed into a preternatural desire to protect it.

## Chapter Thirteen

Once she was back inside her apartment, Fiona headed straight for the bedroom. It was 4:30 in the afternoon, so it was safe to assume that Olivia was now home, assuming she had been at school in the first place. Given the apparent instability of her home situation, Fiona put her odds of regular attendance at less than fifty-fifty.

She had the idea to knock on the wall and call out to her right away but thought it best to listen first. If there were obvious signs that the girl was in her bedroom, then Fiona could go about making contact. The last thing she wanted was to make a bad situation even worse.

Fiona had already felt a twinge of guilt for her role in the situation that led to Olivia's punishment (whatever that was), even though it made no rational sense for her to feel that way. Of course, nothing about the current state of her life made rational sense, so that probably wasn't the best criteria on which to judge.

Just as she'd done when she woke up this morning, Fiona put her ear to the wall, held her breath, and listened. Unlike this morning, there was no offensive reality television show blaring in the background. In fact, there was no noise beyond the low hum of the central heating unit.

After a few moments, Fiona ignored her better judgment and tapped on the wall; loud enough to be heard by Olivia, but quiet enough not to disturb anyone else. With no response on the other side, she tapped slightly harder.

This time she heard something. A light shuffling of feet, perhaps? She dismissed the wishful notion when the fluttering ended almost as suddenly as it began.

"Olivia?" The name was spoken no louder than a whisper, but against the stillness of her bedroom, it sounded very loud. "I just want to know that you're okay. If you don't feel comfortable talking, I understand. Just give me a sign that you can hear me."

Fiona held her breath in anticipation of Olivia's answer. When it didn't come, she released a frustrated sigh and walked out of the bedroom.

Perhaps she would try again. Perhaps she would do the right thing and leave it alone altogether. Perhaps she would break her promise to Iris and move out of Corona Heights before anyone could figure out that she was gone.

That was the ideal scenario, of course, but Fiona could afford neither the potential fee nor the additional blight on her credit score that breaking the lease would result in, so it was also the least likely.

She entered the kitchen to the sound of her cell phone ringing. When she looked at the caller ID and saw that it was Paul Riley, she allowed the call to go to voicemail, then walked to the refrigerator. Before she could open her bottle of water, the phone began ringing a second time. Paul Riley again. Fiona was hard pressed to ignore the call twice.

"Hello?"

Fiona heard nothing on the other end of the line.

"Hello? Paul, are you there?"

Static, followed by dead air, followed by the sound of Paul's voice. By the time she heard it, he was in mid-conversation. "It's entirely up to you, of course. But I think he actually sounded sincere."

"Paul, slow down. I didn't hear anything you said. Your connection is terrible."

More static as Paul spoke. "It shouldn't be. I'm on the landline in my office."

"It's still really hard hearing you. Why don't you call me back?"

"Okay, I'll use a different line."

Paul disconnected. He called back a few seconds later.

"How–'his?" is what Fiona heard when she answered. "An–'etter?"

"It's actually worse now."

More static, then Paul's voice disappeared altogether. A loud ding informed Fiona that the call had been disconnected. When she looked at her phone, she saw NO SERVICE where her four signal bars should have been.

"Oh, God. Please don't tell me I forgot to pay the bill."

After turning the phone off and on several times, she could only manage one bar of service. It was enough to allow Paul's call to come through.

"If I didn't know any better, I'd think you were trying to avoid me," he said from a place that sounded very far away.

"It's not me. It's my phone. I'm not getting a signal in here."

"Well, I'd better be…before I lose…again. I got an… call from—"

"Paul, you're still cutting out," Fiona said as she furiously paced her apartment in search of a spot that would allow a signal to come through. She couldn't find one that gave her more than a single bar.

"I said I…call from Kirk."

Fiona stopped pacing. "Kirk called you?"

"Well…lawyer did, but he…to deliver a message…Kirk."

"Hold that thought," she said as she raced out of her apartment into the hallway. Two bars. "Can you hear me better?"

"Barely," Paul responded from that same faraway place.

Fiona continued down the hall, past 607. Back to one bar. "Still there?"

A garbled response.

She turned down the hall toward apartment 612 and the waiting elevator. She tried to ignore the yellow tape across the apartment door as she walked past it. When she stepped onto the elevator, she lost the signal completely.

*Shit.*

As she stepped onto the first floor, one bar returned. When she made it to the entry door, there were two. It wasn't until she walked outside, past the parking lot, to the back of the apartment building, that the full strength of her signal finally returned.

She immediately redialed Paul's number. He answered after the first ring. "I didn't realize that phone tag was still a thing. But apparently, it is. So, you're it."

Fiona felt relief at the sound of Paul's full, clear voice. "Sorry about that. I couldn't get a signal in my apartment at all. I'm actually standing outside." She took a second to look up at the building. She spotted her east-facing apartment six floors up. Hers appeared to be the only unit with the blinds opened. Even Iris's were shut tight. This meant one of two things: Either no one wanted to be seen, or no one wanted to see the world beyond their window. Either way, the sight gave Fiona the chills.

The sound of Paul's voice refocused her attention. "Are you still there?"

"Yes, I am. You mentioned something about Kirk?"

"Right. I received a call from his lawyer today."

Fiona's stomach tightened as she braced for the bad news. "And?"

"Kirk wants to meet with you, one on one."

She nearly dropped the phone. "What?"

"Apparently, he felt bad about the way your last meeting ended. He wanted to reach out to you personally, but his lawyer advised against it. Can't say I blame him."

"Why does he want to meet with me now?"

"He didn't provide his lawyer with many specifics, only that he wanted to have a personal conversation."

A million thoughts entered Fiona's head at once. *Why the sudden change of heart? What was his angle?* He'd made his feelings abundantly clear during their first meeting. Did he want to rub even more salt in the wound? Perhaps. But she also allowed for other possibilities. Maybe he genuinely felt bad about his actions. Maybe Jacob told him how much he wanted her back. Maybe, just maybe, there was a part of Kirk that still loved her, and he'd finally allowed that part of himself space to breathe.

More wishful thinking. Fiona had already fallen into that trap once. She wasn't going to fall into it again.

"I gave him the chance to be civil. He chose another

route, and that's fine. I'm over it. Right now, my focus is on me. I don't need him for anything."

Paul took a moment to process her words. "Don't you at least want to hear him out?"

"I heard him, Paul. Loud and clear. He can apologize until he's blue in the face if that's even his intention. But he can't undo the damage he caused between us." Despite the emphatic tone of her words, Fiona didn't believe them. But the pain in her heart wouldn't allow her to admit it.

"So, should I inform his lawyer that going forward, all communication between you and Kirk should be strictly through your lawyers?"

"Yes."

"Okay. If that's how you truly feel, I'll call Michael after we're finished."

"Thank you." Fiona began pacing around the children's play area, ducking under the slide, pushing past the rusted swing set, increasing her pace with each step. No matter how fast she walked, she couldn't outrun the feeling that she was making a terrible mistake. Still, she pressed on. "What's next for us?"

"I think we should meet soon to recalibrate our game plan. Any new developments on your end?"

"I went to an AA meeting this morning and may have found a sponsor. It's too early to know for sure, though. I also applied for a job."

"Excellent. Sounds like we'll have a lot to discuss. Let's plan to meet in the next couple of days. I'll check my calendar and get back to you."

"Sounds good." Tired of pacing, Fiona sat down on the edge of the slide. She looked up at the open window of her apartment, suddenly wishing she didn't have to go back inside.

She sat on the slide for a few moments after the call ended.

As she looked around the lot, she saw nothing that impressed her. Thin patches of brown grass surrounded by dirt, an overflowing trash dumpster that was likely home to the neighborhood's wildlife, and several cars that looked too beat-up to be drivable.

This Crown Jewel of Downtown Urban Living was nothing more than a wasteland of abandonment and decay. It was no wonder that she hardly ever saw any of the other tenants; they were probably ashamed to even be associated with this place.

The more time she spent here, the more she understood the sentiment.

When she stood up to go back inside, she looked at the building again. For a moment, her eyes struggled to find the open window of her apartment, even though she was sure she was looking in the right place. She counted from the bottom of the building, six floors up, until she found the window that should have been hers.

But it couldn't have been her window, because the blinds were closed.

Blinking away what must have been a hallucination, she closed her eyes and looked up again.

She found her open window. It was exactly where it was supposed to be, in the same spot she had looked in ten seconds earlier.

*Mind tricks, Fiona. Nothing more.*

What she saw next wasn't so easy to dismiss.

The window next to hers was now open. And in it, as visible as the junked-out cars in the lot underneath it, was the figure of a small child.

Worried that her mind tricks were still at play, Fiona

shook her head to loosen the cobwebs before looking up again.

The child was still there, this time with her hand raised as if she were waving.

Fiona looked around but saw no one else in the lot where she stood. When she looked to the window again, the girl's hand was pressed against the glass, and there was no doubt in Fiona's mind that she was looking at her.

*Olivia* was her first thought, even though the distance didn't allow her to make out any of the girl's features beyond the eyeglasses on her face and the pigtails in her short, dark hair.

Fiona moved toward the building in hopes of getting a better view. She didn't know what Olivia looked like, so there was no way to compare her to the girl she was looking at. She only had the feeling in her gut to go by.

When Fiona raised her hand to wave, the girl responded in kind. As she moved closer, she realized that the girl was smiling. Warmth filled her chest as she smiled back.

Fiona kept walking until she reached the building. Once there, the girl waved one more time, then slowly moved away from the window until she was gone. Fiona stood still in anticipation of her return. When it became clear that she wasn't coming back, Fiona made her way to the front of the building, walked through the empty first floor, and onto the empty elevator, where she landed in the empty sixth-floor hallway.

The first thing she noticed when she exited was that the yellow tape had been removed from apartment 612. She'd guessed this was because the police were now working inside, but the door itself was closed, and she didn't notice police activity anywhere else on the grounds. She lingered in front of the door just long enough to give herself a major case of the creeps before finally moving on.

She had considered the very risky move of stopping in front of 607 on the chance that she could hear any signs of Olivia to go along with the presence in the window. But as she approached, it wasn't apartment 607 that got her attention.

It was her own.

## Chapter Fourteen

Fiona had left in a hurry, her mind focused solely on her cell phone, and it was entirely plausible that she left without closing the door. But as someone with an obsessive-compulsive disorder that sometimes required her to check a door or window multiple times before she felt safe, such a scenario, no matter how distracted she had become, was highly unlikely.

The front door was ajar about four or five inches. She thought there could have been an object on the floor, like a bunched-up mat, that would have prevented her from closing it, something that her hurried state would not have allowed her the time to notice. But she saw no such obstruction when she looked down.

Even though the open door was most likely her own doing, Fiona still hesitated. She pushed the door open a few inches, waited to make sure that nothing stirred, then pushed it open a few more. After a long moment of waiting, she took her first tentative step inside.

*Stop being such a wimp. There's no one in here.*

The declaration wasn't enough to stop an image of Noah—that soulless smile on his face—from flashing in her mind. In the most nightmarish of all scenarios, he was standing in her kitchen (or worse yet, in her bedroom), his hands prepared to carry out the threat that his eyes so subtly communicated.

She pushed the image out of her head as she walked inside, tensing her body for anything.

With each step she took through the apartment, though, the tension subsided. As far as she could see, nothing was out of place, nor did the air feel different, as could happen when there is a foreign presence somewhere beyond the eye's ability to see.

By the time Fiona had concluded her walk-through with trips to the bathroom, her bedroom, and the linen closet, she'd relaxed completely. Whatever had occurred with the door was a fluke, plain and simple, and she felt foolish for thinking otherwise.

She reached for the amulet, clutching it with a tight grip that she hoped would make the transfer of its energy into her weary spirit much smoother.

*Whenever you're ready to rid me of those demons, you go right ahead.*

The soothing warmth of the stone wasn't enough to convince her that such an exorcism was imminent, but it was enough to calm her nerves.

She sat down on the bed to relieve the aching in her feet. It felt like she'd been on them nonstop since moving here, and most of that time had been spent pacing for one reason or another. She struggled to remember what a restful night's sleep felt like. It had been weeks, and she was seriously contemplating a trip to the grocery store for a bottle of Tylenol PM. Anything stronger would mean certain death for her sobriety. Even something as tame as an over-the-counter pain pill brought risk. But at this point in her chronically sleep-deprived state, she was willing to take the chance.

She had thoroughly massaged the knot out of one of her feet and was preparing to dig in to the second when she heard it.

"Hey."

It was a single word spoken in a hurried whisper, loud enough for Fiona to notice, distant enough to know that it came from the apartment adjacent to hers.

Olivia.

"I heard you earlier. Are you still there?"

Fiona rose off the bed and approached the wall. "I'm still here. How are you?"

"I'm okay, I guess."

The brightness in her tone brought a smile to Fiona's face.

"Did you have a good day at school?"

Olivia hesitated before answering, and Fiona wondered if she'd heard the question consistently enough to even know how to answer it.

"School is school. It doesn't really change."

"That's very true. It probably hasn't changed much since I was there, either."

"When would that have been?"

"The olden days."

"You mean when the world was black and white?"

Fiona laughed aloud for the first time that she could remember. "Nope. By then, the world was full Technicolor."

"What's Technicolor?"

*Jesus, maybe I am old.* "Never mind."

Apparently willing to let the query go, Olivia quickly changed subjects. "Have you seen all the police around here?"

Fiona thought about lying but decided instead to downplay the situation. "I have, but I don't think it's a big deal. The police come around sometimes when they want people to feel safe."

"That's not true. They were here because Donald Tisdale died."

Fiona didn't respond.

"It's nice that the police want people to feel safe," Olivia continued, "but I don't think that's possible after what happened to him."

"You know what happened to Donald Tisdale?" a stunned Fiona asked.

Hesitation, then: "Yes."

"Can you tell me?"

"No."

"Why not?"

"My mom says I shouldn't talk about things that I don't know about. She says that's called gossip, and she hates gossip."

"This isn't gossip, honey. Something terrible happened, and the police need to know why. If you know something about a bad thing that happened, telling someone, especially the police, is the right thing to do. Have you or your mom talked to them yet?"

"We heard them in the hallway last night. They knocked on our door a bunch of times, but Noah didn't let my mom answer."

*Fucking Noah.* Fiona had had just about enough of that overgrown bully and resolved right then and there not to tread lightly the next time she saw him. Men like him thrived on inspiring fear in people whom they considered weaker than themselves; in this case, Natalie, Olivia, and now Fiona. He wasn't going to frighten her anymore, and if she had anything to say about it, he wasn't going to frighten Olivia, either.

"You shouldn't listen to anything that Noah says, and neither should your mom. If he cared at all about you, he wouldn't talk the way he does."

"I know he doesn't care about me," a solemn Olivia answered. "But I can't do anything about it. I tried running away last year when I was nine. Instead of walking home from school the way I usually do, I walked in the other direction. I didn't know where I was going. I just wanted to be someplace far away. I was sitting in this park, all by myself. It was getting dark and scary outside. But it still wasn't as scary as it is here. A policeman found me and brought me back home. I got in the worst trouble ever that night. Worse than anything that happened before. Well, almost worse."

Fiona was on the verge of tears. "Do you have any other family you could talk to when you feel sad like that?"

"No. My mom doesn't like it when anybody else is around. She says she doesn't trust other people. She wasn't like that before she met Noah."

In that moment, Fiona devised a two-part plan. The second part of the plan involved a call to Child Welfare. The first required her direct involvement.

"Olivia, do you think we could see each other face to face? Maybe you could come over here or we could meet outside on the playground? Wouldn't that be so much better than talking through this wall?"

"I don't think so."

"Why not?"

"This is the safest way for us to talk."

"I don't understand."

"I really like you, and I don't want you to be in any more danger than you're already in."

"What kind of danger am I in?"

"I'm sure you've felt it in your apartment. The strange things that we talked about before."

"Yes, I've felt it, but you never explained what you think those strange things are."

"What do you think it is?"

Fiona still hadn't come up with a reasonable answer. "I honestly don't know. I just think it's a weird time in my life, and I probably wouldn't be comfortable anywhere."

"Why is it a weird time?"

"You're changing the subject, young lady."

"I've told you about me. Now I want to hear about you. It's only fair."

Fiona bit down on her lip in frustration, but she couldn't argue. "I have a son who I haven't seen in a long time, and it makes me really sad. But I'm doing my best to make sure I can see him again."

"Why haven't you seen him?"

"It's a long story."

"You mean, like, complicated, grown-up stuff."

"Exactly."

"What's your son's name?"

"Jacob."

"What's Jacob like?"

A smile danced across Fiona's face as she envisioned him. "He's a great kid. About your age. Really smart, really kind, really funny. He gets that from me, you know."

"I didn't realize you were funny."

*Few people do,* Fiona thought to herself. "Catch me on a good day, and I'm a regular laugh riot."

"I can't wait for that good day."

"Neither can I."

"So, do you think you'll see your son soon?"

"I hope so. I really miss him."

Olivia was silent for a moment. "I know what it's like to miss people, but when they're gone, they're gone, and sometimes, there isn't anything you can do about it."

"Who are the people you miss?"

Olivia was silent again.

"Are you still there?"

"I am, but I don't want to talk about that."

"Okay, we don't have to. But I would still like for you to think about meeting me somewhere that I can actually see your face."

"I would like that, too. But how do I know I can trust you? My mom always says not to trust strangers, and you're still kind of a stranger."

"Your mom is right to tell you that, but I promise you can trust me."

"She said that was exactly what a bad stranger would say."

"Fair enough. What can I do to convince you?"

"Promise that you'll believe me."

"I've believed everything you've told me so far."

"There's more."

"I'm listening."

"You have to promise first."

Fiona was suddenly worried about what she was walking into, but she also worried that if she didn't walk into it, she'd have no chance of gaining Olivia's trust. "I promise."

"I know who killed Mr. Tisdale."

Fiona could feel the blood drain from her face. "What did you say?"

"I know who did it, and it won't do any good to tell the police...because they'll never catch them."

"Who killed Mr. Tisdale?"

"I can't say it here," Olivia whispered. "We should only talk about it outside."

"I thought you weren't comfortable doing that."

"I changed my mind."

"Okay. What about that spot in the back of the building?"

"Which spot?"

"By the children's playground, the place you saw me standing in earlier when I was on the phone."

"What do you mean?"

"About a half hour ago. I was standing outside. You were looking out the window. We waved to each other."

Olivia was silent.

"Don't you remember?"

"I'm sorry, Fiona."

"Sorry about what?"

"It wasn't me. I wasn't at my window. I never saw you outside. Maybe it was someone else."

"Are there any other girls your age who live on this floor?"

"I don't think so."

Fiona felt something heavy building in her chest, but she ignored it. It didn't matter right now who or what had been in that window. And if no one was there, if the stress of the last few days had degenerated her mental capacity to the point that she was hallucinating, that didn't matter, either. The only thing that did matter was helping this child while she still had the opportunity.

"Do you still want to meet me out there?" Olivia asked.

"Absolutely. When can you go?"

"I don't know. It's kind of hard to leave without my mom seeing. I'd have to sneak out."

The mother in Fiona wasn't in favor of that idea. "Isn't there another way? I don't want you getting in trouble."

"I'm already in trouble. I don't see how sneaking out can make it much worse."

"I'd rather you didn't take the chance. What if I come over and talk to your mom?"

Olivia gasped. "No way. That would be the worst thing to do."

"Why?"

"I thought you said I could trust you. I thought you said you would believe me."

"You can trust me, and I do believe you. I really want to talk more. I just don't want you sneaking out to do it."

"Then I guess we can't talk." Olivia was quiet for a few seconds before saying: "I wanted to believe you, Fiona. I'm sorry that I can't."

"Olivia, wait a second. I—"

"Do you still want to know who killed Mr. Tisdale?"

"Of course, I do."

Olivia began pounding on the wall.

*THUMP THUMP THUMP THUMP THUMP*

"What are you doing? Please stop."

But she didn't.

*THUMP THUMP THUMP*

The noise forced Fiona to back away from the wall.

*THUMP THUMP THUMP THUMP*

When it finally stopped, Fiona called out in anger. "Why are you doing that?"

She could hear Olivia's labored breathing through the wall. "Because I want you to know what you're dealing with, what all of us are dealing with. Because I don't want what happened to Mr. Tisdale to happen to you. Because I want you to run, as fast as you can, the next time you hear that sound. Because the next time you hear it, it won't be from me. I wish I could tell you more, but I don't think I can trust you."

"Olivia, will you please just talk to me?"

"I'm going away now. Bye."

Fiona didn't bother to call out again.

With the pounding still reverberating in her head, she sat down on the bed and began massaging her throbbing temples. There was no longer any space in her mind for rational thought. There was no space for anything except the ever-present desire to sleep away the swirling shitstorm that her life had suddenly become.

Time to get those pills.

She had put on her shoes, grabbed her coat and purse, and twisted the doorknob of her front door when the sound of breaking glass in her bedroom rendered her frozen.

After the grip of fear finally released its hold, Fiona raced into the bedroom just in time to see the second picture frame sliding down the wall. It landed on the carpeted floor with a hard crash, shattering the front glass.

*How is that possible?*

Before Fiona could grasp what she was seeing, the third frame—'Best Mom Ever'—lifted off the wall, suspended in the air by an invisible tether, then struck the floor with a terrifying *thwack* that splinted the wood.

Fiona's muscles seized with fright, leaving her unable to

move, unable to breathe. Her only thought was of the picture inside the frame–Jacob in his Darth Vader costume–her irrational fear that he had somehow been hurt, and her overwhelming urge to save him.

It was with this thought in her mind that she saw the nail slowly inching out of the wall. It dangled perilously by its sharp tip before a loud *pop* sent it hurling to the floor.

An icy chill swept through the room that livened Fiona's numb senses and she scampered to the bedroom door, only to stop at the sound of her name.

"Fiona?"

It was Olivia. Her voice was audible, yet distant, as if the small space between them had widened into a gaping chasm.

"Are you okay?"

Fiona attempted to respond, but the dreadful cold made it difficult to speak. "I…"

When the fourth picture on the wall began to move, she bolted from her bedroom, grabbed her keys, and left the apartment.

She could still hear the faint echo of Olivia's voice as she closed the door.

## Chapter Fifteen

Detective Sullivan stood quietly in Donald Tisdale's living room.

The space felt empty even though nothing had been removed except for the handfuls of evidence that were deemed critical to the investigation.

Sullivan had experienced a similar emptiness in most crime scenes that she revisited. But this one was different.

There was something about Corona Heights in general, and Donald Tisdale's apartment specifically, that seemed almost otherworldly. She felt out of place; like she didn't belong.

Like she wasn't wanted.

The sense of foreboding that had followed her home earlier that morning returned as she and Greer made their way back this afternoon. She thought that by standing alone in the space she so dreaded coming back to, feeling its sensations, listening to its subtle hums and buzzes and ticks, she could ground herself in the reality of it, thereby eliminating its inexplicable power over her.

Sullivan knew right away that the tactic wouldn't work.

She heard the noise the moment she walked into the apartment.

It began as a muted thumping that sounded like footsteps above her. It moved slowly across the length of the ceiling before making its way down the wall in the kitchen and onto the floor underneath her. At that point, she ruled out footsteps as a source of the noise.

She followed the arrhythmic thumping as it skipped across the kitchen floor, into the living room, then finally into the hallway that led to Donald Tisdale's bedroom.

Upon entering the bedroom, her eyes found the stained baseboard where the pool of blood had appeared.

Forensics had performed a DNA analysis that morning that concluded the sample did not belong to Tisdale, which meant that Sullivan's tidy little suicide case had officially been blown wide open.

It was also a confirmation of her fear that Corona Heights was not finished with her yet.

She took note of the phrase *not finished with her yet* and immediately deemed it too dramatic for the circumstances.

Sullivan had combed the bowels of crime scenes one hundred times worse than this one, crime scenes that were still rife with the possibility of *actual* danger, not the made-up kind that was the stuff of the ghost movies that she binge-watched as a kid. This wasn't the Overlook Hotel, for crying out loud. This was a simple crime scene, the same as all the others.

The thumping, which only increased when she entered the bedroom, didn't mean anything, she told herself. Neither did the dark foreboding in her that the noise triggered. The only thing that mattered was finding who had killed Donald Tisdale.

That was, until the thumping got worse.

She listened as the relentless banging spread out on all sides of her, low and slow, like a throbbing heartbeat.

*The heartbeat of the building itself.*

The image made her stomach cramp with fear.

*Thump-thump. Thump-thump.*

Then, just as suddenly as it came, the pulse faded and died out.

"Ridiculous," Sullivan said aloud as she exhaled the full breath she didn't realize she'd been holding in. "It's an old building with really bad pipes. The world is full of them."

Her head now clear, she surveyed the bedroom again. Maybe Tisdale hadn't left a note, but maybe he'd left behind some clue, some reason why–

*Ba-boom*! A force like an earthquake hit the room, tossing Sullivan off her feet as the floor lurched upward, snapping off two of the bedroom floorboards and raking a wide crack down the plaster of the back wall.

"Jesus!"

Now on her back, Sullivan dug her nails into the carpet, like a cat, holding on for survival as the floor began to throb in time with the beat.

*Thump-thump. Thump-thump.*

The reel of the floor knocked an old thrift-store lamp from Tisdale's cheap plyboard nightstand, and Sullivan heard the bathroom mirror crack, then shatter, as she rolled over on her stomach, cowering and covering her head against any other debris.

*Ker-lack*!

The floor seemed to harden suddenly, then flatten, slamming back down with a force that she felt sure would crush the old building like a tin-foil box. Sullivan banged her chin on the floor with the impact and had to shake her head to clear it before she even thought about standing up. Her partner's infamous one-liner escaped her lips before she could stop herself.

"What in the entire fuck?!"

Sullivan scanned the floor and walls for any clue as to what had just happened. The quake seemed like it was over, but she refused to drop her guard as she slowly, deliberately backed out of the room. There may have been work still to do, but she was determined not to spend another second by herself in this apartment.

That was why she felt such relief at the sound of knocking at the front door. Greer had returned, hopefully with Arthur Finley, which meant that the alone time she once coveted was coming to a merciful end.

Greer knocked again before Sullivan could reach the door, turning her relief into irritation.

"Relax, I'm coming. No need to break the door dow—"

When she snatched open the door, Greer wasn't there. Nobody was there. Just a glimpse of whatever had been standing across from her on the other side of that flimsy door, wanting to come in. Whatever had been there, its shape had been small and featureless, like a three-dimensional shadow.

And it moved very fast.

Sullivan felt another chill.

It could have been a child playing a prank, but children playing pranks always gave themselves away with mischievous laughter. Sullivan had heard no laughter, no footsteps padding away in panic. But she still felt the chill. It lingered with a forceful grip, clawing at her insides.

Her stomach felt like she'd just swallowed a three-pound ice block. She began to sweat as a sour fear began to slither up the back of her throat. She tried to swallow, but her saliva flowed like glue.

Sullivan stepped into the hallway. "Hello?" She listened for a response. Hearing none, she slowly rounded the corner where the shadow had disappeared to. "Is someone—"

From her other side, a heavy hand stopped her cold, and despite herself she let out a high-pitched yelp that shrieked down the corridor.

The next sound she heard was Greer's laughter. "Don't worry, Mr. Finley. She reacts like this every time she sees me. It doesn't hurt my feelings as much as it used to."

It took all her willpower to refrain from inviting her partner to go screw himself, but there was a citizen standing next to Greer. Buttoned-up pro that she was, Sullivan wasn't about to lose her cool in front of John Q. Public.

"Didn't you see it?"

"See what?"

"A child, or something, running through the hall."

The smile left Greer's face. "What do you mean a child or *something?*"

"There was a knock at Tisdale's door. I answered, thinking it was you. When I opened the door, I saw this small child or…something…running away."

"What did the child look like?" the man standing next to Greer asked.

Sullivan recounted what she'd seen, which, besides the fast-moving shadow, wasn't much.

The man and Greer looked at one another quizzically.

"We didn't see anything," Greer said.

"It would have run right past you."

"Do you think you could stop saying '*it*'? You're kinda freaking me out."

"I guess you didn't feel the floors shaking, either."

"The floors shaking?"

"Yes."

"We didn't feel any floors shaking."

"How could you not? It literally knocked me off my feet." Sullivan could feel herself losing what little control she had left.

Greer's eyes narrowed with concern. "Clo', are you okay?"

When Sullivan didn't answer, the man standing next to Greer intervened. "We do have several children in the building. When a pack of them get together, it can sound like a freight train tearing through the halls. There's always a morbid sense of curiosity surrounding an event like this, and the kiddos seem to be most affected. I don't know what to say about the shaking in the floors other than an issue with the support beams. I'll have it checked out ASAP. But as far as the knock on the door, I wouldn't doubt for a second that one of the youngsters is behind it."

"It's what kids do," Greer added. "They've got to cope with their fear somehow."

The perfectly logical explanation did nothing to help Sullivan feel better.

"Still, I can imagine it was unnerving," the man said as he extended his hand. "Art Finley."

Greer cut in. "Sorry, with all the excitement, I didn't get a chance to properly introduce you. "Detective Sullivan, this is Arthur Finley. Mr. Finley, Detective Chloe Sullivan."

Sullivan subtly wiped her sweaty palm on the back of her leg before shaking his hand. "Pleasure to meet you, Mr. Finley. I apologize for the theatrics. I assure you that I'm normally very professional."

"No need to apologize, Detective Sullivan. I completely understand. And please, call me Art."

His gentle, kind smile immediately disarmed her. She could now get on with the business of being a homicide detective and not the frightened nine-year-old that had momentarily invaded her body.

"Art has agreed to answer some questions about Mr. Tisdale," Greer said.

"Would you prefer that we talk out here?" Sullivan asked, hoping like hell that he would say yes.

"It's probably not best to be within earshot of the tenants. They're pretty nervous as is."

"Agreed," Greer said. "Would you be okay talking inside Tisdale's apartment?"

Sullivan's face dropped. "It's still an active scene."

"We've collected everything we need. I don't see the harm in it, as long as you agree not to touch anything, Art."

"Promise. Hell, the way I look at it, I'll ultimately be responsible for cleaning out the place when you guys are finished, so it'll be a good primer."

With that, the three made their way inside.

Sullivan stopped before she crossed the entryway, listening for the pulsating rhythm to return. When it didn't, she let out a quiet sigh, and shut the door.

"Have you been having issues with the heating?" Greer said with a shiver as he entered the living room.

"It's been a persistent pain," Arthur responded. "I've been lobbying for a new ventilation system for over a decade now. Mr. Barlow doesn't believe the problem warrants that kind of investment. He doesn't believe in investing much of anything into this place, but that's another story."

Arthur's bright face took on a dark edge as he surveyed

the apartment. Sullivan noticed him shiver, though she attributed that as much to emotion as she had the cold.

"How long have you lived here?" she asked.

"Longer than I can remember. I came in first as a tenant, then, after the old maintenance supervisor died, Mr. Barlow hired me. I'd done some odd jobs around the building, so he knew I was pretty handy."

"You must know this building like the back of your hand by now," Greer said.

"I've gotten to know this old girl really well over the years: the good, the bad, and the oh-so-ugly."

"Same with the tenants?" Sullivan asked.

"Inasmuch as I can. It was much easier back in the day. People moved in, and they stayed for years. Now, with the turnover being so high, the only way I can truly keep track of people is by the number of times I'm called to fix something for them. That seems to be the only time that anyone is interested in conversation. No sense of community like there used to be. Different times altogether, I suppose."

Sullivan nodded her agreement. Different times indeed.

"As we were walking up here, you spoke about your friendship with Mr. Tisdale. Was he close with anyone else in the building?" Greer asked.

"Don kept to himself. He didn't have anything against the people here. He just found over the years that he had less and less in common with them."

"But the two of you were pretty tight."

Arthur's weathered face creased with emotion. "Always." His eyes continued to survey the space before finally landing on the recliner above which Tisdale's hanging body had been discovered.

Sullivan noticed this and watched for any sudden changes in his demeanor. Seeing none, she dismissed his lingering stare as a coincidence and continued her questioning.

"Did he ever speak about anyone else in the building? Anyone he liked, or more importantly, disliked?"

"Don never had a bad word to say about anyone."

"Could there have been anyone who disliked him?"

Arthur eyed her quizzically. "I'm not sure where you're going with this."

"I'm not going anywhere with it, Mr. Finley."

"Art."

"Art. I'm just trying to get a broad picture view of his life here."

"Are you thinking that someone here could have…" He couldn't finish the sentence.

"Like Detective Sullivan said, we're simply trying to understand the bigger picture."

Arthur nodded at Greer before taking a moment to ponder. "Well, I guess there was one thing. Happened some time ago, though."

"What?" Sullivan asked with piqued interest.

"There was this guy, Noah Glasby. Still lives on this floor actually."

"What about him?"

Arthur hesitated as if the memory made him uncomfortable. "So, one day, Don runs into one of the kids who lives on this floor, a little girl in 607. From what Don said, it was a friendly conversation. He'd asked her about school, any fun hobbies she may have had, really basic stuff. Turns out, they shared an interest in drawing. Don was quite the artist, great with nature scenes. I called him our resident Bob Ross. I'd be willing to bet that he still has a few pieces hidden away somewhere. Anyway, she was interested in seeing his work, so he agreed to let her come over on the condition that she got permission from her mother first. So, she asks her mom, and somehow, Noah gets wind of it. That's when all hell breaks loose. He almost beat down Don's door, calling him a pervert and every other despicable name you can imagine."

"Is Noah the girl's father?" Sullivan asked.

Arthur shook his head. "Mother's boyfriend, from what I understand."

"And all of this because Donald Tisdale wanted to show the girl some drawings?" Greer asked. "Seems excessive to me."

"To me too," Arthur concurred. "Noah basically demanded that Don stay away from his family and that if he didn't, the two of them would have issues."

"Did Noah physically threaten him?" Sullivan asked.

"According to Don, there was never an overt threat. He'd retreated into his apartment before Noah could escalate the situation any further. But the threat was implied."

"Were there any altercations after that?"

"No. Don avoided them, and as far as I know, he never talked to the girl again. He was a sweet man. Damned shame that someone would twist his perfectly innocent intentions into something so disgusting. Speaks more to the kind of man Noah is, if you ask me."

Sullivan looked at Greer, hopeful that he had the same thought as she did.

"And you said the girl lived in apartment 607?" Greer asked.

Arthur nodded. "The same as Noah Glasby."

Their next visual exchange confirmed that the two detectives were on the same page.

"What do you say we go pay him a visit?"

Sullivan immediately nodded her agreement. "Right behind you, sport."

"If it's all the same, I'd appreciate it if you didn't mention me in your conversation," Arthur said. "I'm more than happy to help you guys out in whatever way I can. I want to find out what happened to Don as much as anyone. But I have no desire to catch that family's wrath. It's difficult enough dealing with them as is."

"We completely understand, and we would never put you in that position," Sullivan assured him.

Arthur let out a quiet sigh of relief. "Thank you."

"If you don't mind, we'd like for you to stand by in case we need to follow up after our chat with the folks in 607," Greer said.

"Of course. Whatever you need."

After seeing Arthur out of the apartment, Sullivan and Greer made their way down the hall.

"I didn't have much luck with them earlier," Sullivan said as apartment 607 came into view.

"When you were knocking on doors?"

She nodded. "To be fair, I didn't have much luck with anyone. Even when people answered the door, most times I wish they hadn't."

Greer put a hand on her shoulder, stopping both of them before they reached the apartment. A look of concern creased his smooth, chestnut-brown face. "What happened back there, at Tisdale's apartment?"

Sullivan swallowed hard as she attempted to frame her answer.

In her world, there was a logical explanation for everything. She had even found a way to explain the pool of blood that seemed to spontaneously appear in Tisdale's kitchen and bedroom. It was there the entire time. In the rush to declare his suicide an open-and-shut case, every-thing else, including the blood, had been overlooked. Simple.

But what she experienced in his apartment today defied explanation. The thumping in the walls and floor that seemed to move as she did, the knock on the front door, the shadow that slithered away from the door when she opened it; none of it seemed real.

And yet it was. The first issue was admitting that to herself. The second was admitting it to Greer.

The two of them had gotten on nicely in the six months since they'd been partnered. Sullivan's previous partnership hadn't ended well, so Greer's humor, fair-mindedness, and dedication came as a breath of fresh air. She trusted him with her life because the job dictated that she had to. But she'd also come to trust Greer as a person, and she assumed that he trusted her. In her experience, trust was fragile, capable of being shattered by even the slightest indiscretion or misstep.

How would Greer's trust be affected by her belief that what she'd heard and seen in Tisdale's apartment and outside his door was something other than human? Would he ever again trust her to lead the way into a dark alley or active crime scene?

Would he trust the female intuition that she'd fought so hard to convince him was a real thing? He just might. At this point, however, it wasn't worth the risk to find out.

The incident could make for an interesting anecdote over beers one day, where its merits could be dissected, ridiculed, and ultimately dismissed. But for now, she needed Greer's full faith in her ability to help close this case.

She needed to maintain faith in herself, too—faith that

was diminishing a little more with each passing moment spent here.

"Nothing happened that's worth rehashing right now," Sullivan declared as emphatically as she could. "Let's just see what we can find out about Noah."

"Are you sure?" Greer asked with a raised eyebrow of skepticism normally reserved for the interrogation room. "That look on your face. It was like you saw a ghost."

"There's no such thing as ghosts, Marcus. Didn't they teach you that in the police academy?"

With that, she continued down the hallway.

Greer chuckled as he followed close behind. "Sorry, I must have been absent that day."

## Chapter Sixteen

The detectives were greeted by loud music upon arriving at apartment 607, a common occurrence, according to Arthur Finley. Greer smiled and began bobbing his head to the thrashing guitar riffs and rapid-fire drumbeat.

"Metallica, 'Disposable Heroes,'" he said with finger horns raised in the air.

"Funny, I thought this was Megadeth."

"Bite your tongue, young lady."

Sullivan eyed him with amusement. "How do you know so much about it, anyway?"

"What, you don't think a brotha from Park Hill can be a metalhead?"

"Looking at you right now, I don't doubt it for a second."

When the song ended, so did Greer's head banging. "Quick, knock on the door before 'Leper Messiah' starts up."

Sullivan followed his command, silently thanking him

for the much-needed comedy relief. She managed to get in four hard knocks before the next song began.

"Think they heard that?"

Before Greer could answer her question, the door flew open.

The blast from the music hit Sullivan like a sonic wave, momentarily pushing her back. When she regained her bearings, she saw a young woman whose pretty face was marred by a thick layer of black mascara and a pointedly hostile expression. Unable to hear the words she spoke, Sullivan had to rely on her ability to read lips.

"*Can I help you?*" was what she made out.

"Turn the music off first!" she responded in a voice that tested the limits of her vocal range.

The woman's piercing green eyes cut through Sullivan as if her directive meant nothing.

"We said turn it off!" Greer's baritone rose above the music enough to make the woman flinch.

She huffed as she walked back inside to turn off the music. She said nothing to them as she returned.

"Don't you think your neighbors deserve a little more consideration?"

The girl met Greer's question with a contemptuous glare. "Who are you, and what do you want?"

Sullivan displayed her badge without saying anything.

The woman appeared unfazed. "Am I breaking some kind of law?"

"I can cite you for at least three different noise-ordinance violations if you'd like," Sullivan answered. "But I'm not interested in that right now."

"Great. Why are you here, then?"

Sullivan looked at Greer, informing him that this one was all his.

"My name is Greer, and this is my partner, Detective Sullivan. Are you aware of the incident that occurred on this floor?"

"No."

"You haven't heard your neighbors talking about it? You haven't seen us around the building?"

"Like I already said, no."

Sullivan noted the justifiable tension in Greer's jaw and quickly took over the questioning.

"The tenant in apartment 612 was discovered by the building superintendent."

"You mean that creep Tisdale? Is he dead?"

Sullivan couldn't believe the callousness of her tone. "Yes, he's dead."

"And from the sound of it, you really don't care," Greer added.

The woman shrugged. "Should I?"

Sullivan sighed. "What's your name?"

"Why does that matter?"

"Why are you being so evasive?" Greer countered.

The woman hesitated before answering. It was clear that she was accustomed to dealing with people on her own terms and wasn't about to change that for a couple of homicide detectives.

"Natalie Shelby." She blew a tuft of dirty blonde hair out of her face as she fortified her defiant stance. "Why are you talking to me about Donald Tisdale's death? I barely knew the man."

"It sounds like you have pretty strong opinions about his character," Greer said. "What was it you called him, a *creep*?"

"A lot of people thought that about him. Doesn't mean I knew him."

"But you must have your own reasons for agreeing with the sentiment," Sullivan said.

Natalie shrugged off the statement. "Just a feeling I had."

"Based on what?"

"Am I being interrogated or something? Because I haven't done anything wrong."

"We're not implying you did anything wrong, Ms. Shelby," Greer said.

"We're simply asking questions, the same as we did with other tenants in the building," Sullivan followed. "There weren't many who knew Mr. Tisdale. From the sound of it, you did. We simply want to gather as much information about him as possible. There's no reason to be combative."

Or was there?

Natalie crossed her arms, a clear sign that she had no intention of letting her guard down. "Fine. Ask your questions."

Greer looked to Sullivan this time. She promptly took the cue.

"Do you live here alone, Ms. Shelby?"

"What does that have to do with anything?"

"Could you please just answer the question?"

Natalie let out a guttural sigh before answering. "No."

"Who else lives here with you?"

"My kid."

"Anyone else?"

An eye roll, then: "My boyfriend."

"What's your boyfriend's name?"

"Noah."

"Did Noah know Mr. Tisdale?"

"The only person who really knew him was Arthur

Finley, the maintenance guy. Why don't you go talk to him?"

"Because we're talking to you," Greer pushed back.

"I'll repeat it, Ms. Shelby. Did your boyfriend know Mr. Tisdale?"

"Barely."

"Did you or Noah ever have any problems with him?"

"Problems?"

"Confrontations? Disagreements?"

"Is this the standard question you asked everybody?"

Sullivan looked at Greer as she contemplated a suitable answer.

"Yes," Greer lied.

"So, based on your questions, Donald was murdered, and you think somebody in this building did it. Am I right?"

Sullivan looked at Greer again. His eyes made it clear that he wasn't bailing her out a second time.

"Like Detective Greer said, these are standard questions."

"Okay, so you've asked your standard questions. Does that mean you're done with me now?" Natalie already had one hand on the door, ready to close it.

"No," Greer said tersely. "You still haven't answered the question."

Natalie held the door with a white-knuckle grip.

"Do you recall an incident between Donald Tisdale and Noah that involved your daughter?" Sullivan asked.

"Who told you about that?"

Sullivan thought about Arthur Finley and the promise that both she and Greer had made to him. She fully intended to keep that promise, though she understood the potential ramifications he might suffer through the mere mention of the incident. She wished it didn't need to be brought up at all, but Natalie's contemptible attitude forced her hand.

"We talked to a lot of people, Ms. Shelby. Stories tend to float around pretty easily in a place this size."

Natalie's piercing eyes bulged with anger. "These assholes can tell you stories until they're blue in the face, but they're lying. My family, and what happens in it, is nobody else's business because I don't make it anybody else's business."

"Based on what we've heard, you made it other people's business that day. They said that Noah practically broke Donald Tisdale's door down, calling him names, threatening him, all because he wanted to invite your daughter over to his apartment to see some artwork. Do you think that was justified under the circumstances?"

"Yes, I do," Natalie answered without batting an eyelash. "You know what else I think? That you two have asked enough questions, and it's time for you to leave."

"Ms. Shelby, please wait," Greer said in the calmest, most reasoned voice that he was capable of.

"How dare you come here to ask about some random incident that occurred between my boyfriend and that man over *three* years ago. Believe me, if Noah wanted to hurt him, he would've done it then. But he wouldn't hurt him because he's not that kind of man. So, screw you for implying it."

"Ms. Shelby, you're only making things worse by acting this way. Don't allow your mouth to cause the situation to escalate," Sullivan warned. "It won't work out for you."

"Unless you're going to arrest me, we're done. Please go away."

Natalie abruptly concluded the questioning by slamming the door.

Sullivan and Greer looked at each other in stunned silence. It took Sullivan a few seconds to collect herself enough to speak. "You know what I usually say when an interview goes this south this fast."

Greer nodded as he started knocking on the door. "Smoke?"

It was the code word they used whenever something—or in this case, someone—provided the crucial first lead that was always necessary in breaking an investigation.

"No," Sullivan answered as she too began knocking. "Fire."

## Chapter Seventeen

After a long drive that led her nowhere, Fiona had come home to the familiar sound of loud music blasting from Olivia's apartment. For as much as she hated the noise, she also appreciated the distraction.

She'd decided to enter her bedroom straight away, prepared for whatever she would encounter inside. Aside from the broken frames, nothing else appeared out of place.

*Like the broken frames aren't enough,* Fiona grumbled.

She cleaned up the glass without attempting to construct a rational explanation for the horror she'd experienced. She needed to keep her mind calm and her body still. She'd barely been able to control the trembling in her hands, and if she weren't careful, she would lose the ability to control the voices, too.

*Just one, Fiona. To take the edge off.*

She'd just swept up the last fragment of splintered wood when she heard other voices, rising angrily above the music.

When the music abruptly stopped, the voices became clearer.

At first, she thought that Olivia's mother was tuned in to another one of those foul reality shows that she seemingly spent her entire day watching.

But as she listened closer, she realized that the argument wasn't happening on television but in the hallway.

The loudest voice was the most familiar. Olivia's mother. The other two voices, a man and woman, were unfamiliar, but they were no less heated.

She walked to the front door to get a better listen.

*"I already told you, unless you plan on arresting me, I don't have anything else to say!"*

*"Ms. Shelby, you have to calm down."*

*"I won't calm down! You're accusing my boyfriend of doing something that he didn't do, and I'm not going to stand here and listen to it!"*

*"We didn't come here accusing anyone of anything. But the more you yell at us, the more it makes us wonder."*

As she listened more closely, Fiona had come to recognize the second female voice as Detective Sullivan's.

*"When are you expecting Noah back? Maybe we can get a more reasoned response from him."*

She shuddered at the mention of Noah's name. Did this mean that the police were actively looking for him? Could it be in relation to Tisdale's death? It had to be, Fiona quickly concluded. Why else would Detective Sullivan be here?

She opened the door just wide enough to see Sullivan's partner in the hallway. He stood near the wall, clearly agitated.

When Fiona opened the door wider, it creaked loud enough to interrupt the exchange. With the attention suddenly on her, Fiona slinked back behind the door, but it was too late. She heard Natalie's voice before she saw her face.

"See, this is what I'm talking about. Nobody around here can mind their own damned business."

Fiona's heart nearly leaped out of her chest. She felt guilty, embarrassed, and fearful all at the same time. "I'm sorry, I didn't mean to—"

Sullivan's partner cut her off. "It's okay, Miss. We apologize for disturbing you."

Detective Sullivan stepped away from Natalie's door just enough for Fiona to finally see her. "Hello, Ms. Graves."

Fiona nodded. "Again, I didn't mean to interrupt. I was just heading out," she said, a lie fueled by her angst.

"Really? She just happened to be leaving? Please, she's barely even dressed. Fucking nosey, like all the rest of them."

Fiona still couldn't see Natalie's face, but she could feel her voice. It reverberated off the walls. She imagined what the sound of that voice had done to Olivia over the years, how much pain it caused, how much fear it inspired.

It was this thought that brought her into the hallway, against all better judgment. This conversation was none of her business, just like Natalie said. But it also gave Fiona the perfect opportunity, one that she feared would never come again. She had to seize it.

"Have you spoken with Olivia yet?"

"Who is Olivia?" Sullivan asked.

Before Fiona could answer, she got her first glimpse of Natalie.

Standing all of five foot one and weighing next to nothing, Natalie Shelby was certainly not impressive physically. But what she lacked in size, she more than made up for with her voice; and right now, its raw power was in full force.

Unfortunately for Fiona, that power was now directed squarely at her.

"What did you say?" Natalie barked as she took a step toward her.

Detective Sullivan blocked her path. "Who is Olivia?"

"Natalie's daughter," Fiona said.

"Why in the hell would you bring up my daughter?"

Detective Sullivan turned to Fiona, waiting for an answer to the question.

*Cat's out of the bag now. May as well let it roam free.* "I talked to her."

"What? When?"

Fiona kept calm. "Twice in the last twenty-four hours."

Natalie bristled. "No, you didn't!"

"Yes, I did," Fiona said to Sullivan. "And she told me things."

Natalie was still yelling, but Fiona tuned her out, keeping the focus on the detectives instead.

"What did she tell you?" Sullivan's partner asked.

"I'm sorry, Fiona. This is Detective Marcus Greer," Sullivan said.

Fiona acknowledged him with a nod before answering his question. "Among other things, she told me that she knew who killed Donald Tisdale."

Her words took the air out of everyone in the group, and for a long moment, no one spoke.

"You're a goddamned liar!" Natalie finally said as she approached Fiona again.

Thankfully, Detective Sullivan's size and obvious strength created a significant deterrent.

"You need to calm down, Ms. Shelby. Right now."

Something in Sullivan's tone must have hit the right nerve because Natalie stopped dead in her tracks. This time, when she spoke, the octaves were lowered significantly. "She's lying. There's no way she talked to my daughter."

"I did," Fiona insisted.

"How?" Detective Greer asked.

"Through the wall in my apartment. My bedroom is adjacent to hers. She actually called out to me first."

"Through the wall? Jesus, do you know how weird that sounds?" Natalie scoffed.

"There's nothing weird about it. Your daughter obviously needed someone to talk to." Fiona turned to the detectives. "Maybe you should ask Natalie what her daughter has experienced that would make her say the things that she did."

Sullivan turned to Natalie. "Where is your daughter now, Ms. Shelby?"

Natalie didn't answer.

When Fiona looked into the apartment, she saw something move. A small shadow disappearing behind a corner. As she waited for the shadow to return, Fiona heard Detective Sullivan's question again.

"Where is your daughter?"

Natalie finally answered. "She's not here."

Fiona's eyes remained focused on that corner.

"Where is she?"

Then she saw it. A tiny head peeking from around the corner. It was bathed in darkness, but Fiona knew exactly what she was looking at.

"She's right there!" Fiona pointed inside the apartment. As soon as she did, Olivia disappeared.

"What are you talking about? She's at her father's house," Natalie said incredulously.

"She looked right at me," Fiona countered. "She was

standing behind that corner." Fiona pointed to the spot again, but nothing was there.

"We'd really like to talk to her, Ms. Shelby," Detective Greer said. "If she knows anything about Mr. Tisdale—"

Natalie cut him off. "She doesn't."

"Why don't you let us find that out," Detective Sullivan said.

"Because she's not here!"

"I'm telling you, I saw her," Fiona reiterated.

Sullivan turned to Greer. They nodded in silent agreement.

"Ms. Shelby, if you don't mind, I'm going to take a look," Sullivan said as she gestured to the apartment.

Natalie stepped in front of the door. "I do mind!"

"Then call her out here," Greer demanded.

"I can't call her because she isn't in there."

The detectives looked at Fiona again.

"She's there."

Sullivan nodded. "Ms. Shelby, I'm just going to have a look."

"Like hell you are." Natalie made a move toward Sullivan but was restrained by Greer. "This is illegal! You can't just go in there!"

"Ma'am, we're performing a welfare check on your daughter, which means we can absolutely go in there."

Sullivan slowly entered the apartment. "Olivia? If you're here, can you come out, sweetie? We're with your mom. Everything is okay. We just want to talk."

Fiona could feel the heat of Natalie's venomous stare. She refused to look back, keeping her eyes instead on Detective Sullivan as she combed the apartment, stopping first in the living room, then the kitchen, before finally making her way toward the back corner of the apartment.

"Olivia?"

Fiona held her breath as Sullivan disappeared behind the dark corner.

"Are you in here, sweetheart?"

Light suddenly filled the dark corridor. Fiona could see a shadow but couldn't tell if it was Sullivan's or Olivia's. Within seconds, the light was off, and Sullivan had emerged from behind the corner.

"Well?" Greer said as she approached.

Sullivan shook her head. "No one's in there."

Fiona's mouth flew open in shock. "What? That can't be."

"I'm afraid it is, Ms. Graves. I checked every corner of the apartment, including the girl's bedroom. There was no indication that she'd been there."

"I told you," an emboldened Natalie shouted. "Now, can you please leave?"

Fiona was too stunned to move. "I don't understand. I know I saw something."

"You didn't see anything," Natalie scoffed.

"But I talked to her not even two hours ago."

Sullivan looked at her with eyes that were surprisingly sympathetic. "I'm sorry. I don't know what else to tell you."

"We'd like to speak with your boyfriend, Ms. Shelby," Greer said. "Do you know when he'll be back?"

"He works crazy hours, so I hardly ever know when he's coming home. He may not show up until next week for all I know."

"Well, whenever he does show, have him call us."

Greer gave Natalie a card, which she snatched out of his hand.

"When will Olivia be back?" Sullivan asked.

"Like I said, she's with her father, has been since yesterday. I don't know when she'll be back. But you'd be wasting your time anyway. She doesn't know the first thing about Donald Tisdale."

Fiona shouted *Liar!* in her mind but kept quiet.

"Fine," Sullivan said. "Just make sure you have Noah contact us. We're still in the midst of our investigation, so we'll be around the building. It won't be difficult to contact us."

"Wonderful," Natalie replied dismissively. "Anything else?"

"No, but we need to make sure that the situation is okay here before we leave."

Natalie looked at Fiona. "Everything is fine."

"Is that the case, Ms. Graves?" Greer asked.

Fiona hesitated. "Yes."

"We don't want to be called back here," Sullivan said to Natalie. "If we are, I can guarantee you we won't be happy."

Unfazed by the detective's warning, Natalie walked inside her apartment. "Can I go now?"

Sullivan nodded. "Thank you for your time."

Natalie's narrow, angry eyes took dead aim at Fiona as she closed the door.

"Are you sure you're okay, Ms. Graves?" Greer asked.

"I honestly don't know."

"What did you see in there?" Sullivan asked.

"Apparently, nothing."

Sullivan persisted. "You're positive about that?"

"It's been a rough few days. I've barely slept, and it's obviously getting to me."

Sullivan and Greer exchanged a look.

"You made some serious claims about Ms. Shelby's

daughter and Donald Tisdale," Greer said. "Why don't you tell us more about that?"

"I only know what I heard her say."

"That she knew who killed him."

Fiona nodded.

"When did she tell you this?" Sullivan asked.

"Earlier this afternoon."

"But you heard what her mother said. Olivia has been with her father since yesterday."

"And you believe that?" Fiona asked incredulously.

"Frankly, we don't know what to believe, Ms. Graves. So far, none of this is adding up."

"It doesn't add up to me, either. But I know what I heard. Olivia's voice was as clear to me as yours is now. I didn't just make it up in my head."

"No one's saying you did," Greer insisted.

"Then what are you going to do about it?"

"Without knowing for sure where Olivia is, we only have her mother's word to go on."

"How do you even know there is a father? She could've made the whole thing up."

Sullivan nodded. "Anything's possible, and we can keep pressing if need be. But Olivia hasn't officially been reported missing, nor do we have cause to suspect that her welfare is in danger."

"You haven't heard what I have."

"But are you certain of what you heard, Ms. Graves?" Greer asked. "Olivia wasn't in the apartment."

"Like I told you, I wasn't imagining things."

"Perhaps you weren't. But it's going to take more than your word to justify pressing Ms. Shelby. It's going to take us hearing from Olivia herself."

"So, that's the end of it?"

"We don't want to doubt your story," Sullivan said. "We just need to hear it from her."

Fiona nodded and began the walk back to her apartment. She felt thoroughly defeated.

"Is there anything else we can do for you?" Greer's offer felt forced.

"No," Fiona said as she opened the door. Before she could enter the apartment, Sullivan called out to her.

"Ms. Graves?"

"Yes?"

"Do you still have my card?"

"Yes."

"Good. Call me if you need anything, even if it's just to talk."

Fiona didn't think much of the offer until she looked in Detective Sullivan's eyes. They communicated an understanding that couldn't be stated with words. In Sullivan's eyes, she saw validation, she saw belief, and she saw proof that she wasn't crazy after all. In an instant, she knew exactly why Sullivan had made the offer.

"Thank you, Detective Sullivan. I'm glad you understand."

"I absolutely do, Ms. Graves."

## Chapter Eighteen

Fiona had barely settled back into her apartment when she heard a knock on the door. It was a gentle knock, one that said *I come in peace*, which meant it was likely not Natalie, but she was still nervous as she approached.

"Who is it?"

"It's Iris."

Fiona looked through the peephole and saw Iris standing there in her housecoat and slippers. Relieved, she quickly opened the door.

"I heard shouting and had a sinking feeling that you were involved. Are you okay?"

"I'm fine," Fiona answered, not meaning it.

"I wanted to come out the second I heard her voice." Iris made a silent gesture toward Natalie's apartment. "But I feared my presence might only make things worse."

Fiona agreed, but she took comfort in the fact that Iris had her back. "Come in," she said.

"Thank you. I'm not too keen on the idea of stirring up

that tornado of a woman again."

Fiona gently closed the door behind her.

"Quaint little place," Iris said as she surveyed the apartment. "Nice to see you're not a hoarder like me."

Fiona felt a twinge of embarrassment. "It's not much, I'm afraid."

"It's home, and for now, that's all you need."

Fiona didn't agree but nodded anyway. "Can I offer you anything? Coffee, water?"

"Water would be nice."

Fiona went into the kitchen to retrieve two bottles. When she came back into the living room, Iris had taken a seat on the futon.

"Thank you, dear," she said as she opened the bottle and took a sip. "Feels like déjà vu all over again, doesn't it?"

Fiona joined her on the futon. "It sure does. No offense to your wonderful company, but one late-night meeting was more than enough for me."

"Me too. I'm not sure how much more of this excitement I can take."

The amulet around Fiona's neck suddenly felt warm. When she touched it, Iris smiled.

"I see you're still wearing it. Is it everything it's cracked up to be?"

"I can't lie. There's something to it. I find myself reaching for it all the time. The warmth is comforting."

"It's supposed to be. It's similar to a mood stone in that it responds to the energy it receives from you. If it gets warmth, it gives warmth back. It clearly likes your energy. Scares me to think of how it would respond to that poor, lost soul next door."

Fiona's thoughts shifted back to the confrontation.

"I've been through a lot of stuff, Iris. I've encountered

some tough customers, especially in my rehab days. But I've never experienced anything like that. She's completely unhinged."

"You're right about that."

"With the way she was carrying on, I honestly thought she was going to get herself arrested."

"They should have arrested her. I think everyone in this building has had enough of that family."

"Don't you mean Natalie and Noah?"

Iris looked at her with blank eyes.

"Olivia hasn't done anything," Fiona explained. "It's not her fault that her mother is such a witch. If anything, the people here should rally around that little girl."

Iris was quiet.

"Don't you agree?"

"I have to be honest. I'm sick of the entire lot. They've been a constant source of trouble around here. It's no reflection on Olivia. I understand that she's just a child and shouldn't be judged by her parents' actions, but Natalie's overbearing need to protect her contributes to a lot of the problems."

"Throw the baby out with the bathwater. Is that what you're saying?"

"When you put it like that, it sounds rather harsh."

"It is harsh."

Iris smiled. "Touché. I've always had an issue framing my arguments properly. I'm not nearly as heartless as I sound right now, believe me."

Fiona wanted to.

"Speaking of Olivia," Iris continued, "What was that strange business about her not being in the apartment?"

Fiona visibly shook as she thought about it. "Did you not hear the part that led up to that?"

"Not all of it. And based on the way you're shaking right now, I have to assume it wasn't good."

"It wasn't good at all."

Iris edged forward on the couch, taking Fiona's hands in her own. "Tell me."

"I talked to Olivia again."

"You did? When?"

"Earlier today, same circumstances as before."

"Through your bedroom wall."

Fiona nodded. "She told me that she knew who killed Donald Tisdale."

Shock caused Iris to release her grip on Fiona's hands. "You can't be serious."

"I'm afraid I am. She wanted to tell me who but said she was afraid that someone would hear her, so we agreed to meet outside."

"And did you?"

"No. Olivia said she had to sneak out in order to meet me. I wasn't comfortable with the idea. When I told her that, she completely shut down. It was like she didn't want anything else to do with me. Then something else happened."

"What?"

"Before she went away, she asked me if I still wanted to know who killed him. Of course, I said yes. Suddenly, she starts pounding on the walls. I told her to stop, but she wouldn't. It got louder and louder until I could hardly hear anything else. When I asked her why she did it, she said it was because she wanted me to know what I was dealing with. She said she didn't want the same thing that happened to Tisdale to happen to me. She said that she wanted me to know what that danger sounded like, so the next time I heard it, I would know to run."

Iris sat back on the couch. "Oh my."

"It gets worse. A little while later, I was on my way out of the apartment when I heard breaking glass in my bedroom. When I went in there, I saw that every single picture that I'd hung on the wall had fallen to the floor. The frames were shattered to pieces."

"How does that happen on a carpeted floor?"

"Exactly."

Iris made no effort to hide her dismay. "What did you do?"

"I freaked out and left the apartment. I drove around for the longest time hoping to find someplace else to stay. There wasn't any place else, so I came back here and tried to forget the whole thing ever happened."

"You're a lot braver than you give yourself credit for. I'd be petrified to come back."

"Believe me, I was. I still am. But what am I supposed to do? I can't move out. I can't afford a hotel."

"You can stay with me," Iris offered. "At least until you sort things out."

"I wouldn't want to impose on you like that. Besides, I don't know what there is to sort out. I don't even know if what I'm experiencing is real or not."

"Of course, it's real. Why would you think otherwise?"

Fiona hesitated, thinking hard about whether she should say what was really on her mind. She had only just now come to terms with it, and giving it voice threatened to send her over the edge. "Everything I've experienced with Olivia, the conversations, her pounding on the walls, I'm not sure if any of it even happened."

"Because?"

"Because, apparently, there is no Olivia."

"I don't understand."

"It's the answer to your question about the strange business with Olivia not being in her apartment. Before I went out into the hallway, I overheard the detectives asking Natalie about an incident with Noah and Donald Tisdale that involved Olivia. They wanted to speak to Noah about it, but Natalie claimed he wasn't there. The conversation got my attention because of my run-in with him earlier today."

"What run-in?"

"A conversation for another time. Anyway, when I went out there and saw how crazy Natalie was acting, my first concern was for Olivia's safety, especially given what she had already told me. When I mentioned this, Detective Sullivan asked Natalie to bring her out, which she flat-out refused to do. When the detective pressed, Natalie said that Olivia had been at her father's house since yesterday. I knew that wasn't true because I had just talked to her. So, Detective Sullivan went into the apartment to check, and Olivia wasn't there."

"She checked everywhere?"

"Apparently so. She said that it looked as if no one had been in her room for quite some time."

"What did you think when she said that?"

"First, I thought that Natalie was lying, that she was hiding Olivia somewhere. But the more I thought about that, the less sense it made."

"So, the next logical conclusion was that you imagined everything?"

"I never said there was anything logical about my conclusion."

"Good, because frankly, it sounds ridiculous."

Fiona hadn't heard Iris speak in such blunt terms before, and it stung.

"Tell me how you really feel."

"I'm sorry to be so direct. I only say that because I know that you aren't imagining things. Those conversations happened. I'm as sure about that as I am that the two of us are talking right now."

"Then how do you explain the fact that Olivia wasn't in the apartment?"

Iris didn't have the immediate answer that Fiona had hoped she would. "I guess I can't. But that doesn't mean I'm wrong."

"What does it mean?"

"It means that we have to figure out what's going on."

"And how do we do that?"

"We go over there and demand answers."

"Forget it. I'm not stirring up that hornet's nest again."

"You don't have to. I can handle her myself."

Iris rose from the couch, but Fiona grabbed her arm before she could get farther. "Please, just let it go."

"Fine," Iris said before sitting. "What do you suggest we do then?"

"Nothing. It's out of our hands. Detective Sullivan told Natalie that she planned to follow up with Noah about his confrontation with Donald Tisdale. Maybe something will come from that."

"I seriously doubt it."

"Why?"

"Because it wasn't much of a confrontation."

"You know what happened?"

"I wasn't here at the time, but the building talks."

*Does it ever*, Fiona thought. "I only got bits and pieces of the story, but I did hear the detectives say that it involved Natalie's daughter. What was Olivia's role?"

"It wasn't Olivia."

"Who was it?"

"Natalie's other daughter."

Fiona gasped. "She has another daughter?"

"Yes. I believe her name is Eva. Apparently, she was never around much. Lived with her father most of the time. Anyway, she was eight or nine when it happened. She had befriended Donald over their mutual love of drawing. He invited her over to see some of his work. Perfectly innocent. But Natalie and Noah turned it into something sick and twisted. Noah told him to leave her alone or else. He complied because he didn't want any trouble. Less than a month later, she went to live with her father and thankfully never came back. I heard that he got full custody of her."

"Is this the same father that Natalie claims Olivia is with?"

Iris shook her head. "From what I understand, Olivia's father died before she was born."

Fiona's face dropped with sadness. "That's terrible."

"The poor girl hasn't caught many breaks in her young life."

"So, Natalie was lying."

"Of course, she was. That's why we need to confront her."

"Like I said, that's something the police need to handle. I'm not insensitive to what's going on, far from it. But I have my own issues to deal with. I don't think I have the strength to take on anyone else's."

Iris's tension immediately subsided. "I'm sorry, sweetheart. Your son is the only thing you should be focused on. I should have been more mindful of that."

"It's okay, Iris. I understand your urgency, and I want to help Olivia. I'm just not sure what I can do."

"You're right. It is best to leave it to the police. Noah

certainly has issues, but they may be barking up the wrong tree when it comes to him and Donald. Let's just hope they discover something else."

"Let's hope so. Speaking of Noah—" Fiona's sentence was suddenly interrupted by a high-pitched ringtone.

"I'm sorry, dear, that's me," Iris said as she fumbled in her pocket before pulling out a small flip phone. "I've been expecting an important call from my Quinn. Hopefully, this is him." She flipped open the phone, saying, "Hello?" a few octaves higher than her normal speaking voice. "Quinn, are you there? I don't hear anything. Let me call you back."

She disconnected the call and redialed. After a few seconds, she spoke into the phone. "Quinn, can you hear… Yes, I know it's a terrible connection. Where are you? Honey, you keep cutting out. I can't hear a word you're saying." She frowned at Fiona. "It went dead again."

Fiona thought back to the earlier issue with her own cell phone. "How many service bars do you have?"

Iris looked at her phone. "None."

"That happened to me too. I had to go outside to finish my call."

"Well, I'm certainly not doing that. I'll just have to keep trying. Maybe I'll have better luck in my own apartment." She stood. "I'll feel a lot better leaving here knowing that you're okay."

Fiona forced a smile. "I am."

"Are you sure? I can always call Quinn back later."

"I'm sure."

Iris hesitated for a moment before saying, "Okay. I'm off then. Thank you for accommodating my intrusion. I promise that our next meeting will be under much better circumstances. Perhaps we should plan a trip out, maybe grab some lunch."

"I'd like that."

"Wonderful. You take care, okay? I mean it."

"I will, Iris. And thank you."

After a warm hug, Iris left. Fiona stood by the door until she heard the three lock clicks that assured her Iris was safely inside her apartment.

When she closed the door, she walked into the kitchen to retrieve her own cell phone from the kitchen counter. She had no bars either.

On a whim, she dialed Kirk's cell phone number, beginning with the 206 area code that she assumed he still used.

She held her breath as she pushed the last digit. It was beyond stupid, and she knew it. But what did it matter? The phone didn't work anyway.

When the call rang through, she gasped and promptly hung up.

*Dammit, that wasn't supposed to happen.*

Thoroughly disgusted with herself and her chronically reckless decision-making, Fiona put the phone back on the counter and began the trip to her bedroom for what promised to be another restless night. Halfway there, her cell phone rang. She raced back to the kitchen and picked up the phone–Kirk's number.

"You've got to be kidding me."

Her thumb hovered over the answer button for four long rings. On the fifth, she slid the button to the right. Her voice trembled as she answered. "Hello?"

She heard the low hum of distant static before the line went dead.

Her body ached with the dull pain of emptiness as she turned off the phone and made her way to bed.

## Chapter Nineteen

Fiona had no memory of falling asleep, nor did she remember dreaming. All she knew for sure was that for seven glorious hours between 10:30 p.m. and 5:30 a.m. there was nothing but deep, penetrating, restful darkness.

She awoke that morning to the faintest sliver of predawn light peeking through her window. Though the light was enough to confirm the promise of a brand-new day, it wasn't yet enough to illuminate her bedroom.

Thankfully, the sleeping pills had done their job. She woke up physically rejuvenated, and for the first time in days, Fiona felt that she could approach the day with energy and focus.

But the pitch-blackness that enveloped her room made it tough to get out of bed. So instead of taking advantage of her newfound energy and getting a jumpstart on the day, she pulled the covers over her shoulders, sank as deep as her air mattress would allow, and focused on that thin sliver of light in her window until she drifted back to sleep.

This time, she did dream.

As had been the case in nearly every other dream she had, Jacob's was the first face that she saw.

Dressed in a black suit and tie, he stood outside her apartment, jiggling the door handle, frustrated that he couldn't get in. In his free hand, he held a bundle of fresh flowers—the yellow marigolds that had always been Fiona's favorites.

She could see him from inside the apartment, but she couldn't get out of bed to let him in. He twisted the handle, pushed on the door with his shoulder, but it wouldn't budge. Suddenly, his eyes grew fearful and he began sobbing.

"*Mom, let me in. Mom, please.*"

The soft whimper registered in Fiona's ear with the force of a megaphone. But still, she couldn't move.

Finally, with one last strike of his shoulder, Jacob came through the door.

He smiled with relief as he stepped inside the dark apartment, the bright marigolds beaming in his hand.

"*Mom? Are you here?*"

"*Yes, honey. I'm here, in the bedroom.*"

Fiona once again attempted to get out of bed, but she was still unable to move.

"*Mom, I'm here. Where are you?*"

Jacob's voice sounded distant, though Fiona could clearly see him.

"*I'm here. Just follow Mommy's voice. You'll find me.*"

He started sobbing again.

"*I can't find you. Why won't you come to me?*"

Fiona attempted to lift herself out of bed, but something pushed her back down—a heavy hand that she couldn't see. The harder she fought, the harder the hand pushed back.

*"Please, don't."*

*"I have to go, Mom. I can't stay here."*

*"Jacob, no. Please wait!"*

Without saying another word, he turned around and walked toward the door.

*"Don't go, Jacob. I'm coming."*

The invisible hands that held her down on the bed pressed harder, and she suddenly found it difficult to breathe.

*"Please don't leave me."*

Jacob reached for the doorknob. Before he turned it, he looked back into the darkness. The marigolds were no longer in his hand.

*"I miss you, Mommy. Why did you have to go?"*

He opened the door and stepped through it.

The hallway was just as dark as her apartment, and Fiona instinctively knew that once Jacob entered it, she would never see him again.

She tried to call out one last time, but there was no air left in her lungs.

The last image she saw of Jacob was the ghostly white silhouette of his face against the pitch-black of the hallway.

He smiled again. This time, there was nothing bright about it. This time, it was dark, contorted, and malevolent.

Then, in an instant, he was gone, and she was some-place warm, looking up at a bright blue sky.

Fiona thought for a moment that she had finally landed on that sun-filled sandy beach. Then she looked down and saw the marigolds spread out on top of her. The soft fabric of her favorite sundress clung to her cold body. Once again, she couldn't move, bound on all sides by an obstruction that she didn't see.

It was only when she saw Kirk's face, and the shovel in his hand, and the mound of dirt that he was preparing to toss on her, that she realized what the obstruction was.

She tried to stop him, but lungs that were devoid of air couldn't produce much noise. The bright sky disappeared with each mound of dirt that Kirk heaped on top of her until there was nothing left but darkness and the sound of wheezing as she struggled through her final breaths.

When she was in the dark void, she heard a young, soft voice.

*"No, it's not time yet."*

Fiona didn't recognize the voice, but it comforted her, nonetheless.

*"Wake up."*

She rose with a furious start, gasping for air. Quickly realizing that there was no danger, no invisible hands crushing her chest, she steadied her breathing.

She looked around the daylit bedroom, trying to reorient herself. It was just a dream—all of it. There was no Jacob, no marigolds, no casket, no mounds of dirt burying her alive. It was another day, a new day. And she still had the chance to make everything right.

Relieved beyond anything she had ever felt before, Fiona made her way out of bed and into the bathroom. The feeling of rejuvenation that she'd woken up with earlier was gone, replaced with a fierce exhaustion. She carefully avoided looking in the mirror for fear of how her face would display that exhaustion. She instead kept her focus on a hallway photo of her mother holding a newborn Jacob. It was the one photo that had thus far managed not to fall off the wall it had been nailed to.

But there was still something wrong. She couldn't pinpoint what that something was until she approached it.

The tilt of the photo appeared minor at first, but the closer she got to it, the more askew it became. She never saw it move; it was almost as if the microscopic changes happened every time she blinked. For every blink, it seemed, there was a one-degree turn until, by the time she stood directly in front of it, the photo had rotated a full forty-five degrees.

She stared at it for a long moment before touching it, her head tilting in unison with a sideways Jacob.

"What the hell is this?" she asked herself. Her tongue felt thick, and she slurred the words. She was used to the feeling, though this time, it wasn't the result of alcohol. Fearing what the words would sound like should she say anything else, Fiona kept quiet as she turned the picture to its rightful position. It fell easily back into place.

She gave no conscious thought to how the photo had ended up in that position. The answer, she knew, was not readily available. And even if it were, she was better off not knowing.

As she walked back into the bathroom, she heard a slow creaking sound. Her eyes immediately fell on the door that she had just walked through.

*I must have brushed up against it,* she concluded, completely ignoring the fact that the sound had originated in another area of the apartment entirely. She had turned on the faucet for her daily wake-up call when she heard the creaking again. This time, she couldn't ignore it.

She shut off the water and listened.

Another creak. This one louder.

Fiona froze with fear, unsure of what to do. She wanted to lock the door, hide in the shower, and wait until whatever was opening the door decided to leave. Better yet, she could squeeze through the tight bathroom window and take her chances with the six-story drop. It was certainly better than the nightmare alternative that she had already decided was inevitable.

But what if it wasn't? What if it was nothing more than her overcooked imagination having its way again? Was she prepared to spend the rest of the day cowering in her shower because of a threat that most likely didn't even exist?

Fiona answered the question by slowly making her way out of the bathroom and into the hallway. When she rounded the corner into the living room, she froze again, instantly wishing that she had chosen the window.

Her front door was wide open.

Beneath the distant sound of televisions and muted chatter from other apartments, Fiona heard something else.

"*Hey!*"

An excited whisper.

"*Come here, quick! I want to show you something!*"

Then, mischievous, youthful laughter.

"*Come on, Fiona! Hurry up! You're gonna miss it!*"

She ran for the door to the sound of light, quick footsteps closing in from behind her.

By the time the screaming in her mind traveled to her mouth, it was nothing more than a labored moan.

Her momentum was stopped cold as she crossed the doorway. Heavy hands on her shoulders. She closed her eyes and screamed. Then she fought.

"Miss, calm down!"

Fiona pushed until she broke free of the grip. Only then did she open her eyes.

She immediately recognized the man from his pictures, but she didn't register him as friend or foe.

Iris's son held his hands up. "I'm sorry. I didn't mean to grab you like that, but you almost knocked me down running out of your apartment. Is everything okay?"

Still unsure of what to make of his appearance in front of her door, Fiona backed away.

He stepped back, too, holding his hands higher in the air. "My name is Quinn. My mom lives right here. I was just leaving her apartment when you came running out of yours. Is someone in there trying to hurt you?"

"I don't know," Fiona answered warily.

"Is anyone else in there?"

"I don't know."

Quinn looked at her with eyes that were understandably confused. "Do you want me to check?"

Fiona nodded as she backed away another step.

"Okay." He tensed as he walked into her apartment.

Fiona continued to edge down the hall until she was in front of 607.

"Is someone in here?" Quinn's voice was strong and unwavering. "If you are, come out."

Iris suddenly emerged from her apartment. "Quinn, is that you?"

When she stepped into the hall, her eyes immediately found Fiona. "Sweetheart, what's the matter?"

Fiona motioned to the open door of her apartment.

"Is Quinn in there?"

Fiona nodded.

Iris quickly moved toward the door. "Quinn? What's going on?"

Within seconds, he emerged from the apartment.

"There's no one in there," he said to Fiona. "I checked everywhere."

"What's this about?" Iris asked again.

When Quinn shrugged, Iris turned to Fiona.

"What's wrong, sweetheart?"

Fiona looked at Iris, then at Quinn, then at Olivia's apartment, then at her open front door, and suddenly she knew exactly what was wrong.

"Pretty much everything."

## Chapter Twenty

"There's no issue with the door that I can see," Arthur declared as he completed the inspection that Iris had requested.

That wasn't news to Fiona. She knew there was nothing wrong with the door, except that someone, or something, had opened it and entered without her consent. But as had been the case when she saw the shadowy figure inside Olivia's apartment, it was apparently all in her mind.

"You're positive you locked it?" Arthur asked Fiona in a tone that suggested the fault was somehow hers.

"Yes," Fiona answered confidently. Her OCD would never allow her to overlook such a thing, but she thought it best not to burden anyone with that particular bit of trivia.

"Looking at the door, I can tell you that no one forced their way in. I don't really know what else to say beyond that."

"Maybe you should get a deadbolt," Iris suggested. "I have two of them. It's the only thing that helps me sleep at night."

"I don't need a deadbolt."

"Are you sure?" Arthur asked. "It won't be a problem. I can have it installed in ten minutes."

"Please, Fiona," Iris reiterated. "If you don't do it for your sake, do it for mine. I don't want to be up in the middle of the night worrying about you."

Fiona knew that whatever she experienced in her apartment wasn't going to be deterred by a deadbolt, but she decided to play along for the sake of getting everyone off her back. "Fine."

"Great. Can you get that done today, Artie?" a relieved Iris asked.

"Sure. Whenever Fiona is ready."

"I'll let you know," Fiona said, knowing that she would never follow through.

"Sounds good. Well, if you guys won't be needing me anymore, I have a few other errands to run around the building."

"Thanks for coming," Iris said.

"Yes, thank you," Fiona added.

"My pleasure. Sorry I couldn't find anything more definitive for you. Strange things happen sometimes. Things we can't explain. I guess this is one of those situations."

"Guess so," Fiona answered with a tired voice.

"The important thing is that you're safe now. You'll let me know when you're ready for that deadbolt?"

"Of course."

Arthur tipped his cap to the group. "I'm off, then. You folks be sure to have a good day."

"We will," Iris declared as she escorted him into the hallway. "And thanks again." When she came back, she closed the door, making sure to lock it, then she walked over to Quinn, who had silently watched the exchange from the living room. "Fiona, you're more than welcome to stay with me until you get that deadbolt installed."

Fiona shook her head. "I'll be fine."

"Shaking your head while answering in the affirmative is a dead giveaway that you're not telling the truth."

"I'm fine, Iris."

"I certainly wouldn't be. Would you, Quinn?"

He shifted nervously, clearly embarrassed by the sudden attention. "We can't tell her how to feel, Mom. We weren't here."

Fiona appreciated the voice of reason.

Iris did not. "Anyway," she said with a glare before turning back to Fiona, "I would feel much more at ease if you stayed with me for a while."

"That won't be necessary. I'd make a terrible house-guest, anyway."

"Fine. Then I'll stay with you."

"Sorry, but I'm an even worse host," Fiona replied. When she looked at Quinn, he smiled.

"Well, you have to let me do something. I can tell the stress is getting to you. Whether you saw something in here or not—and I believe you did—it doesn't really matter at this point. You need a change in scenery, even if it's temporary, just to let your mind breathe a little."

Iris was right about that, but her apartment wasn't the change that Fiona had in mind.

"I appreciate it. But all I want now is to move forward with the day. I have a lot to do and not a lot of time to do it."

Iris nodded. "Your son. I understand. But with all of the strain you're feeling right now, do you even have enough left to give to him?"

As much as the question bothered Fiona, she knew it was valid. She also knew that if this conversation was ever going to end, and she desperately needed it to, she would have to lie. "I have more than enough to give him."

Iris tapped Quinn on the shoulder and motioned toward the door. "We'll leave you to it then. I'm not happy about it, but if you insist that you're okay, I have to accept that."

"I insist," Fiona replied, forcing another smile.

Iris hugged her as they entered the hallway. "If you need anything, you know where I live."

"I certainly do."

Fiona turned her strained smile to Quinn. He responded with a smile of his own.

"I'm sorry again about our abrupt meeting," he said. "I wish it was under better circumstances, but I'm glad everything is okay now."

Quinn was anything but the silent, brooding type that the photos on Iris's mantel suggested. He was down-to-earth, considerate, and fully present. But there was also strength. Emotional strength to deal with his loving, but overbearing mother. Bodily strength–his broad, sturdy shoulders suggested lots of time in the gym–to handle any threats that came his way. He made Fiona feel safe, physically at least. But her heart feared how easy it would be to lose herself in the deep blue sea of his gaze, the security of his tight embrace, the hypnotic pull of his easy smile. She couldn't afford to lose any parts of herself, even if, in this moment, it was the only thing she wanted to do.

"I'm the one who came running out of my apartment like a raving lunatic," Fiona said with a nervous swipe at her tousled hair. It's me who should be apologizing,"

"A handshake will do."

She felt a charge of adrenaline as his large hand wrapped around hers. The feeling was not unwelcome.

"We'll let you run along now," Iris said abruptly.

Though her expression gave nothing away, Fiona could only pray that she hadn't picked up on the semi-flirtatious exchange. She knew from personal experience that mothers had a powerful sixth sense when it came to their sons. And Iris was more plugged in than most.

"Thank you again." Fiona put a hand on her shoulder and was relieved when Iris cupped it with her own.

"Anytime." Then she turned an eye to Quinn. "And as for you, young man, you still need to take me to the store."

"Ready when you are, Mother," he replied with a courteous bow.

Iris beamed at her son's gesture. "Let me grab my coat and purse."

Just as the pair began the short walk to Iris's apartment, the door to 607 opened.

Fiona held her breath in anticipation of who would walk through it. When she saw Noah's now-familiar black work boots and rolled-up blue jeans, her chest tightened.

He looked surprised by the sight of them but quickly pushed the expression away, replacing it with the narrow-eyed suspicion that was much more at home on his war-beaten face. What kind of war he was waging, Fiona wasn't sure. But his look suggested that the fighting was far from over.

Then something unexpected happened. His face softened, allowing one side of his mouth to curl up in a tight smile. What happened next nearly knocked Fiona off her feet.

"How's it going, Quinn? Been a while."

Quinn didn't return the smile, but his eyes were clearly receptive to the greeting.

"It's going okay. Busy as ever."

"I hear that. Off to work myself. See you around." When Noah's eyes shifted to Fiona and Iris, his tight smile dissolved. He looked like he wanted to say something not at all friendly, but Quinn's presence forced him to swallow it. Through pursed lips, he instead said, "You ladies have a wonderful day."

Determined not to engage him, Fiona looked away.

Iris, however, wasn't willing to let him off so easy. "In the two-plus years I've lived next to you, that has got to be the first friendly word I've heard you utter to anyone. This must be a wonderful day indeed." Then she turned a dubious eye to her son. "So, how long have you two gentlemen been acquainted?"

Quinn appeared nervous to answer. "We–"

Noah quickly jumped in. "I helped him once when he was dragging some things out of your apartment, Mrs. Matheson. Your son's a good man."

"I'm aware of that. But you're not, which makes it odd that you would want to befriend him."

"Mom, relax," a flustered Quinn chided. "It's not that serious."

"Exactly, Mrs. Matheson. It's not that serious," Noah echoed with a grin. He clearly relished the sudden tension his presence created.

Iris wasn't fazed. "You should probably run along now. It would be positively awful if you lost your job because we made you late for work. Wouldn't that be awful, everyone?"

Fiona and Quinn looked at one another with the same mortified expression.

"Yes, it would be awful," Iris continued.

"Right. Well, on that charming note…" Noah turned and walked down the hallway.

Fiona was about to let out a sigh of relief, but Iris's voice stopped it.

"One more thing, Noah."

He turned to acknowledge her with his best *fuck you* smile on display. "What's that, Mrs. Matheson?"

"Did those detectives ever catch up to you?"

The smile went away. "What detectives?"

"The ones who were here looking for you last night. I heard they wanted to talk about Donald Tisdale."

"Is that what you heard?" Noah's hard stare fell on Fiona.

"What are you looking at her for? I'm the one who asked the question."

Quinn began pulling on Iris's arm. "Let's go, Mom."

Iris pulled free of his grip, then turned back to Noah. "You're not going to intimidate anyone else around here, do you understand? Not me, not Fiona, and certainly not that innocent little girl. One of these days, you'll finally be exposed for the terrible human being that you are. And if it takes those detectives knocking on your door every single day to find that out for themselves, I'll make sure they have a reason to come back here every single day."

"Looks to me like I'm the only one being intimidated here," Noah said smugly. "I don't hear Quinn saying that I intimidate him." He looked at Fiona. "I don't hear you saying it, either. Of course, your issue is that you have trouble minding your own business. But I thought we'd hashed that out already. I guess I was wrong."

Fiona knew that he was talking about her confrontation with Natalie, but she refused to add fuel to this already raging fire by speaking on it.

"All I'm doing is defending my family's integrity," Noah continued. "If you consider that being intimidating, well, I think you're all being a little too sensitive."

"Just heed my words, Noah Glasby," Iris said sharply.

Noah bowed his head in mock deference. "Yes, ma'am. Your *threats* are heeded. Again, you folks have a wonderful day." Without saying anything else, he turned down the hallway toward the elevator. He glanced back at the group as he rounded the corner, still smiling.

Iris immediately directed her ire at Quinn. "What do you think you're doing, befriending that psychopath?" she asked, jabbing him with a hard elbow.

"I just said hi to the guy a couple of times. I didn't think it was a big deal."

"Well, it is a big deal. You've been around here long enough to know what kind of people they are. They're not stable, and I don't want you associating with them in any way, shape, or form. You got me?"

Iris was scolding this grown man like he was a seven-year-old child. And for the briefest of moments, Quinn played the part.

"Fine. I got you." He cowered under the weight of his mother's rebuke. Fiona felt sorry for him, but quickly realized that she probably would have reacted the same way if it were her son.

"Now, can we please get to the store? I don't want to have crowds to contend with, especially after this nonsense."

Quinn's broad shoulders slumped as he started down the hallway. He didn't acknowledge Fiona as he passed.

"I'm sorry for all of that," Iris said as she put a gentle hand on Fiona's shoulder.

"No problem," she replied, suddenly feeling intimidated

herself. She had been caught off guard by Iris's intensity, but she also felt gratitude that the intensity had been used in her defense.

"Are you going to be okay?"

"I'll be fine. I have some errands to run today, so I'll be busy out in the world."

"Good. The last thing you need to do is stay cooped up in here. I should give you my cell phone number in case you need me while I'm out. Let me grab a pen. I think I have one on that table near the door. Hold tight." She took a hurried step toward her apartment before Fiona stopped her.

"Not necessary, Iris. I'm okay. You need to run along so you can beat the rush."

The thought was enough for Iris to abandon her pursuit. "You're right. I should get going. I still need to talk some sense into that rock-headed son of mine anyway. Take care, sweetheart."

"You too."

She watched as Iris and Quinn shuffled off toward the elevator. Iris spoke to him in a hushed but stern tone. Fiona could only thank the heavens that it wasn't her on the receiving end of those words.

Before she could walk back into her apartment, she heard the muted sound of applause coming from 607. Random outbursts of numbers followed the applause. *"Six seventy-five!"* Then: *"Five hundred!"* Then: *"Eight-fifty!"* Rising above the outbursts, a female voice declared her own number. "I'm gonna go with eight-fifty."

More applause as the male game show host repeated the number, "Eight-fifty." A loud ding confirmed the number. "And the actual retail price is…"

Before Fiona couldn't hear the number, her attention

shifted to something else. Another voice. This one was more familiar.

"Why would you do that?"

At first, Fiona thought that Natalie was simply protesting the game show contestant's bid. Then she heard something else.

"I don't know how many times I can tolerate having this conversation with you. Don't talk to people you don't know."

Fiona didn't hear a response.

"Not another word," Natalie continued. "You don't speak. You listen. Got it?"

Fiona edged closer to the door, careful to avoid the peephole. The background noise of the television dissolved into nothing as she tuned her ear to Natalie's voice.

"You don't know that woman. She could be a danger to you, to us."

Silence.

"I don't care if you think she's nice. I've talked to her, and so has Noah, and I can promise you she isn't nice."

Fiona didn't need an advanced degree to know that Natalie was talking about her. She felt angry that someone with such a horrible disposition would have the nerve to judge her character, but she let it go, focusing instead on what she hoped would be the sound of Olivia's voice. Despite Natalie's continued dialogue, Fiona never heard it.

*Must be a phone call,* she quickly concluded. Perhaps Natalie wasn't lying when she said that Olivia was away. It would explain the one-way conversation. Unfortunately, it would leave many other things unexplained.

"Is there anything else you need to say? Or have I finally made myself clear?"

Silence.

"I'm glad you understand. Just make sure we don't have to talk about this again, okay?"

Fiona took a step toward her apartment in anticipation of Natalie ending the phone call.

"Now go to your room and lay down for a while. If you're too sick to go to school, you're too sick to be up watching television. I'll make breakfast soon."

Fiona saw strobes of white-hot pulsating light in her immediate field of vision, fear so potent that it manifested itself in physical form.

"We don't have pancakes. You can have cereal like you always do."

More silence as Natalie listened to a response that Fiona couldn't hear.

"Whatever. Do you know how many children in the world would kill for a handful of dried rice? Let alone that bowl of refined sugar you call breakfast? Be thankful for what you have. No more arguing about it. Just go, and I'll call you when it's ready."

All Fiona could hear after that was the exuberant screams of game show contestants as they clamored for the double-wide hot tub that none of them would ever have use for.

She walked back into her apartment on wobbly legs, barely making it to the kitchen counter to retrieve her phone before collapsing in an exhausted heap on her futon.

"Please, God. Please let it work." Fiona closed her eyes and silently repeated the prayer before turning on her cell phone. She smiled at the sight of five signal bars. Full strength. "I owe you one," she said with a look to the sky. In reality, it was far more than one, but she'd stopped counting years ago. She hoped He had too.

Fiona never got around to storing Paul Riley's contact

information in her phone, so she had to dial his number manually. Her hands shook so violently that she misdialed three times before finally connecting. After being informed of her call by his assistant—the young, sharply dressed kid she'd met a few days ago—Paul answered on the first ring.

"Good morning, Fiona. How are you?" Unlike their last conversation, his voice came through loud and clear.

"Not good, Paul. Not good at all."

"What's the matter? Did something happen?"

"Yes."

"Tell me."

"I can't. Not here. Would it be possible to stop by your office sometime today?"

"I have an open hour this afternoon between one and two."

"Great. I'll be there."

"Okay, but can you give me at least an idea of what this is about?"

"I may need some legal advice outside of my custody situation."

"What kind of advice?"

"Advice on what my rights are as a tenant, and how I can protect myself if I'm forced to break my lease early."

"I'm sorry, but I'm not understanding."

Fiona attempted to answer but choked on the words as a giant knot formed in her throat.

"Are you okay, Fiona? You're kind of freaking me out here."

She composed herself long enough to force out the nine words that she had repeated in her mind since the first night she moved in; words that, up until this very second, she hoped she would never have to act on.

"I can't spend one more night inside this apartment."

## Chapter Twenty-One

"Tenant rights isn't exactly my area of legal expertise," Paul Riley said as he and Fiona entered his office. "But I was able to research the potential options that someone in your situation might have."

"And?"

"Unfortunately, you don't have many."

Fiona's heart sank. "Are you saying that I'm stuck there?"

"No one can force you to stay. You can leave the apartment anytime you want. But if you leave before the lease expires, it's going to cost you a lot of time and money, neither of which you can afford to lose."

"But I read somewhere that exceptions can be made for unsafe living conditions. That place isn't safe."

"That particular provision only applies if the building itself is unsafe. Say, for instance, the heat stops working in the dead of winter, and the owner refuses to fix it. Structural deficiencies are another example."

"What about batshit crazy neighbors? Is there a provision in the state code for that?"

Paul started to smile but wisely pushed it back. "I'm afraid not."

"So, what am I supposed to do?"

"Have you brought the issue up with your landlord?"

Fiona shook her head. "He's got bigger problems right now. My personal comfort is probably on the bottom of his priority list."

"Yeah, I read about what happened. They're saying it was a suicide, right?"

"I don't think they know any more than you or I do."

"Well, I still don't think it would hurt to give him a call. At the very least, he can talk to your neighbors, maybe offer some kind of conflict resolution."

"These aren't the kind of people that respond to conflict resolution. Besides, it isn't just the neighbors."

"What else is it?"

"Strange things are happening there."

"In your apartment?"

Fiona nodded, unsure if she was ready to say more.

"Give me an example."

"Just one?"

"Is there more than one?"

Fiona nodded again.

"Okay, start with the worst."

"Aside from the fact that a man was most likely killed in an apartment on the same floor as mine, I think the building might be haunted."

Paul's eyes widened. "Say that again?"

"I can't speak for the entire building, but I can say for sure that my apartment is."

The smile that Paul had successfully suppressed before

was now on full display, more the result, Fiona suspected, of nervousness than amusement. "What leads you to believe that?"

Fiona ran a blow-by-blow of each unexplained event that occurred since she moved in, from the pictures to the strange thumping noises to the conversations with Olivia to the voice that called her name this morning.

"I know how it all sounds," she said in response to Paul's furrowed brow of skepticism. "Trust me. If it wasn't for the stories that my next-door neighbor Iris told me, I would have dismissed it as complete bullshit, too."

"Does Iris think your apartment is haunted?"

"She thinks it's cursed."

Paul shook his head. "Jesus, you do need to get out of there. It sounds like you're surrounded by a bunch of loons."

"I can't dispute that. But I also can't dispute what I've personally witnessed."

"And the girl, Olivia. Is she the same one who you heard crying a few nights ago?"

"Yes."

"And you've had several conversations with her since then, but you still haven't seen her?"

"I thought I saw Olivia inside her apartment when the detectives were there, but her mother insisted that she was away."

"Do you think you've been talking to a ghost, then?"

"I don't know what to believe about that place. That's why I need to leave. If she is a ghost, if she isn't a ghost; either way, the situation is unmanageable, and I don't want any part of it."

"But you told me that you fear for her safety."

"I do."

"*If* she's real."

This exchange was beginning to feel more like a cross-examination than a conversation. "Why do I get the feeling you don't believe me?"

"It doesn't matter if I believe it. What matters is that you believe it. I'm just trying to figure out why."

Fiona tensed. "I didn't realize I was paying for a lawyer *and* a therapist."

"I'm no therapist, Fiona."

"Then why are you acting like one? I didn't come here to have you analyze my experience. I came here to get advice about my lease."

"And I provided that. But you've said some things that are frankly a little troubling, and as your lawyer, it's my job to understand your state of mind... so that when it's time for a deposition, I'm not blindsided by some attack on you from Kirk's lawyer."

"What kind of an attack?"

"An attack on your mental and emotional stability."

Fiona nearly fell out of her chair. "Are you implying that I'm mentally or emotionally unstable?"

"No, but if what you're telling me ever becomes part of a public record, and it will if these are the conditions under which you break your lease, you can bet that Kirk's lawyer will imply it. Unfortunately, with your track record, it wouldn't take much for the court to side with him."

"I can't believe what I'm hearing."

"I'm sorry to be the one to break it to you, but as your lawyer, *that* is my job."

"So, this is you're not-so-subtle way of telling me to stay in that hellhole apartment."

"Absolutely, at least until a custody decision has been rendered. You've only been here for a week, yet you've already found an apartment, joined an AA group, and are well on your way to finding a job. That will speak volumes to the court about your readiness and commitment. What do you think it would say if you break your lease after one week because you think that ghosts are haunting your apartment building? Do you think the courts would still consider you ready and committed? Not a chance. And what would be the end result? Everything you've worked so hard to build would go to shit. Gone in an instant."

Fiona was so angry that she hadn't felt the tears streaming down her face until she saw them dot her blouse. She wiped them away with the back of her hand, not bothering to reach for the box of tissue on Paul's desk.

"Can I ask you something else?" Paul said in a solemn tone.

"Why not?" she responded, thinking that he couldn't possibly say anything worse than he already had.

She was wrong.

"How have you been coping since the meeting with Kirk?"

After fighting to compose herself, Fiona could only manage a three-word answer. "Not very well."

Paul nodded like he expected that answer. "We know what your coping mechanisms were in the past, and we know how destructive they were. Has that changed?"

"Of course, it has."

"Are you sure? I need to know." The complete lack of belief in Paul's tone was enough to finally send Fiona over the edge. She stood up from the chair with a clenched fist, prepared to either storm out of his office or punch him in the face. "Are you suggesting that I'm drinking again?"

"I'm not suggesting, Fiona. I'm asking. There's a difference."

"I'm not drinking, okay? I'm scared." Fiona began pacing the office before finally deciding to walk out. "I can see that it was a mistake coming here. Sorry for wasting your time with my drunken, babbling nonsense."

Paul rose from his chair before she could leave. "Fiona, wait. I'm sorry. I didn't mean to come across like that. Please don't leave."

Fiona stood in the doorway, hesitant to reenter the office.

"I'm not doubting you," Paul continued. "I'm here to fight for you in every way possible. Right now, that fight is for your integrity because that's the only hand you have to play. Ultimately, the court doesn't care what kind of house you live in, what kind of car you drive, or what kind of job you have. What they really want to know is that you can be trusted to provide a stable environment for Jacob. But when you start talking about ghosts and curses…Let's just say that's not going to sit too well. There are still a lot of battles to fight. Your living situation shouldn't be one of them."

"So, you're saying I shouldn't do anything about it? That I should just stay there and wait for God-knows-what to happen?"

"If you can hang on until we have our day in court, yes, that would be my legal advice."

Fiona felt deflated as she reentered the office and sat back down. "How long am I going to have to wait?"

"Well, there could be a way to expedite things."

"And what is that?"

"Have you given any more thought to taking Kirk up on his offer to talk? In my experience, the most successful custody cases end when the two parties can come together on a mutually agreed-upon course of action rather than relying solely on the courts. His meeting request could signify that he's open to such a negotiation."

"I don't think I could bring myself to call him after what happened the other day," Fiona declared, completely glossing over the fact that she called him last night in what amounted to a drunk dial. "How do you know that he doesn't want anything more than to humiliate me again?"

"I don't know, and neither will you unless you call."

"I'll have to think about it."

"Think hard. Despite the way things turned out, the two of you were married once. You loved each other once. I can tell you from years of doing this that the love never completely goes away, even in the nastiest situations. You need someone to talk to who doesn't charge you by the hour." Paul cracked a smile, and this time, Fiona reciprocated.

"This session should be free."

"You may be a sympathy case, but you're not a charity case. No free rides this go 'round."

"I don't care how much I have to pay you. I just want this all to be over."

"Call Kirk."

"And what about my apartment? How am I supposed to live there?"

"If it's really that bad, get a hotel room until you can figure something else out."

"Believe me, I've thought about it. But I can't afford a hotel room and my rent."

"Then my advice would be to lay low and wait it out. If Olivia tries to reach out to you again, don't respond. It sounds like she's playing games. But if she isn't, if something else truly is going on, you can't make it your problem. The more energy you give to that, the less you'll have for

Jacob. This may be your best and last opportunity to make things right with him, and if you miss out on that, the regret will make what you're experiencing right now look like child's play. Don't let that happen."

Fiona rose from Paul's desk, determined to take his advice. She would find a way to deal with Corona Heights, and its strange noises, and its unhinged tenants, if that's what it took to get Jacob back.

She thought about the knocking on her bedroom wall, and the falling pictures, and the persistent voice of warning that said: *Something is very wrong inside that apartment.*

*That may be,* her voice of reason countered. *But you'll still find a way.*

"I won't let it happen," Fiona answered, absolutely believing it.

She didn't know it then, but Corona Heights–and its strange noises and its unhinged tenants–had very different ideas.

## Chapter Twenty-Two

After spending a good portion of the afternoon scouring the depths of a depleted job market, Fiona canvassed seven motels before settling on one that fit both her limited price range and minimum standard of cleanliness and safety.

The Red Lodge Inn didn't provide much: a bed, a basic bathroom with clean towels, and a decent view of Denver's eclectic, and sometimes sketchy, Colfax Avenue. But what it had going for it most was that it was nowhere near Corona Heights.

She dreaded being back there, even for the ten minutes it would take to pack clothes and toiletries for the two days that she planned to spend at the motel, but she took comfort in the fact that she'd finally found a safe space to get a decent night's sleep.

Perhaps some time in a different environment would help her get the perspective she needed to make the situation in Corona Heights work.

At least, that was what Fiona told herself. The truth of

the matter was that she simply didn't want to be scared anymore.

She returned to the building to pick up a change of clothes. *I'll be quick,* she promised herself as she navigated the quiet corridors with her head down, avoiding eye contact with the handful of tenants she passed.

From what she saw, they were all normal-looking, well-adjusted people. None of them looked unbalanced like her immediate neighbors, or frightened of the air they breathed like she was.

She wondered if they lived in some other part of the building altogether, sequestered away from everyone else. She silently cursed the thought of their good fortune, while at the same time holding to the optimistic promise that their warm presence provided.

She was determined to carry that optimism with her as she approached the creaky elevator that would carry her up to the sixth floor and the cold abyss that was her apartment. She would think of these normal people as she quickly packed her clothes, hoping it would make the abyss seem a little less dark and endless. While she was away, she would formulate a rock-solid plan to become one of those normal people, and if she was fortunate, that plan would succeed.

"It will absolutely succeed," Fiona declared aloud, unconcerned if anyone heard her.

She repeated the line as she entered the elevator, and once more when she stepped onto the sixth floor.

She was preparing for a fourth go when Quinn suddenly emerged in the hallway.

He dropped a large black trash bag to the floor as he closed Iris's door. Then he picked it up, hoisted it over his shoulder, and slowly made his way in Fiona's direction.

They quickly made eye contact. It was uncomfortable,

and Fiona had to fight the temptation to reverse course back to the elevator before he could catch up. Instead, she put on a smile as they met.

"Looks like you're packing quite the load," Fiona said as she glanced at the heavy-looking bag. She immediately closed her eyes in horrified embarrassment, praying that Quinn didn't take the double entendre the way she did.

*God, you're a world-class idiot sometimes.*

If Quinn did read more into the reference, his tired expression didn't show it. "My mom's weekly purge," he said with a limp smile.

Fiona nodded, eager to shift the focus away from his load. "She has a sizable collection of things in there."

"Too much, if you ask me. She only agrees to these purges because I basically force her to. She holds on to a lot of stuff that she doesn't need, and if I wasn't here to tear it away from her, you would probably see her on that *Hoarders* show."

The thought made Fiona sad. Iris held on to those things as a way of staying connected to a past that she refused to let go of. Fiona did the same thing. Instead of hoarding physical items like Iris did, she hoarded guilt, regret, and idealized memories. The methods may have differed, but the outcomes were equally devastating.

"You're a good son, Quinn. I can see how much she appreciates what you do."

"It's not always easy with her. Sometimes she's down-right intolerable. But I'm all she's got. I'd never turn my back on her."

Fiona hoped that Jacob would one day say the same thing. Right now, she couldn't be sure. "She's lucky to have you."

Quinn nodded, not as warmed by the thought as Fiona

expected he would be. After an awkward silence, he grimaced as he shifted the large bag to his other shoulder.

Fiona took the cue. "I won't keep you. That thing looks like it weighs a ton."

"Yeah, I should probably get going. I need to get some rest for the second round tomorrow."

"Good luck with that."

"Thanks. I'll need it."

The two of them exchanged uneasy smiles before Fiona walked away. She only made it a few steps before Quinn called out.

"Hey, Fiona?"

"Yes?"

"I'm sorry for that exchange earlier with my mom and Noah."

"Don't worry about it."

"Mom explained some things to me after the fact about the situation between you and him. I want you to know that the two of us aren't friends. I hardly know the guy. If he ever bugs you again, let me know and I'll—"

Fiona interrupted before he could finish. "I appreciate that, Quinn. But it's not a big deal. Really."

"Are you sure? Because some of the stuff my mom said…"

"I'm sure," Fiona answered, ignoring the sudden shift in Quinn's demeanor. Eyes that were once bright and friendly became narrow and distant. The sight gave her a chill that she didn't expect.

"Okay. Well, if you change your mind, just tell my mom, and I'll—"

"I won't change my mind. But thank you."

The light in Quinn's eyes returned just as suddenly as it had disappeared. "Fair enough. You have a good day then."

He looked over her shoulder and pointed at something. "By the way, there's a package at your door."

Fiona looked down the hall and immediately saw the gift bag in front of her apartment, unsure of why she hadn't noticed it before. "Strange. I wasn't expecting anything."

"Must be your lucky day," Quinn said with another tired smile before continuing down the hallway.

*Why don't I feel lucky?* Fiona thought as she approached her apartment.

The plain pink bag was placed neatly in the center of the doorway. The red and white tissue paper covering the top of it gave no clue as to the contents inside, but as she got closer, she could see an envelope attached to one of the handles with her name clearly written in black ink.

Hesitant to remove the paper, she picked up the envelope first.

Aside from her printed name, there was nothing else written on it, no postage, no return address. She opened the envelope with nervous fingers and slowly pulled out the card.

*To Fiona. I hope there are no hard feelings. But in case there are, consider this a peace offering. Let bygones be bygones?*

It was signed with an illegible scrawl that she had a difficult time deciphering as an actual language, let alone a name.

She put the card back in the envelope and turned her attention to the bag. Something deep inside of her, the powerful instinct that she still refused to call a guardian angel, told her not to look in it. She ignored the instinct, removing the strands of tissue one by one until she saw the gold bottle cap.

Fiona retreated from the bag in horror, only to be

pulled back to it by the force of a curiosity that masked itself as denial.

*This can't possibly be what I think it is.*

She needed one more look at the cap for the reality to truly set in.

It was the same brand of Bushmills whiskey that she'd bought a few nights earlier only to pour down the sink in a fit of disgust and regret.

But somehow it was in her hand, filled to the brim, begging her to open it a second time.

*This time, you won't pour me down the sink,* she could almost hear it say. *This time, you'll let me help you, the same as I always have. You need me, Fiona. That's why I came back.*

She knew it wasn't the same bottle, just like she knew it couldn't actually talk. But she couldn't deny its immediate and overwhelming power to render everything else around her invisible.

Momentarily blinded by her tears, Fiona felt around on the floor until she found the bag. She shoved the bottle inside without giving it another thought, fumbled with her keys until she finally lined them up with the lock, and rushed inside her apartment. She closed the door with such force that the dog three apartments away began barking.

Despite the frantic whispers that tried to convince her she was overreacting, Fiona ran into the bathroom, opened the bottle (refusing to acknowledge how much the rushing scent of oak and pepper made her mouth water), and poured its contents down the toilet.

"Fuck you!"

Shattering glass punctuated the sound of her guttural scream as she threw the bottle against the shower, streaking the tile and nearby wall with the remnants of brown fluid. The alcohol that she tried so desperately to get rid of now filled the bathroom with spoors of metallic dryness that burned her nostrils every time she breathed them in.

Fiona knew she needed to clean up the mess before the smell settled in permanently, but she was rendered immobile by the torrent of thoughts that suddenly flooded her mind.

The only person who could've left that bottle was Noah. He'd seen her in the liquor store buying that exact same brand. He was in her AA meeting the very next day. He knew how vulnerable she was, and he knew just what to do to exploit that vulnerability. It all made sense.

Except for the card.

The handwriting was delicate, not like she imagined his would be. And the signature, if it could be called that, was unlike any she had ever seen. If Noah wanted to send a message, why would he attempt to do so anonymously when Fiona would immediately trace it back to him anyway?

Or maybe it wasn't Noah at all. Maybe the handwriting was Natalie's. That would explain the feminine script, and possibly the obscure signature.

But Natalie didn't strike Fiona as someone who had either the cunning or the patience to strike in such a passive-aggressive way, no matter how much damage it had the potential to do. She was more apt to break the whiskey bottle and slice Fiona's throat.

So, if it wasn't Natalie, where did the bottle come from?

The possibilities made Fiona's head spin in much the same way a glass of the Bushmills would have, and she suddenly felt the overwhelming urge to lie down.

"Just for a minute," she told herself as she walked into her bedroom and plopped down on the air mattress. "Then you need to clean up this mess and get the hell out of here."

She massaged her forehead in a vain effort to make the spinning stop, but the violent tornado of thoughts and images continued to swirl, raking its mortally destructive blow across her already fragile psyche.

There was nothing left to think about now. No more tears to shed, no more treaties to negotiate with Corona Heights or the so-called human beings in it, no more fear of what Paul, or the courts, or Kirk thought of her, no more hanging on until she had her day in court.

The only thing she could do now was leave. If there were consequences to be had, she would gladly accept them. There wasn't a single conceivable outcome, short of never being able to see Jacob again, that could be worse than the hell this place had become.

"Time to go!" Fiona shouted as if she were trying to communicate with someone on the other side of her bedroom. Or perhaps she was trying to communicate with the apartment, and indeed the building *itself*. "Screw you, and screw what you're trying to do to me. It's not working. It'll never work. Go screw with somebody else."

Forged by the spirit of her words, Fiona rose from the air mattress, took her suitcases out of the closet, and began stuffing clothes inside them. She would come back for the rest of her things after she found a storage unit to put them in. Hell, she would leave them behind altogether if she had to. They had most likely been tainted by the foul energy of this place, anyway. And if that were the case, they belonged here.

After filling the first suitcase, she quickly moved to the second. As soon as she unzipped it, she heard her name.

*"Fiona?"*

She assumed that the voice was coming from inside her head, the same as she assumed when she first heard it three nights ago.

*"Are you really leaving?"*

And similar to then, she quickly realized that she was wrong.

"You can't leave."

For the first time since they'd been communicating, Olivia wasn't whispering. Her voice was strong, confident, and unafraid of being heard. But it couldn't have been her. She was nowhere to be found when Detective Sullivan looked for her.

"I need to see you, Fiona."

Fiona dropped the suitcase. "Olivia? Is that really you?"

"Of course, it is."

"But I thought you were gone. I came over to your apartment. A detective went inside to find you, but you weren't—"

"My mom wanted you to think I was gone. But I was here the whole time."

"Why would she do that?"

"She doesn't want me to see you."

"Why?"

"Because of what you know, or at least, what she thinks you know."

Fiona's head started spinning again. "I don't understand. What am I supposed to know?"

"The truth of what happened."

"To Donald Tisdale?"

"Not just him."

"Who else, Olivia? Tell me."

"If you let me come over, right now, I can show you."

Fiona felt a wave of panic rising in her chest. "But your mom…"

"She's not here. But I don't have much time before she comes back. If you want to see me, it has to be now."

Fiona heard her cell phone ringing in the kitchen. She ignored it. "Okay."

Olivia's voice brimmed with excitement. "I'll be right over."

Fiona heard light, eager footsteps as Olivia ran out of her bedroom. She followed suit, quickly making her way out of her own bedroom and into the living room where she waited in front of the door. As she stood there, she heard a ding from her cell phone. Whoever called had left a message.

Fiona was determined to stay put until Olivia arrived, but after a few moments, her curiosity won out and she walked into the kitchen to retrieve her phone. She swiped the home screen, fully expecting to see Paul's name. What she saw instead made her entire body tremble with dread, sadness, and hope, all at the same time.

She barely heard Olivia knocking on the door as she listened to the message.

The sound of Jacob's voice managed to drown out the entire world.

## Chapter Twenty-Three

"Hi, Mommy. It's Jake. How are you?" His voice sounded just like Fiona remembered it. Mature and articulate but with the perfect amount of bashful charm. "I'm good, and so is Daddy. We really like it here so far."

After a few seconds of silence, Fiona heard Kirk's voice in the background, coaching a tentative Jacob on what to say next.

"Do you miss Mommy?" Kirk asked him.

"Yeah."

"Then tell her."

Jacob was back on the phone. "I miss you, Mommy. I hope you miss me too."

"Oh, honey, I miss you every day." Fiona spoke the words as if Jacob were there to hear them.

"Tell Mommy you've been thinking about her," Kirk instructed.

"I've been thinking about you. I want to see you soon."

Fiona tried to respond, but the heavy emotion that rose in her chest didn't allow her to speak.

"Anything else you want to say?"

"Uh…no."

"Okay, then tell her goodbye."

"Bye, Mommy. I miss you and love you, and I can't wait to see you."

"Bye, honey. I love you so much. I'll see you soon. I promise." Fiona thought the words, but she wasn't sure how many of them made it out of her mouth.

Jacob's voice was suddenly replaced with Kirk's. "Um, hi, Fiona. How is it going? Jake has really been asking to talk to you, so we called." His voice was just as tentative as Jacob's had been, but Fiona was thrilled to hear it nonetheless.

Out of her other ear, she heard the knocking on the door.

She'd been aware of it for the entire time that she listened to the message, but she couldn't move to answer it.

"I know things got a little heated between us the other day, and I just wanted to say that I'm sorry. I know I could've handled it better, and I…"

"Are you here, Fiona?"

Olivia's muted voice briefly rose above Kirk's, then faded.

"…really meet up again, this time without the lawyers if that's possible. Just let me know if…"

"Fiona? Why won't you…"

"I feel like I'm rambling now. Again, I'm sorry for the way I acted. Talk to you soon."

The moment the message ended, Fiona replayed it. She breathed in the sound of Jacob's voice—every phrase, every word, every syllable—until it filled her entire being. It was the best feeling she'd had in years, and she wanted nothing more than to stand there and bask in it until she worked up the courage to call him back. But as soon as the message ended again, her attention suddenly fell on Olivia.

She quickly walked to the door. "I'm so sorry. I'm coming right now." But when she opened it, Olivia wasn't there.

"Oh, shit."

Fiona stepped out into the hallway but saw no sign of Olivia there either.

She was prepared to go back inside with the hope of reaching Olivia through the bedroom wall again when she glanced over at her apartment door.

It was open.

Fiona approached it without giving herself a chance to rethink the notion.

There were no signs of movement inside that she could see. The television was off, as were all the lights, except for a single beam emitting from the back hallway.

She took a step inside the doorway, knocked, and listened.

Still no movement.

By the time Fiona took her next step, she was inside the apartment.

"Hello?"

She waited for a response.

Hearing none, she advanced a few steps farther, allowing for her first real glimpse into the lives of the people who had come to dominate so much of hers.

Her first sensation was fear. The second was light-headedness, possibly the result of the marijuana smell that permeated the apartment. It was legal here, as it had been in her home state.

*That doesn't give them the right to smoke it in front of her.*

Fiona was aware of the hypocrisy of her judgment, considering the perilous situation she'd put her own son in. But it didn't matter. All she could think about was the cruel injustice of a world that gave these monsters free rein to be horrible parents while she had to fight with every ounce of her being for the chance to even talk to her child.

Pushing the useless thought aside, she continued in, walking past a living room cluttered with fast-food wrappers and empty beer cans, and a kitchen filled with dirty dishes and an overflowing trashcan.

On the walls were various pictures of two young girls. They were together in some, standing arm in arm during various events: birthday parties, Christmas mornings, Halloween costume parades. In others, they were separate. One was older than the other by a few years, but they were spitting images.

One picture, in particular, captured Fiona's attention. It showed a much younger Natalie in her hospital bed with a newborn baby in her arms. Next to her on the bed sat the older sister, much smaller than she was in some of the other pictures. Long tendrils of copper-colored hair swept across her pale, freckled face on either side, shielding her eyes from the gaze of the camera. Her smile, strained like Natalie's, revealed the growth of a first tooth.

Fiona concluded that one of the girls was Olivia, while the other was the sister who Iris claimed now lived with her father.

As her eyes drifted along the wall of pictures, Fiona came upon one that stopped her cold.

It was in its own space, tucked away from all the others. If she hadn't been looking closely, she might have missed it altogether. But now that she'd seen it, nothing else seemed relevant.

Natalie was in the same hospital room. But this time, she was sitting in a rocking chair, and there was not one baby in her arms, but two, both wearing the same pink-and-white beanies. The older sister stood off to the side, with only half of her tiny body visible in the frame.

Fiona covered her mouth, but she was too late to stifle the audible gasp that escaped from it.

She began looking around the living room in a frantic search for more pictures that she may have missed. It wasn't long before she found them, packed in an old Kodak envelope on top of a nearby bookshelf.

She quickly sifted through the large stack of random photos before finding the one that she was looking for..

The twin girls, no more than four or five years old, wore matching overalls and pigtails. They looked exactly alike, save for two minor differences: one of the girls wore glasses, and the other wasn't smiling. The subtle differences were apparent in all the other pictures that Fiona saw of the pair. As the girls progressed in age, the differences became less subtle.

She compared the latest picture of the twins to the most recent picture of the older and younger sisters. The younger sister (minus her twin) had aged only a year, possibly two, between the pictures. But then Fiona noticed something else, something that she had completely missed before. The younger sister, the twin without the glasses, hadn't smiled in *any* of the pictures, and in a few of the more recent ones, she could barely look at the camera. It was then that the stark contrast between this girl, her twin sister, and her older sister became obvious.

But three sobering questions remained: Why was this

little girl always so sad? What happened to her twin sister? And which one of them was Olivia?

Fiona had hoped for an immediate answer to the last question as she walked out of the living room toward the single beam of light that she assumed was coming from Olivia's bedroom.

After a few steps, she stopped and looked behind her. The apartment door was still open.

She could have saved herself the inevitable trespassing charge by leaving right then, but instead, she closed the door, took a deep breath, and turned her attention back to the light.

"Olivia? It's Fiona. Can you please come out?"

Fiona took the silent response as a cue that Olivia was upset.

"I'm sorry I didn't come to the door. I had just gotten a really important phone call, and I…" Fiona stopped herself. "That's no excuse. I'm really sorry. Can we still talk?"

Fiona took her first step toward Olivia's bedroom. But before she could take her second, the beam of light went out.

Her eyes grew wide with fear as she attempted to adjust them to the dark space.

"Olivia?"

She took another few steps toward the bedroom before she heard from a place that seemed very distant: "Go away."

Fiona continued toward the voice. "Olivia, please don't be mad at me. I just want to talk."

"No, you don't. You're just like my mom. Every time I try to talk to her, she ignores me. And you did the same thing." Olivia's voice seemed more remote now, despite Fiona being directly outside her slightly ajar bedroom door.

She saw nothing but black as she looked through the narrow opening. "I'm not ignoring you, okay? I want to talk."

Fiona jumped as something stirred in the darkness.

"Olivia, please."

"Fine. I'll talk to you. But you have to promise something first."

"What?"

"You have to promise that you won't get scared and move away like you almost did today."

Fiona swallowed hard as she attempted to formulate a rational justification for the blatant lie that she was about to tell. She searched the deepest recesses of her conscience but couldn't come up with a single thing. She lied anyway.

"I won't leave."

"Do you promise?"

"I promise."

"Okay, you can come in."

Fiona slowly opened the door, revealing more of the pitch-darkness of the bedroom.

Her eyes darted aimlessly from one end of black space to the other until she finally found a tiny sliver of sunlight that edged its way in through a corner of the drawn window shade. It was only then that she was oriented enough in her surroundings to notice the dark, spindly mass holding perfectly still in the corner.

## Chapter Twenty-Four

"Olivia? Is that you?"

After a tense moment of silence, Fiona heard: "Yes."

She let out a sigh of relief that was louder than she'd intended. "Can you please turn on a light? I can't see."

"Noah took the lightbulb out."

Not believing her, Fiona slid her hand across the wall until she came upon the light switch. When she flipped it, nothing happened.

"He says I keep it on too much, says I waste too much electricity that I don't pay for. But it's the only way I can sleep."

"What about the light that was just on? Where did that come from?"

"It was this."

Fiona was suddenly blinded by the harsh glare of an LED bulb.

"Got it."

Olivia quickly turned off the flashlight. "Sorry. I forget how bright it can be."

As Fiona blinked away the residual strobes, she heard footsteps creaking across the floor. In the next instant, she was blinded again, this time by sunlight as Olivia let up the window shade.

"Is that better?"

When Fiona opened her eyes, the first thing she noticed was the glasses. The dark, oval-shaped frames looked similar to the ones she'd noticed in the photos, only now they seemed a size too small for Olivia's face.

"Noah and my mom always like for the shades to be down. I only opened the window because they aren't here."

"Where are they?" Fiona asked as she blinked away the last floating dot of light.

"Noah is at work. And my mom...I don't know where she is. But I'm sure she won't be gone for long, so we shouldn't waste too much time."

With her vision fully restored, Fiona finally got her first good look at Olivia.

She was long and lean, appearing much taller than the girl in the photos. Instead of the short pigtails present in many of the shots, her dark brown hair was long and rich, with finely trimmed bangs that nearly touched the top rim of her glasses.

She wore a faded Taylor Swift T-shirt and loose black leggings. She looked like any other normal adolescent girl that one would see on the street hanging out with her friends, gossiping about boys, laughing and joking, and loving the utter simplicity of her life. But nothing about this adolescent girl's life was simple or normal.

"Is it okay if I sit?" Fiona asked.

"Sure. Why don't you sit there?" Olivia pointed to a twin bed that had been stripped of its sheets and blankets.

It was then that Fiona noticed the makeshift sleeping area that Olivia had made on the corner near the wall, which consisted of a pillow, a flat sheet, and a plain white comforter piled on top of a *Dora the Explorer* sleeping bag.

"That's where I sleep now," Olivia confirmed.

"But it looks like you have a perfectly good bed right here."

"I'm more comfortable there."

"Why?"

"Because I'm closer to you."

Olivia adjusted her tight glasses, and when she looked up at Fiona, she smiled. But it didn't take long for her brave face to falter under the weight of sadness.

She did her best to hold the smile, even as her mouth began quivering. "It's been different since you moved in. I don't feel as scared as I used to, back when your apartment was empty."

Fiona did her best to hide her own sadness. "What made you so scared?"

"Lots of things." Olivia's eyes suddenly drifted to the amulet hanging around Fiona's neck. "What's that?" she asked, pointing to it.

Fiona held on to the warm stone with a tight grip. "It was a special gift from a friend."

"It's really pretty."

When Fiona saw the look of admiration in Olivia's gentle eyes, she only had one thought. "Would you like to wear it?"

Olivia's face brightened with excitement, then fell just as quickly. "But you said it was a gift. Won't your friend be mad if you let me wear it?"

"Of course not," Fiona said, lifting the chain off her neck. "She would want to help you just as much as she helped me. Besides, it's already served its purpose. Come on, let's make sure it fits."

Olivia was suddenly hesitant. "How would it help me?"

"Well, it helped me feel brave. It helped me not want to run or move away when certain things happened."

"Certain things?"

"You know what I'm talking about."

Olivia nodded.

"After I started wearing this, those things didn't feel quite so scary."

That wasn't entirely true.

"Will it do that for me?"

"There's only one way to find out." Fiona held out the necklace.

The tension faded from Olivia's face as she stepped toward it. When she put her hand out, Fiona dropped the necklace in it.

Olivia smiled as she squeezed. "It feels so warm."

"I've been told it's a mood stone, meaning that whatever energy you give to it, it gives back to you. It's giving you warmth; that means it likes your energy."

Olivia's smile suddenly flattened. "I wonder how it would react to Noah. Or even my mom?"

Fiona knew it was best not to respond.

"I bet it would be so cold for Noah that it would freeze his entire hand." Olivia's smile returned at the thought.

Fiona smiled too. "How about I put it on for you."

Olivia handed her the amulet, turned around, and lifted her long hair. "I sure hope it fits."

Fiona clasped it and turned her around. The stone sat just below the base of her sternum. "Fits beautifully."

"Really?" Olivia ran to her dresser mirror, holding the stone in her hand like it was the most prized possession she'd ever owned. "I love it. Thank you."

Fiona walked up behind Olivia, looking at her in the mirror. "You should only thank me if it helps you feel braver."

"It's already helping." Olivia's eyes brightened with curiosity. "How does it do that?"

"I honestly don't know. All I know is that it works."

Olivia turned back to the mirror. "I guess you can't really question magic."

"No, I guess you can't."

The brightness in Olivia's eyes was suddenly replaced with concern. "But if you aren't wearing this anymore, won't you get scared again? Won't you want to leave?"

"I promise I'll be fine. I'm a lot more worried about you."

"You don't have to worry about me. I have this now," Olivia answered with a brave smile that didn't look at all manufactured.

"That's all I needed to hear. Now, do you mind if we sit? I'd like to talk to you about something else."

Olivia sat down at the edge of the bed. "I need to talk to you too."

Fiona sat at the opposite end, taking long, deep breaths in a vain effort to calm her nerves. "Me first."

"Okay."

There were so many things Fiona wanted to say that her mind scrambled to find the appropriate starting point. "How do you handle the constant noise from Noah and your mom?"

"I have my headphones and my music. That helps me

not hear the arguing. I mean, I still hear it, but it's not as bad. I also stay in my room a lot."

"But honey, you shouldn't have to do that. This is your apartment too."

"He doesn't think so. He always tells me that until I start paying the bills, I don't have the right to say anything."

"And your mom lets him talk to you like that?"

"She can be just as bad as he is. Sometimes worse."

"What does *worse* mean?"

A faraway thought momentarily distracted Olivia. "I don't feel like talking about it."

"Are you ever able to talk to anyone about it? Friends, maybe?"

"What friends?"

"How about teachers?"

Olivia cast her eyes to the floor. "Nobody understands. Sometimes I don't think they even want to understand. So, I don't bother them with it."

"Well, I'm here, and I want to understand. Help me do that."

Olivia suddenly rose to her feet and walked to the window. "I need to look out for my mom's car. Like I said, I don't know when she'll be back, and the last thing I want is for her to see you here."

*Trust me, kid. It's the last thing I want too,* Fiona thought. "Don't worry about that now. Come sit."

Olivia watched the parking lot for a few more seconds before finally retaking her seat on the bed. "No sign of her. I'll look again soon, just to make sure."

"Okay. But for now, why don't you tell me what you know about Donald Tisdale."

Olivia let out a deep, labored sigh. "He was killed."

"How do you know that?"

"I just know."

"You have to be more specific."

"He was killed because he wasn't a nice man."

Fiona struggled to manage the frustration in her voice. "Do you know who killed him?"

After a long hesitation, she nodded.

"Who was it?"

"I'm worried that you won't believe me."

"I know it's a scary thing to talk about, but you have to trust me."

Olivia's eyes suddenly welled up with emotion.

Fiona put a gentle hand on her cheek to wipe away the tears. "You don't have to be afraid anymore. I'll protect you."

After taking a moment to compose herself, Olivia nodded. "I believe you. But I'm still scared."

"Scared of what?"

"Scared to tell you who killed him."

"Okay. Let's start with something else."

"What?"

"Tell me why Donald Tisdale wasn't a nice man."

"Because he hurt people."

"How do you know that?"

"I just know."

"Did he ever hurt you?"

Olivia shook her head.

"Then who did he hurt?"

"You know."

"What do you mean? How would I know?"

"Because you've heard it."

Fiona felt her frustration rising again. "I don't understand."

Olivia stood up from the bed, walked over to the corner

of the room where her bedding was, and hit the wall with an open palm.

"That."

She then closed her hand and began pounding on the wall with all the force she could muster. "I know you've heard it!" she shouted with a fury that seemed to grow with each strike.

"Yes, I have. Now please stop."

Olivia complied. Exhausted from the display, she sat down on her makeshift bed to catch her breath. "She does it because she's trapped here and she's trying to get out. But she can't."

"Who?"

Olivia reached into her sleeping bag and pulled out a folded piece of paper. She unfolded it, studied it for a moment, then stood, refolded the paper, and brought it to Fiona.

She gasped the instant she opened it.

The immaculately detailed hand-drawn portrait depicted a young smiling girl staring longingly out of a window onto the busy street below. It was titled *Lost in Dream*, with the neatly scripted signature of *D. Tisdale*.

Aside from the incredible craftsmanship, one detail caught Fiona's attention immediately: the girl, with her short pigtails and oval-shaped eyeglasses, looked just like Olivia.

Fiona's mind immediately went to the conversation that she overheard between Detective Sullivan and Natalie about an incident between Donald Tisdale and Noah. Iris had suggested that it involved Olivia's older sister, but Fiona questioned that now.

"Donald Tisdale drew this?" she asked, already knowing the answer.

Olivia nodded.

"When?"

"I don't know. It was a while ago, I guess."

Fiona handed the drawing back. "You must really like it if you've kept it all this time."

Olivia's soft face suddenly hardened. "Not so much."

"Then why do you have it?"

"Because it helps me remember what she looks like."

The sudden revelation washed over Fiona like a tidal wave, and if she wasn't already sitting down, she would have been knocked completely off her feet.

## Chapter Twenty-Five

"Your sister," Fiona said with a shudder. "This is your twin sister."

Olivia nodded. "Her name was Hannah."

"Was?"

Olivia walked back to her pile of bedding and slipped the drawing back into its rightful place inside the sleeping bag. "This picture is one of the few things that helps me remember her. And these." She pointed to the eyeglasses she was wearing, eyeglasses that Fiona now knew belonged to her sister. "She had an extra pair."

She also now knew that the little girl who never smiled in any of the pictures was Olivia. It was finally coming together. But the end result wasn't any less jarring. "I'm sorry, honey. I'm so very sorry."

Olivia took her seat on the bed. The tension in her features was gone, replaced with something that was neutral and unfeeling. "My mom says that things sometimes happen in life that don't make sense. That's the one thing she's ever said to me that I know is true."

"Can you tell me what happened to Hannah?" Fiona asked hesitantly. "I know it's really hard to talk about, so I understand if you can't…"

"She's dead," Olivia answered without any identifiable emotion.

Fiona gave herself a moment to recover from Olivia's blunt response. "How did it happen? Does it have something to do with that picture? With Donald Tisdale?"

She knew the answer long before she asked the question. But as had been the case with every other difficult circumstance that arose in her life, denial was the safest, most readily available option.

Unfortunately, there would be no conceivable way to deny the words that Olivia spoke next.

"Hannah always talked about how much she liked his drawings, and she wanted him to teach her. My mom and Noah said she couldn't talk to him, but she ignored them and went to see Mr. Tisdale anyway. She started telling me about all these cool drawings that he had of the mountains and forests and things like that. Then he told her to go stand by the window so he could draw her.

"She said it was the coolest thing ever, and she wanted to have it. He told her that the only way she could keep it is if she promised to come see him again so he could make more drawings of her. So, she did. I told her that she shouldn't do it, that Mom and Noah would be mad. But she said they were wrong about him. He wouldn't hurt a fly. She begged me not to tell anybody, so I didn't. Then she went to school one day while I was home sick, and she never came back." The thought made Olivia tremble. "I guess she was the one who was wrong about him."

There wasn't any defense in Fiona's vast arsenal to shield her from the heartbreak that she felt at that moment.

She struggled to find an appropriate follow-up question. "Was your sister ever found?"

"No."

"Then how do you know that she died?"

"It's been almost three years. She wouldn't just leave and never come back. She would never leave me."

"Did the police ever think that Donald Tisdale had anything to do with Hannah's disappearance?"

"No."

"Even with the drawings?"

"Nobody will ever believe it was him, especially now that he's dead."

"Then why are you so certain?"

Even with the long silence that Olivia used to mentally prepare herself, she still struggled to formulate the words. "Because…she showed me."

Her disbelief thoroughly suspended, Fiona didn't hesitate as she asked the question. "How?"

"She comes to me in my dreams. Tells me things. Shows me things. She comes to me when I'm awake sometimes, but it's a lot scarier, so I tell her not to do it."

Before Fiona could even consider a response, Olivia rose from the bed and walked to the window. When she turned back to Fiona, all the color had drained from her face. "You have to go."

"What's the matter?"

"My mom's here. You need to leave, now!"

Fueled by her sudden rise of panic, Olivia grabbed Fiona by the hand and forced her off the bed. "Hurry."

With the panicked girl leading her by the hand, Fiona scurried out of the bedroom and into the dark hallway, but the sound of muffled conversation stopped them before they could get any further.

"Oh, my God, she's here," Olivia cried.

The next sound Fiona heard was a key sliding into the door.

"Hide!"

"What? Where?"

Olivia quickly led them back into the bedroom. "In the closet."

"But wait, how am I supposed to–"

Olivia cut her off mid-protest. "Just go. You'll be safe in here until I can get you out."

Without another word exchanged between them, Olivia pushed Fiona into the closet and closed the door. Olivia's footsteps quickly moved across the floor before suddenly coming to a stop. Fiona heard the sound of the shades being drawn. Next came the rustling of Olivia's makeshift bed.

Natalie's booming voice streamed in from the living room. "Yeah, I just got home. No, it went fine. Jesus, why is it so dark in here? Hold on, Noah. Olivia? Where are you? I hope you're still in bed."

Footsteps in the hallway led to the opening of Olivia's bedroom door. "Are you asleep?" Natalie asked in a compassionless tone.

Olivia responded with deep breathing meant to signify that she was.

Natalie sighed as she closed the door. Heavy footsteps then moved through the hallway and into the living room, where her telephone conversation resumed.

"Yeah, I just checked on her. She's still asleep, thank God. I swear, I can't deal with the whining anymore." She paused. "Christ, Noah. I don't know what's wrong with her. She's always sick with one thing or another. You know that. But if she misses much more school, the goddamned truancy cops are gonna show up at our door." Another long pause. "I don't know if they're still looking for you. I haven't seen those detectives around here all day, so I seriously doubt it. What could they possibly want, anyway?"

Natalie's footsteps echoed through the wall as she began pacing. "Of course, they shouldn't suspect you. No one is telling them anything about you. Stop being so damn paranoid." After listening to a response that she apparently didn't like, Natalie began screaming into the phone. "I'd like to see you try it, Noah! I really would! Whatever, I'm done! Have a nice day, prick!"

Natalie continued talking after that, but it was apparent that the conversation was now with herself.

"If he even thinks about putting his hands on me again, I swear to God…"

Her voice grew louder as she began pacing the hallway outside Olivia's bedroom door. "I'm so tired of this shit, all of it. I could end everything in five seconds; I don't think he understands that. But I'll do it. I've done it before. I can easily do it again. Bastard wouldn't even see it coming." There was a sudden bang as Natalie hit something. "Just like that."

Fiona held her breath as Olivia's door slowly creaked open.

After a few seconds, Natalie closed it and started walking down the hall, hitting the walls and knocking objects to the floor. "Just like that!"

Her angry tirade culminated with the sound of a heavy door slamming shut.

Fiona thought for a moment that Natalie had left the apartment. Then she heard more yelling.

As the nightmare scenario played itself out in Natalie's bedroom, Fiona barely gave any thought to the fact that she was trapped inside the closet of an apartment that she had no business being in, with no reasonable hope of getting out without a fight that she wasn't the least bit prepared to take on.

All she could think about was how she was going to make sure that Olivia didn't meet the same fate as her sister. Because from everything that she could see, it was only a matter of time.

Suddenly, as if she were reading Fiona's mind, Olivia whispered confidently, "Don't worry. We'll find a way out of this. Just hold on a little bit longer."

Crouched uncomfortably in the blinding darkness of that closet, Fiona wanted to believe her. But the thin thread that she had been hanging on to ever since she first arrived here finally snapped, plunging her into a black hole of nothingness that felt like it went on forever, and ever, and ever.

## Chapter Twenty-Six

"Maybe you should let me run point this time," Detective Greer suggested as he and Sullivan prepared to reenter Donald Tisdale's apartment. "Ghosts and goblins don't scare me one bit. I'll take rattling chains over an AK-47 pointed at my head any day of the week."

Sullivan was more than happy to take Greer up on his offer, even if she didn't appreciate the humor. "I never said anything about ghosts."

"Okay. So explain to me what you saw at the door."

Hesitation as she considered her answer.

"Is *it* still an acceptable description?"

"Not really."

"Then I couldn't tell you. Maybe it was a kid. Maybe it was a figment of my overwrought imagination."

"And the shaking floor?"

Sullivan didn't hesitate this time. "That was real. And it wasn't buckling support beams like Finley said."

Greer's brow furrowed as if he were preparing to protest.

"Look at me," Sullivan barked. Her jaw was rigid, her eyes tight and focused. Hers was a face that said *Pay attention if you know what's good for you. This is serious business.* Perps had been on the receiving end of that look hundreds of times. This was the first time that Sullivan had used it on her partner. She hoped it would be the last. "Something unnatural happened in here. For a split second, I thought the entire building was going to fall down on top of me. Only me, and no one else. That's not hyperbole, Marcus. Only me."

Based on the widening of Greer's eyes and the subtle fluttering of his chin, Sullivan's look of serious business was enough to convince him.

"Alright," was all he said.

"There's a giant crack on the bedroom wall if you want further proof. Oh, and if that's not enough, the bathroom mirror shattered. Fun times."

"I believe you, Chloe."

Sullivan looked into his eyes and knew it was true. She allowed her stiff jaw to relax. "I wish I could explain it, but I can't."

"And you won't have to. Not to me or anyone else if that's what you choose. Unless it's somehow pertinent to the investigation, which I doubt, this stays between us."

"Thank you, partner."

"You're welcome. Do you feel safe going back in there?"

Sullivan took in a deep pull of air, and she felt better. "Absolutely. We've still got work to do."

"Glad to hear you say that." Greer put his hand on the doorknob and pushed it open. "Too soon to say ladies first?"

Sullivan felt the makings of a smile as she walked past

him and into the apartment. "Just when I thought chivalry was dead."

She felt the chill the moment she walked in. When she glanced at Greer, it was obvious that he felt it, too. "It may not be a ghost, but it's damn sure something."

"You ain't lyin'," Greer said. "Apparently, that ventilation issue hasn't been addressed."

Sullivan walked to the thermostat. "Sixty-eight degrees."

"Coldest sixty-eight degrees I've ever felt."

"You ain't lyin'."

Greer chuckled. "Where should we look first?"

"The only thing that Arthur Finley said was that the drawings were stashed away in the apartment. He never said where."

"I'm pretty sure there isn't much new ground to cover after forensics had their way with the place. So, remind me why you think this is even remotely worth our time?"

Sullivan wanted to credit her intuition again, but she feared that the card wouldn't play nearly as well as it did twenty-four hours ago. "Because the techs could have found the artwork and not thought twice about it. And if there are still pieces in here, even something small that we could have originally missed, they might give us our only insight into who Tisdale was. I've read that you can tell a lot about the mindset of an artist based on the work they produce."

"Yeah, I could tell after one look at *The Potato Eaters* that van Gogh was more than a few spuds short."

Sullivan smiled. "That painting is kinda creepy, isn't it?"

"More like nightmare-inducing. I always thought it should have been called *The People Eaters* because I'm positive that girl was cutting into a loaf of cooked brain."

Something turned in Sullivan's stomach that caused an

involuntary activation of her gag reflex. "You should really shut up now."

"I'm just saying. Are we doing this because you think we can find some weird shit like that in Tisdale's collection?"

Sullivan hadn't consciously considered that before, but now that Greer had suggested it, she was intrigued by the possibility. "Let's just focus on finding the drawings before we start psychoanalyzing them. This may very well amount to nothing, and if it does, at least we can say we tried."

"The good news is that we don't have much space to cover. I'll start poking around in here."

"Okay. I'll start in the bedroom. We can flare out from there until we meet in the middle."

Greer started in a small pantry space in the kitchen, while Sullivan moved down the hallway to Tisdale's bedroom. Thankfully, there was no thumping inside the walls or ceiling this time, only the disquieting stillness of a recently abandoned space.

If Tisdale had any artwork in his bedroom, it wasn't on display. In fact, the only ornamental touch in the entire room was a poster-size calendar on the wall above the bed that featured the city skyline framed by a burnt-orange sunset. It was titled *The Magic of Denver*. Tisdale had faithfully crossed out each passing day of the year, all the way up to his last on April 12.

Sullivan took her flashlight to the wall in search of nail holes where his work may have been previously displayed and taken down, but she found none.

After scanning the open areas of the room, she ventured inside the closet. When she turned on the light, she immediately noticed a tall trunk in the far-right corner, tucked behind a neatly hung row of work uniforms. When she cleared out the uniforms, she realized that the trunk had been turned vertically with the lid faced against the wall. The presence of powder residue told her that forensics had conducted a surface examination of it. If they found anything inside, it obviously wasn't enough to justify moving it out of its original position.

Still, Sullivan felt compelled to look.

She attempted to move the trunk out of the corner, but after several tries, it wouldn't budge. There was something very heavy in there. And despite the forensic team's apparent lack of interest in it, Sullivan's adrenaline spiked when she considered the possibilities.

"Marcus, come in here," she yelled from inside the closet. "I think I found something!"

Greer quickly made his way into the room. "What is it?" His eyes briefly surveyed the long, jagged crack on the adjoining wall before he stuck his head in the closet.

Sullivan pointed to the trunk. "There's something heavy in here. I'm having a hard time moving it."

Greer motioned for her to come out of the closet so he could slide in. "Let me have a try."

He grabbed the top edge with one hand and gave it a yank, but the trunk only moved a few inches. "So, it's like that, huh?" he told the unyielding object. "You're not getting the best of me that easy." This time, Greer took the edge with both hands, set his feet, and drove them hard into the floor. The trunk moved a few inches farther. He set his feet again and pulled. After several more goes, he finally moved it far enough out to allow him the space to push it the rest of the way. Once it was finally out of the closet, it took both of them to set it down horizontally.

"What the hell is in this thing?" a thoroughly winded Greer asked.

"We're about to find out," Sullivan answered as she removed the latch and flipped the top open.

The pair stood frozen as they stared at piles upon piles of magazines. The visible issues ranged from vintage editions of *Reader's Digest* to recent copies of *Art in America.*

Greer sighed as he began digging through them. "So, this is your smoking gun? A trunkful of the *Watercolor Artist* and *Popular Photography*? Hopefully, there are a few *Playboys* in here or something. That way, we'd know the guy actually had blood pumping through his veins."

Sullivan shook her head as she joined him in combing through the magazines. It didn't take long to figure out that there was nothing to find here, but they continued digging until they reached the bottom of the trunk.

"Well, this was a major waste," Greer said as he fanned through the last magazine, a *New Yorker* from 1992.

"There's no way we would've known unless we looked," Sullivan said defensively. "At least we confirmed that he really was into art. Unfortunately, it looked like he was far more interested in reading about it than actually doing it."

"Story of his life, I bet."

Sullivan looked around the bedroom, at its no-frills décor, and bare walls, and crisply made bed, and neatly organized closet, and she indeed saw the story of Tisdale's life. He was simple. He was predictable. He was bored. And he was all alone.

"Hell of a sad story."

Greer nodded his agreement. "What do you say we get this back in the closet? There may be some keepsakes here that his next-of-kin might be interested in."

Tisdale had a younger sister in Des Moines. She was appropriately devastated by Sullivan's call but informed her that she was bedridden and wouldn't be able to make the trip out. With no one else to claim him, Tisdale's personal effects would most likely be turned over to the state. Still, Sullivan saw no need to leave the trunk in the middle of the bedroom. "You do the pushing. I'll navigate."

Between the two of them, they guided the trunk back into the closet with relative ease. But when Greer attempted to give it a final push into the corner, it caught on something. He pulled it back a couple of feet and pushed. It caught a second time.

"Chloe, can you look in there?" a frustrated Greer asked. "The trunk keeps getting stuck."

Sullivan looked in the corner but couldn't find any obstruction. "There's nothing in here. Just keep trying."

Greer pushed again, getting only a few inches before running into the unseen barrier. Sullivan crammed inside the tight space. When they both pushed, the trunk began to move. Then there was a loud crack, like the splintering of wood, and the left front of the trunk suddenly dropped into the floor.

"What the hell was that?" Greer asked in a slight panic as he rushed to pull the trunk out of the hole.

Sullivan quickly moved in, shining her flashlight on the floor. "You've got to be kidding."

Greer moved the trunk out of the closet and rejoined Sullivan. "Is that what I think it is?" he asked as he looked at the floor.

Sullivan nodded and moved closer. She estimated that the small opening measured no more than two feet by two feet. The edges of the floor where the hole had been cut where jagged, creating an uneven fit for the plywood covering.

"Piss-poor construction," Greer said. "But it's definitely a trapdoor."

"He must have kept the trunk here because the door didn't close all the way," Sullivan speculated. "It was open just enough for us to tear it off the hinge when we forced our way through."

"Brilliant summation, my dear Watson. So, what the hell is it here for?"

"Let's find out." Sullivan kneeled in front of the shallow opening. When she pointed her flashlight inside, she saw the edges of a large, black notebook.

"The elusive artwork?" Greer asked.

"Could be."

"Okay, step back so I can get the door off."

Sullivan nodded and backed away.

"Just make sure you keep the light on it," Greer said. "If there's something alive in there, I want to see it before it has the chance to crawl up my leg."

The door had been designed to be flipped up and to the right so that it could rest on the wall. But since it had been torn away at the hinge, Greer had to carry out the entire door. He set it down on the opposite wall and allowed Sullivan to move in.

"Well? Any creepy-crawlies down there?"

Sullivan shined the flashlight into the hole. Instead of one large notebook, she now saw four, along with a small composition pad and an envelope that looked to contain photographs. Fortunately, there were no creepy-crawlies. "You're safe, Detective."

"That's a relief," Greer said with an exaggerated sigh. He bent down for a closer inspection of the items. "These are definitely sketchbooks," he said before retrieving one of them. "Let's see where Mr. Tisdale's artistic sensibilities led him."

He couldn't hide his disappointment as he flipped through a series of blank pages.

"Or not," Sullivan said, equally disappointed.

Greer looked as if he had given up on the pursuit entirely when he suddenly stopped flipping. "Holy..."

"What is it?"

He didn't say anything for a few seconds as he stared at the page.

"Marcus?"

Greer looked at her with a grim expression.

"Please don't tell me we have another group of potato eaters on our hands," Sullivan said with a nervous smile.

Greer's hand trembled slightly as he handed her the notebook. "It's way worse."

## Chapter Twenty-Seven

The sketch was a detailed recreation of the crime scene as Sullivan and Greer first discovered it, right down to the noose dangling in the doorway and the chair situated underneath it. The only thing missing from the sketch was Tisdale himself. The bottom-right corner had been signed: "*D Tisdale–Apr 6th.*"

"This was dated one week ago," Sullivan said.

"He obviously planned it out ahead of time."

"Looks that way." But something wasn't right. Sullivan continued studying the sketch until she figured out what that something was. "What do you think this is," she asked Greer. "Directly behind the chair near the floor."

After looking at it for a long time, Greer drew the same conclusion that Sullivan had. "It looks like a small hand wrapped around the doorframe."

Sullivan nodded. "And perhaps the shadow of a head peering around the corner?"

Greer took the book and flipped to the next page. This

sketch of the doorway wasn't as detailed as the last, but it did reveal a closer view of the hand. The shadow was also more apparent now. Based on its scale in comparison to the doorway and chair, it belonged to a child.

"Well, Dr. Freud, here's your chance to psychoanalyze," Greer said solemnly. "What does this tell you about Donald Tisdale's mindset?"

Sullivan didn't offer an answer as she took the book back from Greer and flipped to the next page. The formless shadow now loomed in the middle of the doorway, its face framed by two red dots that were apparently meant to represent its eyes.

The shadow took more form on the next page. The red eyes were larger now, with a jagged line that looked like a snarl outlining its mouth. The black mass grew larger and more frighteningly detailed with each subsequent sketch until the last page in the book revealed what it actually was: a young girl whose ghostly features were contorted with malevolent anger.

It was the same young girl who Sullivan thought she saw running away from Tisdale's apartment door. She was as sure of it as she had been of anything in her life. But she locked the revelation away in the deepest part of her consciousness that she could access.

"What the hell is that?" Greer asked.

Sullivan answered the only way that she could right now. "I have no idea."

She put the book aside and reached for the next one. It was filled with the nature sketches that Arthur Finley had spoken of. There was also a sketch of the exterior of Corona Heights. Its massive spires, sharply slated roof, and intricate stonework loomed over the desolate surroundings like something out of a nineteen-century gothic novel.

Sullivan wondered if that was what the building really looked like, or if it was more the result of artistic embellishment. She had never surveyed the exterior closely enough to know for sure, but it certainly felt accurate based on how she felt every time she came inside.

Greer put the second sketchbook aside and reached for the third. It was blank.

That left one more.

"Please, Lord, let there be something in this one aside from mountains and evergreen trees," he said in what Sullivan assumed was a lame attempt at a prayer.

Despite the terrible execution, Greer's appeal was answered.

This book appeared to pick up where the first one left off, showing what looked to be the same girl but with brighter, more appropriately human features. Gone were the flaming red eyes and crooked, evil grin. The girl depicted in this sketch looked content as she stared out of a window onto a bustling scene of activity outside. This drawing was the only one to have a title: *Lost in Dream,* and it was signed by Tisdale and dated December 16.

The book revealed more sketches of the same girl, mostly head portraits. In one, the small, inverted outline of a man was visible as a reflection through the girl's eyeglasses. The detail was breathtaking, even if the subject matter was inexplicably disturbing.

"Do you think it's his granddaughter?" Greer asked, eager to grasp at any logical explanation that he could.

"No one we've talked to, including his sister, ever indicated that he had children. So I highly doubt it's his granddaughter."

"Then, who is she?"

Sullivan put the last sketchbook aside and reached for

the envelope. As she'd suspected, it contained a large stack of photographs. She split the stack, giving one half to Greer while she kept the other.

They began flipping through them simultaneously and with equal speed, desperate to find any real-world clue that could shed light on who the girl may have been.

It was Greer who found the first photo. "I think we got her."

When Sullivan saw the photo of the young girl sitting alone on Tisdale's couch, she grabbed the last sketchbook to compare it with the drawings. From the glasses to the pigtails to the easy, trusting smile, it was an exact match.

"Keep looking," Sullivan said as she turned back to her own pile. "There have to be more."

And unfortunately, there were.

The girl was photographed on Tisdale's couch on four separate occasions, the trusting smile on her face appearing to diminish in each one. Then came the photos of Tisdale and the girl together. Some were on the couch, where they sat side by side; others were in the recliner–the same one that he used to assist in his own hanging–where she sat in his lap. She looked uncomfortable in some and outright frightened in others. The scene was unseemly at best. At worst?

"Dammit, Marcus. This isn't good."

"It's beyond not good," Greer responded before handing Sullivan another photo.

She almost didn't take it for fear of what she might see, but the job demanded that she divorce herself from any emotion that may interfere with her ability to assess the situation objectively. So, after she took the photo, she closed her eyes and clenched her stomach, prepared to assess whatever she saw with a clear mind and an objective heart.

She opened her eyes to a close-up shot of the girl sitting on Donald Tisdale's lap. Tisdale was kissing her on the cheek as she appeared to recoil in disgust. The rest of the photo almost failed to register with Sullivan, either because of the shock that she felt when she saw it, or the brief, but necessary, denial of its very existence.

Arthur Finley sat beside them, his hand on the girl's knee, kissing her cheek at the same time Tisdale was.

Before Sullivan had time to fully process what she was seeing, Greer held up the next photo. The entire image was scribbled in black with the ink of a ballpoint pen.

Her breath caught as she tried to speak.

"I already know what you're going to say," Greer murmured. "This one could be really bad."

Sullivan swallowed hard, but the knot in her throat only tightened. "Yeah. Do you think forensics can do anything with it?"

"God, I hope so." He took a deep breath before turning over the last photo. "This is another shot of the girl by herself. Look where she's standing."

The image showed the girl in the hallway standing in front of the closed door of an apartment. The only visible numbers were *60*, but Sullivan was quickly able to surmise the rest.

"Apartment 607. Do you think this could be Natalie Shelby's daughter?"

"Makes total sense with the story we heard about Noah going after Tisdale for trying to befriend the girl."

"It might also explain why Natalie didn't give two shits when we told her that Tisdale was dead."

Greer carefully studied the other photos. "There's something about this girl."

"What?"

"I don't know. I just feel like I've seen her. I can't place it, but she definitely looks familiar."

"Could you have seen her around the building?"

Greer looked at Sullivan with heavy eyes. "No. It was someplace else." Failing to connect his thoughts, he shook them away. "Never mind. I guess it's not important right now. Who do you want to talk to first?"

"I'd love to hear what Arthur Finley has to say about this," Sullivan answered, fighting to contain her mounting anger.

"Let's go," Greer answered, making no effort whatsoever to contain his. "But after that, we need to find Noah. It might be time to revisit your theory about what happened here."

Sullivan appreciated the acknowledgment, but she could take no satisfaction in it. "Afterward, we should bring forensics back in here for another round. Somehow they missed all of this."

"How are we going to explain the cracked wall and broken bathroom mirror?"

"We aren't," Sullivan answered firmly.

Greer nodded his understanding. "We can always let them discover it for themselves, act like it all just appeared out of thin air."

"That sounds familiar."

"Right. The blood on the kitchen floor."

"Blood that didn't match Tisdale's, or anyone else's in our registry."

Greer's eyes lit up, as if he were hit with a sudden revelation. "Do you think the blood could've belonged to…" He stopped short of finishing the sentence.

"What?"

He stared at the pictures, and suddenly Sullivan knew exactly what he was about to say. She didn't want to finish the sentence either.

"Let's just find Finley," she said instead.

"Right behind you, sport."

## Chapter Twenty-Eight

Though there was no good way to accurately measure time in the endless black void of that closet (for all she knew, time could have stopped altogether), Fiona estimated that it had been about twenty minutes since she last heard anything from Natalie. Her epically irrational rant had come to a merciful end before that, but the pacing, punctuated by grunts and mumbled curses, continued. Her once furious energy seemed to ebb with each deliberate step until, finally, there was nothing.

Olivia had been quiet the entire time, afraid, like Fiona was, of making even the slightest noise. But when Fiona heard the rustling of her bedding, followed by those first tentative footsteps across the creaky floor, she knew it was time to move.

"Are you okay in there?" Olivia whispered from outside the closet door.

Fiona was alive, and that was enough. "Yes."

"I think it might be safe to leave now. I'm going to make sure. Stay here until I come back, okay?"

*Do I really have a choice?* "Okay."

With that, Olivia slowly made her way out of the bedroom, the floor groaning under the weight of each uncertain step.

Fiona knew there wouldn't be much time to formulate the story she was going to tell Sullivan after she called the detective from her apartment, but she had to come up with something, because making that call was the only way she could ensure Olivia's safety. And right now, keeping her safe was the only thing that mattered.

Olivia was gone for only a few seconds before she tiptoed back into the bedroom.

Fiona waited impatiently for a status update. When Olivia didn't offer one, she took the chance and whispered. "Hey, what's going on?"

Silence.

"Olivia, what are you doing?"

The floor creaked as light footsteps drew closer to the closet door. When they stopped, Fiona held her breath.

She heard a hand touch the doorknob a few seconds before she heard it turn. It gave her time to slink back into the closet as far as she could. Just as she hit the wall, the closet door opened—only a crack.

*Natalie.*

Fiona could no longer hold her breath, so she covered her mouth to mute the noise of her heavy breathing.

The door hung open, allowing the darkness of the bedroom to spill inside the closet. The void expanded until she could no longer tell where she ended and it began.

Fiona had not only become part of the void, she *was* the void.

When she mouthed Olivia's name, she could almost see

the word leaving her body like a fine white mist that evaporated particle by particle until it no longer existed.

Fiona jumped as the door opened a little more. The floor buckled. Then she heard a voice.

"Why are you trying to take her away?"

The voice was soft, young, like Olivia's.

"She can't leave."

But it wasn't Olivia's.

"I won't let her leave."

The door opened more.

"You can't take her."

Fiona knew she should have felt fear at that moment. Instead, she felt an inexplicable sadness.

"I'm trying to help her." She didn't remember forming the words, or even thinking them. They were simply there.

"I need her to help *me*."

The voice was Hannah's. There was no way that Fiona should have logically known that, but much like the words she spoke before it, the thought was simply there.

"Help you do what?"

"Get him."

"Who?"

"The other one who hurt me. He's close."

"It's not safe here. Olivia has to leave, and so do I." Fiona attempted to say more, but the sudden swell in her throat wouldn't allow it.

The voice that she prayed was only in her mind suddenly went silent.

Then she heard footsteps approaching from the hallway. Olivia was coming back.

Before Fiona could make her first move out of the closet, she heard a heavy hand take hold of the doorknob.

The last thing she heard before being rocked by the sound of the closet door slamming shut was the word "No!"

## Chapter Twenty-Nine

Arthur Finley's apartment was located on the first floor, directly across from the laundry room. Among the many complaints that he expressed to Sullivan and Greer about his Corona Heights experience, his apartment's high visibility was easily the number one gripe. He argued that when tenants were reminded of his whereabouts every time they washed their clothes, it made it much easier to call on him to unclog that minor backup in the sink or change the lightbulb that flickered every time they opened the refrigerator. Sullivan now wondered if his unreasonable desire to keep a low profile was based on something else entirely.

Greer volunteered to knock on the door before she could even ask.

In her experience, the vast majority of people who avoided answering their doors did so because they were convinced that the person on the other side was either trying to sell them something or cure them of the original sin of being born with flesh and blood and wanton lust.

Greer's heavy hand was enough to beckon even the most sinful of souls out of their dark hiding places, so it wouldn't be easy for Arthur to dismiss him as just another lost soul selling salvation, or a lazy tenant who wanted to recruit him for some menial task. He would know that the person at his door meant business. And if he got a bit of the piss scared out of him in the process, Sullivan knew that would be okay, too.

*Let 'er rip big fella.*

As usual, he didn't disappoint.

After the last echo bounced through the narrow corridor and faded away, Greer turned to her with a sheepish grin. "Do you think I overdid it that time?"

"Under the circumstances, my friend, I'd say it was just right."

Arthur Finley was visibly flustered as he answered the door. "Hello, Detectives," he said as he struggled to corral the bow tie dangling loosely from his neck. His formal evening wear was a startling departure from the standard handyman attire that Sullivan had grown accustomed to seeing.

"I've never tied one of these in my life. Damn foolish of me to wait until now." He attempted a smile, but his frustration wouldn't allow him to wear it for long. "Can I help you guys with something?"

"We'd like to ask a few questions if you have a moment," Greer answered coldly.

"I'm afraid it's not the best time. My son's wedding is this evening, and I need to get to the church beforehand for family pictures. I'm sure my ex-wife is already there, impatient as ever. I'm not too keen on getting the death-eyes from her any more than I already do."

"We'll be as brief as possible, Mr. Finley, but we can't

promise that you'll make it there on time," Sullivan said, matching Greer's frosty tone.

"Didn't I tell you to call me Art?" he responded with a nervous smile. "What's this about, anyway?"

"May we come in?"

Arthur looked like he wanted to say no. "Sure, if you don't mind me running around like a chicken with its head cut off. I took my cufflinks out of the box this morning, and I haven't been able to find them. I sure hope Derek makes this marriage thing a one-time deal. I couldn't possibly go through this nonsense again." His nervous smile returned.

When Sullivan and Greer said nothing as they entered the apartment, the smile went away.

Sullivan stood in the middle of the living room to address Arthur, while Greer lingered in the kitchen, casing the apartment for anything that could raise even the most minor warning flag.

There wasn't much to see aside from a few pictures with the young man that was presumably his son, various pieces of hockey memorabilia from some bygone era, and a tall bookshelf lined with police procedurals and true-crime books.

On the surface, it was probably not enough to pique Greer's interest even a little bit. But as Sullivan now knew all too well, the most interesting parts of Corona Heights existed far below surface view.

Arthur attempted another pass with the bow tie. "So, what can I help you with?"

"We were hoping you could shed some light on the friendships that Donald Tisdale may have had with anyone in the building aside from you," Sullivan began.

"I already told you, he didn't have any friendships. Not real ones, anyway. He got along with people just fine, but it never seemed to progress beyond the casual acquaintance stage."

"Why do you think that was?" Greer asked.

"Because he didn't trust people."

"And why did he have issues trusting people?"

"The truth is I don't really know why he had trouble forming close friendships. All I know is that he and I got on well enough."

"It sure seems that way," Greer said, pacing the kitchen.

"Look, I'm happy to cooperate with you in any way that I can. But I'm not sure why we need to cover this ground again. Donald was a private man who liked to keep to himself. It never bothered anyone that he didn't invite them over for coffee or engage in the latest building gossip. Frankly, he didn't have much interest in that stuff. He lived his life exactly as he wanted to, and if you ask me, there's nothing wrong with that."

"There isn't anything wrong with a man pursuing his solitary interests," Greer concurred. "Hell, I wish I had some hobby that allowed me to disconnect from the world every once in a while."

"It's never too late to try something new, Detective."

Greer nodded and began pacing the kitchen again.

"It's funny you should bring up Tisdale's solitary interests," Sullivan said to Greer before turning back to Arthur. "That's actually why we're here."

Arthur stopped fiddling with his tie. "Go on."

"You mentioned to us in passing once that Mr. Tisdale possibly had some artwork stashed away in his apartment."

"Right. I mean, I can't be 100 percent sure of that, I just figured—"

"We found it."

"In a trapdoor inside his closet," Greer added.

Arthur suddenly started in on his tie again, this time with visibly nervous fingers. "Strange place for it."

"We thought so, too," Sullivan said. "Until we saw his sketches. Then it didn't seem strange at all."

Arthur kept his energy on the tie that he had no chance in hell of tying.

"Are you familiar with them?" Greer asked.

"I don't recall seeing anything other than his nature pieces."

Greer reached inside the messenger bag that he'd carried on his shoulder. He pulled out the two sketchbooks. "Maybe we can refresh your memory." He gave the sketchbooks to Sullivan, while he kept the photo envelope.

Sullivan flipped to the first sketch of Tisdale's living room. "Looks similar to the way we found his apartment when we first came in, right down to the knot pattern of the noose. What do you make of that?"

Arthur tried to speak, but his voice failed him.

Sullivan then flipped through the rest of the book, ending with the sketch of the menacing shadow. "Pretty creepy stuff, if you ask me."

"Seriously creepy," Greer echoed.

"Do you have any thoughts on what could have inspired this?"

"Absolutely not," a wide-eyed Arthur replied. "He never mentioned having drawings like that, and he damn sure never showed me any of them."

Sullivan opened the second sketchbook. "What about these?"

The color instantly drained from Arthur's face.

"What's wrong?" Greer asked in an unfeeling tone.

Arthur fought hard to compose himself. "Nothing. It's

just strange seeing these, knowing that my friend drew them and he's not here anymore."

The sentiment didn't move Sullivan one millimeter. She'd had enough of the back and forth. It was time to ask the question. "Do you know who the girl in the drawings is?"

The moment Arthur lifted his chin and stuck out his chest, Sullivan knew he was preparing to lie.

"Can't say that I recognize her." He looked at something to the right of Sullivan as he said the words. Further proof in her mind that he wasn't telling the truth. Though she hated it at the time, the one-week body language seminar she took in the academy had become an invaluable weapon in her investigative arsenal.

Greer reached into the envelope and pulled out the first photo of the girl and Tisdale. "What about her?"

Arthur stared at it for less than a second. "Sorry, but no."

"Take a closer look," Greer said as he held the photo up.

"I don't recognize her," Arthur answered, his irritation slowly mounting.

Sullivan motioned for Greer to hand her the envelope, eager to take the kill shot herself. She took a deep breath before showing him the photo. Everything was about to change, and she had to make sure she was ready.

The sense of calm that came over her as she exhaled told her that she was.

"Then what's your explanation for this?" Sullivan walked over to Arthur and handed him the photo. "Take a good look."

Arthur studied it for a long time without saying anything.

"Mr. Finley?"

He looked up at Sullivan with eyes that had suddenly turned red. "Where did you find this?"

"The same place we found the sketches."

Arthur turned it face down before giving it back. "I know what you might be thinking about that, but—"

"What are we thinking about it?" Greer interrupted.

"That it looks…I assure you, it's nothing."

Sullivan was quickly losing patience. "Who is she?"

"Her name is Hannah. Hannah Shelby."

"Natalie Shelby's daughter?"

"Yes."

"The same daughter who Natalie's boyfriend didn't want around Tisdale?"

Arthur nodded. "But Noah completely overreacted."

"Did he?" Greer said. "From the looks of those photos, he may not have reacted strongly enough."

"There's nothing to those, Detective. Hannah was simply a friend."

"I assume there's nothing to this photo, either?"

Sullivan watched the last remaining color drain from Arthur's face as she held up the blacked-out image.

"I have no idea what that could be. But I'm sure it's nothing."

"For your sake, I hope you're right," Greer said. "Because our forensics team will scrub it, and if it's anywhere near as bad as we think it could be…"

"It isn't!" Arthur insisted.

"Then why did you lie to us about knowing her?" Sullivan said.

Arthur stammered hard before finally answering. "I didn't mean to lie, I…I knew the issues that it caused with Noah and Hannah's mother, and I just…" He paused to collect his thoughts. "She was a really sweet child who was fun to be around. Not like most of the adults here."

"What do you mean *was* a really sweet child?" Sullivan asked.

"I didn't mean anything by it. Look, that picture was nothing more than the three of us clowning around. If you're here to suggest that it was anything more than that…"

"We're not suggesting anything, Mr. Finley," Greer said. "But when you lie about something so important, you can imagine how that would raise some suspicion."

"Well, I can assure you that the suspicion isn't justified."

"Thank you for the reassurance, but if it's all the same, we'd like to decide that for ourselves," Sullivan chided.

Arthur's cheeks flushed. "Fine. Have your suspicions. But I need to get to my son's wedding, so…"

"We understand, Mr. Finley, and we'll get out of your hair for now. We just want to make sure there isn't anything else you want to tell us about Donald Tisdale's relationship with Hannah, or anyone else for that matter. This might be your last chance."

Arthur's irritation finally boiled over. "I've told you everything I know, Detective Sullivan. Now, if you don't mind, I'd like to leave before I'm late."

Sullivan looked at Greer. "Do you have anything else?"

Greer shook his head. They both knew that without a smoking gun in the drawings or photos, there wasn't much else they could do with Arthur Finley until they talked to the girl.

"Thank you for your time, Mr. Finley. Depending on what Hannah Shelby tells us, we may need to call on you again."

Arthur walked to his door and opened it, clearing the

path for Sullivan and Greer to leave. "I understand, and as always, I'll be happy to help in any way I can."

"We're counting on that," Greer said as he and Sullivan made their way out the door.

"Enjoy your son's wedding," Sullivan said, taking care to sound as insincere as possible.

Arthur didn't even bother to fake a smile as he closed the door on them.

Greer did the smiling for him. "Dead to rights?" he asked Sullivan with a pat on her back.

"Let's make sure the girl doesn't corroborate his story before we call the judge," Sullivan warned.

"He's guilty of something."

"Whatever that something might be, what does it have to do with Tisdale's death?"

"Maybe nothing. Maybe everything. Whatever the answer, I feel like we're close to figuring it out."

As they entered the elevator for their short trip to the sixth floor, something made Sullivan tremble.

"What's the matter?" Greer asked. "The cold still getting to you?"

The chill that permeated Tisdale's apartment was nonexistent down here. When Sullivan trembled again, she realized that the reaction had nothing to do with a change in the temperature.

"You're right about one thing, Marcus."

"What's that?"

"We're definitely getting close."

## Chapter Thirty

"Fiona, why did you close the door so hard?" Olivia asked with a frantic whisper as she pointed her flashlight inside the closet.

Fiona scrambled to her feet. "We have to go."

"I know, but you have to be quiet. My mom is asleep now, but she wakes up really easy. So, when you follow me out, don't make a sound. Walk on your tiptoes if you need to."

"Where is she?"

"In her bedroom. But it's right by the front door. If you bump into anything, she'll hear. If you turn the doorknob too hard, she'll hear. Understand?"

"Yes."

"Okay, let's go."

Olivia took Fiona by the hand and slowly led her out of the bedroom. The floor buckled with each agonizing step.

When they made it into the living room, Fiona was nearly leveled by the smell of marijuana wafting out from Natalie's bedroom.

"Just plug your nose," Olivia suggested. "That way, it won't make your head feel funny."

At that moment, Fiona almost wished that Natalie would wake up so she would have an excuse to beat the living crap out of her. Olivia squeezed her hand, and the thought went away.

She released Fiona's hand when they reached the front door. Olivia looked at her with nervous eyes as she brought her index finger up to her mouth. "Shh." One last reminder to keep it together until they got out safely. Fiona was doing her best to comply.

After Olivia unlocked the door, she reached for the doorknob and gave it a gentle turn. It wouldn't open.

She gave it another turn, this time with more force. It still wouldn't budge.

"Did you unlock it?" Fiona asked in a soft whisper.

"Yes." The nervousness in Olivia's eyes quickly became panic as she began pulling at the door. "Why won't it open?"

Fiona doubled-checked that the door wasn't locked, then took hold of the doorknob and began pulling as hard as she could. It wouldn't open for her, either.

"What's wrong with this door?"

"I don't know," a frantic Olivia whispered. "What are we gonna—"

A loud knock interrupted her before she could finish the question. A second knock quickly followed.

Olivia began tugging at the doorknob again. "Oh, no. Please don't do this. Please."

After the third knock, they heard stirring in Natalie's bedroom.

"Please, Hannah, you have to let us go." When Olivia pulled on the doorknob, the knocking started up again, increasing in volume until it penetrated the entire space around them.

There were tears in Olivia's eyes now. "I'll do whatever you want, just let us leave," she pleaded, though her whispers were barely audible.

A groggy voice from the other room. "What's going on in there?"

"We have to do something."

Olivia ignored Fiona and kept her focus on the door. The pounding intensified. "I'll do it. I promise. Just please stop this."

The instant she said that, the pounding ceased. Fiona felt a pulsating wave of energy move through her as the door clicked.

When Olivia pulled this time, it opened. Fiona took her by the hand and ran out into the hallway. As she gently closed the door behind her, she heard from inside, "Olivia, what the hell are you doing out there?"

They ran into Fiona's apartment.

Once safely inside, Olivia was suddenly overcome with emotion, and she ran to the couch. She was sobbing uncontrollably by the time Fiona reached her.

"It's okay, honey. You're safe now." Olivia struggled to catch her breath, and Fiona feared that she would hyperventilate. "You have to calm down."

"I can't. We're not safe." The words came out in spastic bursts. "Not until it's finished."

"What?"

Olivia stopped sobbing long enough to look at Fiona. "I'm not supposed to tell you."

"Well, I'm not waiting around here for anything. I'm calling the police, and we're getting you out of here."

Fiona stood up from the couch and made her way into

the kitchen, where her phone was. "Please, God, let it work," she pleaded before picking it up. Her heart sank at the sight of the words NO SERVICE. She stuffed the phone in her pocket, grabbed her car keys, and ran back to the couch.

"Come on. We have to leave."

Olivia was no longer crying. "No, we can't."

"What are you talking about?"

"We can't leave. I made a promise to my sister, and I have to keep it."

"There's no time to debate this. We have to go, now."

"I said no!"

The raw force of Olivia's voice sent Fiona reeling backward.

Suddenly, she heard Natalie's muffled voice through the wall. "Olivia, where are you? Stop playing games and get out here!"

Fiona grabbed Olivia by the shoulders. "Let's go."

"No!" She broke free of Fiona's grip and slowly backed away from the door. Her eyes narrowed to slits. "Not until it's finished." Her voice had a trace of menace to it now.

Ignoring the new fear that she suddenly felt, Fiona took Olivia by the hand and led her to the door. When she pulled on the doorknob, it wouldn't turn. Fear immediately overtook her, and she started pounding on the door. "Open, goddamn you."

She was stopped cold by the sound of a voice.

"Olivia!" Natalie was standing in the hallway now. "Are you out here?"

Fiona had just turned around to tell Olivia to keep quiet when she was suddenly knocked to the floor. Before she could attempt to make it back to her feet, the walls on all sides of her began vibrating, as if hundreds of powerful, unseen hands were attempting to break through. Fiona struggled to her feet, only to be pushed down again. The walls began to crack, and Fiona was convinced that the ceiling was going to crumble on top of her.

"I have to go now, Fiona!" she heard Olivia shout over the deafening rumble. "It won't be over until I do!"

Fiona turned to stop her, but she wasn't there. She looked behind her just in time to see Olivia's shadow disappear into her bedroom.

"Olivia, wait!"

Fiona finally got to her feet. But before she could make it to the hallway, her bedroom door slammed shut. The instant it did, the apartment fell into silence. No vibrating walls, no crumbling ceiling. The only sound that Fiona could hear as she approached the bedroom was the residual ringing in her ears.

"Olivia?"

Silence.

She put her hand on the doorknob, expecting that it would be locked. To her surprise, it turned. She took a deep breath to steady her nerves. "I'm coming in."

Fiona opened the door.

The shriek came before her mind even had the chance to process what she was seeing. When the horror finally settled in, she shrieked again.

The bedroom was completely empty. Her furniture, her pictures, her clothes, even the window coverings, were all gone. The walls looked like they had recently been painted with a fresh coat of white. Brand new, except for a small section of exposed drywall on the area adjacent to Olivia's bedroom.

Fiona could smell the paint as she walked into the room. She felt the floorboards cracking under her feet, the same as it always had. She felt the sun's warmth on her face as she approached the open window. She felt the firm structure of the walls as she reached out to touch them. Yet the entire scene felt like a movie that the real Fiona was observing from someplace very distant. None of it was real. It was either the construct of a waking dream or the vivid hallucination of a mind that had finally lost its grip on reality.

When an unfamiliar male voice began calling out from the living room, she concluded that it couldn't have been real, either. But it made her jump, nonetheless.

"When will you be back to paint it?"

"Sometime tonight," another male voice answered. This voice sounded familiar, but Fiona struggled to place it.

"Well, you need to be quick about it. We can't assume that Barlow won't just randomly show up with some young couple ready to rent the place. This needs to be finished."

"Everything is fine," the familiar voice said. "Even if he does come in here, it's not like he'll start digging through the damned walls."

"I hope not. We went through a lot of trouble for this."

"I know we did, and it'll be okay. Now stop worrying, and let's get out of here."

The front door opened and then closed.

In the silence that followed, Fiona heard something else. A voice that she immediately recognized.

"*See me.*"

As if being led by something invisible, Fiona walked to the area of exposed drywall, kneeled in front of it, and listened.

"*Here.*"

When pressed against the drywall, her hand immediately went through. She began ripping it away piece by piece until the hole it had covered was fully exposed.

Sensing that something was inside, she reached down into the narrow space between her wall and Olivia's, feeling around blindly until her hand found something.

It was cold and brittle.

When she attempted to pick it up, it started moving.

Fiona tried to move her hand out, but the cold and brittle thing grabbed her hand and squeezed.

She didn't know for sure that it was a hand until she felt its nails digging into her flesh.

Fiona screamed as the nails dug in deeper.

She pulled her hand out and immediately cradled it; applying pressure that she hoped would stop the bleeding. But when she looked at her hand, there was nothing there: no blood, no nail marks. The only discomfort she felt was the pressure that she had applied with her other hand.

When she looked up, the hole was gone. So was the exposed drywall. The wall had been completely painted over with the dingy off-white color that she always knew was there.

When she stepped backward, she nearly tripped on the pair of running shoes that she always left in the middle of the floor. Unsure if they were real, she bent down to pick them up. They felt real.

She threw them in the corner, and they landed with a gentle thud on top of the air mattress. Everything was exactly as she remembered it before her dream.

*But was it a dream? And if it was a dream, and I was asleep, why am I standing?*

The sound of drawers opening and closing in the kitchen interrupted the thought.

Fiona ran out of her bedroom to the sight of Olivia

standing near the front door. She held something in her right hand but shielded it from view.

If Fiona hadn't known better, she would have thought that she had just woken up from a night of heavy drinking. Her thoughts were scattered, her memories fractured.

How long had she been in her bedroom? How long was she separated from Olivia? Were there really men in her apartment? Why did her hand suddenly throb with searing pain?

"Olivia, what are you doing?" Fiona asked as she struggled to get her bearings.

"I'm sorry. I have to do it."

"Do what?" Fiona tried to walk toward her, but her legs felt like cement.

"Kill the other one who hurt my sister." Olivia turned around to reveal the object in her hand. It was little more than a common steak knife, but in her hands, it looked much larger.

"Olivia, please don't do this."

"The sooner I do it, the sooner she can finally leave." Olivia reached for the door and opened it. "If I don't see you again, I'm sorry. But at least you'll be safe now."

Fiona's legs finally came to life, and she sprinted toward the door. "Olivia, don't!" But it was too late. Olivia closed the door behind her before Fiona could reach it.

She flung the door open, expecting to see her running down the hallway, but she was nowhere to be found.

"Olivia?"

At the sound of that, Natalie suddenly emerged from her apartment, a deranged look in her eyes.

"Olivia, are you out here?" When she saw Fiona, her face burned red with anger. "Is she with you?"

Fiona was just about to answer yes when Detectives Sullivan and Greer appeared in the hallway.

Natalie immediately turned to them and began pointing at Fiona. "I'm glad you're here. This bitch is trying to kidnap my daughter!"

Fiona noticed Greer move a hand slowly toward the gun holster attached to his hip. "Step back, Ms. Shelby," he warned. "Right now."

"Why are you telling me to step back? She took Olivia!"

Sullivan approached the pair, her attention on Fiona. "Ms. Graves?"

"She was in my apartment, but—"

"See? I told you she has her! What are you waiting for?"

"Quiet, Ms. Shelby," Sullivan ordered. Then, to Fiona, "Why was she in your apartment?"

"Because she was afraid to be in there," Fiona answered, pointing at Natalie's apartment. "I was on my way to find you, but before I could, she ran off."

"That's bullshit!"

"Ms. Shelby, we're only telling you one more time," Greer said, his hand still parked on his hip.

Sullivan moved closer to Fiona. "Where is Olivia now?"

"I don't know, but we have to find her. I'm worried she's going to do something."

"What?"

"Hurt someone."

"What the hell are you talking about?" Natalie blurted out. "She wouldn't hurt anybody."

"I think you're wrong about that."

"Tell us who, Ms. Graves," Sullivan said.

"The other person who killed her sister."

"Her sister?"

Fiona nodded. "Her twin sister. Hannah."

The group looked at Natalie, who had inexplicably become quiet.

"What is she talking about, Ms. Shelby?"

Natalie's lips quivered as she attempted to answer Sullivan's question. "I don't know."

"Yes, you do," Fiona replied bitterly. "I saw Hannah's picture."

Tears began streaking down Natalie's face. "But she's not...She's still out there somewhere. I know she is."

Greer pulled a photo out of the envelope he was carrying and walked over to Natalie. "Is this Hannah?"

Natalie took the photo. She broke down the moment she saw it. "Where did you find..."

"My God, I remember where I've seen her," Greer interrupted.

"Where?" Sullivan asked.

"A missing persons case from almost three years ago. If I recall correctly, her classmates last saw her getting off the school bus at her normal stop, but she never made it home. It was thought that she was abducted before she got here, but she was never found."

"And she's still out there," Natalie insisted.

"Not according to Olivia," Fiona countered, doing so as delicately as she could. Despite everything, the anguish on Natalie's face affected her. "And she promised to kill the other man who was responsible."

"The other man?" Sullivan asked.

"Olivia said that Donald Tisdale was the one who killed Hannah and that there was someone else with him. Wherever she's going, it has to be inside the building."

Sullivan looked at Greer. "It is."

Greer nodded his agreement.

"Where is she?" Natalie asked frantically.

Greer had already started down the hallway by the time Detective Sullivan answered. "Arthur Finley's."

Natalie took off behind Greer and Sullivan as they ran to the elevator.

By the time Fiona's unsteady legs allowed her to catch up, the elevator was already on its way down to the first floor.

Rather than wait for the elevator to make its way back up, Fiona decided to take the stairs. She wasn't completely confident that her fatigued legs could handle the six flights, but she had to chance it.

Accessing the staircase meant passing Donald Tisdale's apartment. The thought made her heart jump, but she pressed on. She kept her head down, and her ears tuned inward as she came upon it. *It's just another apartment, Fiona. Don't pay it any attention.* But as she walked past, something did catch her attention.

"Hey."

A soft voice from behind the door.

Fiona stopped, despite every cell in her body begging her not to.

"Fiona, is that you?"

The voice sounded like Olivia's.

*That doesn't mean it* is *Olivia.*

"Fiona, I know it's you. I can see you through the peephole."

*But what if it* is *her? I can't just walk away.*

Fiona turned to the apartment door. "Olivia?"

"Yes, it's me."

"What are you doing in there?"

"Hiding from my mom. She's not with you, is she?"

"No."

"Is anyone else with you?"

"No."

"Then come in, quick."

Fiona heard the click of a lock, then saw the door open a few inches.

"Hurry, before they come back."

Fiona put a hand on the doorknob.

*What are you doing? You can't go in there.*

She pushed the door open a few more inches.

*No. Go get Detective Sullivan. You can't be in there by yourself.*

She pulled the door closed.

*But what if she runs away again? What if someone doesn't find her this time? It'll be your fault because you turned your back on her.*

She reopened the door a few inches and waited.

There were no more voices to counsel her.

"Fiona, get in here. What are you doing?"

*Wasting time being frightened of nothing*, she told herself, knowing it wasn't true. There was a lot to be frightened of.

But she walked in anyway, hoping beyond all hope that the guardian angel she had thus far refused to acknowledge was walking in with her.

## Chapter Thirty-One

In the space of twenty minutes, Arthur Finley went from being an unreasonably proud father celebrating his only son's wedding day to wanting to curse his own existence and everyone who had ever been a part of it.

He began by cursing his ex-wife, whose unrestrained financial demands forced him to live in this shithole in the first place, and ended with Donald Tisdale, whose perverse obsession led to the inescapably dire situation that he found himself in.

In the nearly three years since it happened, Donald never provided an acceptable explanation, saying only that the girl's death was a "tragic accident."

He insisted that he never touched her in any sexual way, and Arthur had no choice but to believe him. But the remaining details of what occurred that day had apparently followed Donald to the grave, a fact that didn't make Arthur unhappy.

If guilt was the true catalyst for his suicide, it would have been easy to leave behind a confessional where he recounted the sordid details, expressed regret, offered prayers for Hannah and her family, and made the obligatory request for forgiveness. But that didn't happen. And because of that, Arthur believed that the entire incident, and his unfortunate role in it, would find a proper burial right alongside Donald.

But he was wrong.

Donald did leave a confession. It may not have been a detailed explanation, but it was enough to lead Detectives Greer and Sullivan to Arthur's doorstep with questions that he wasn't adequately prepared to answer. And it was all because of one throwaway—and in hindsight, ridiculously stupid—comment about Donald possibly keeping artwork somewhere in his apartment.

Arthur was completely unaware of the trapdoor and the contents inside of it. If he'd been thinking, he would have checked the apartment for anything that could have even remotely incriminated him. But as had been the case in so many other instances, Arthur wasn't thinking.

He wasn't thinking when he agreed to Donald's unusual request to keep his friendship with Hannah a secret.

He wasn't thinking when he took those pictures of the two of them, or when he agreed to be in one himself (what a colossal, life-altering mistake that was).

He wasn't thinking when he agreed to help dispose of Hannah Shelby's body after Donald thought it more prudent to dismember and scatter its parts rather than face the consequences of his actions.

He wasn't thinking when he decided to protect the false image of Donald as a kind, caring, loyal friend who never bothered a soul.

And now, because he wasn't thinking, because he initially lied to the detectives about knowing Hannah, he found himself in a world of trouble, and short of taking the coward's route that Donald chose, there wouldn't be an easy way out of it.

Not that he deserved one.

Arthur may not have killed her, but his complicity after the fact was equally horrific. He understood that, just like he understood that justice, in one form or another, would eventually come for him. After three long, miserable years of waiting, perhaps the call had finally come.

For now, he had his son's wedding to attend, even if it was the last place in the world he wanted to be.

As much as he tried, he couldn't shake the image of Sullivan and Greer showing up at the ceremony and hauling him off in handcuffs before his son and future daughter-in-law could even exchange their vows. How was he going to explain this to him? How was he going to explain it to anyone?

He pushed the question out of his mind as he straightened the bow tie that took him over an hour to get right, put on his suit coat, and headed for the door. He would work on his smile while he was in the car. Right now, the expression seemed more remote to him than the dimmest star in the farthest reaches of space.

Just as he reached for his keys, there was a knock on the door. He'd initially considered not answering it, fearing that the detectives had already come back to collect him. But he knew that avoiding them would do no good. Even if he did run, they would eventually find him. His guilt-riddled conscience would make sure of it.

He looked through the peephole expecting to see them but instead saw nothing. He quickly shrugged it off, telling himself that it must have been an impatient tenant who decided to try to change the dead battery in the smoke detector by himself this time.

At least someone had taken mercy on him today. Arthur smiled at the thought.

A second knock at the door erased the smile before it had the chance to settle on his face.

This time, he didn't bother to look through the peephole, deciding instead to call out, "Who is it?" in the least hospitable voice that he could summon.

"Mr. Finley?"

The young girl's voice stopped Arthur cold.

"I was wondering if you could help me?"

He looked through the peephole and again saw nothing.

"Who is it?" he asked with a sudden nervousness that he couldn't explain.

"Olivia Shelby from apartment 607. I need help."

Ignoring the blaring instinct that told him to do otherwise, Arthur opened the door. Gasping at the empty space in front of him, he quickly looked down the hallway to his right, then to his left.

No one was there.

"I'm down here."

Her voice was distant now.

"Where?"

"The storage cellar. I needed a place to hide until I got help."

"The storage cellar?"

"Yes."

*How is that possible?* he thought.

The storage cellar was locked, and he was the only person aside from the building manager who had the key.

Then he was struck by another thought: *If she's in the cellar, how can I hear her voice so clearly?*

"Because I'm not actually down there, yet," Olivia said from a place that suddenly didn't sound so distant.

"How is that—" Before the screaming in Arthur's head could subside long enough to allow him to fully respond, the voice called out to him again.

"But don't worry. I have a key too. Turn around and see."

When he did, he saw a brief flash of brilliant white light that quickly faded into nothingness.

When he came to, he was still in darkness. There was nothing binding him to the floor, but he couldn't move. His head and back hurt, and he was freezing cold.

He heard knocking. Then he heard someone calling his name. It was Detective Greer.

And he sounded very far away.

## Chapter Thirty-Two

Sullivan and Greer arrived at Arthur Finley's apartment to find the door partially open. Despite Greer's repeated calls, Arthur didn't answer.

"Why would he leave without closing his door?"

When Sullivan pushed the door open, she saw Arthur's car keys on the floor. "Good question."

"Well, I'd say this gives us enough probable cause to have a look around," Greer said as he picked them up.

Sullivan nodded her agreement then turned to Natalie. "We don't know what we're dealing with yet, so you need to stay here while we go inside."

"If he's doing anything to my daughter, you'd better make damn sure that you find him before I do," Natalie warned.

She had been understandably hysterical for the entire elevator ride down, but Sullivan was growing tired of the threats.

"You'll stand here, quietly, and let us do our job, or you

can go back up to your apartment and wait. Do you understand?"

Natalie indicated her understanding with an exaggerated eye roll.

Greer advanced inside. After one last glare at Natalie for good measure, Sullivan followed.

"Mr. Finley, are you in here?" Greer's baritone voice bounced off the walls of the empty space and echoed in Sullivan's ears, and she immediately knew.

"He's not here."

"Again, why would he leave without closing his door?"

"I don't think he left," Sullivan said, pointing at the car keys in Greer's hand.

"So, where is he?"

"I don't know. But something tells me we'd better find him qui–" Sullivan stopped. She heard something. Faint. Difficult to make out.

"What is it?"

"I don't know." Then she heard it again. More definitive this time. "Do you hear it?"

"No."

"Someone is screaming."

"Where?"

Sullivan began moving around the apartment. "I don't know."

Greer began moving around with her. "I still can't–"

"Shh." Sullivan suddenly stopped, dropped to her knees, and put her ear to the floor. "Here."

Without saying anything, Greer dropped to the floor, put his ear down, and listened. His wide-eyed glance back to Sullivan indicated that he'd heard it too.

"Where is it coming from?"

"There must be a basement level that we haven't seen yet."

"Do you think it's—"

Greer was interrupted by Natalie's sudden appearance in the doorway. "Get out here, quick!"

By the time Sullivan and Greer got to their feet, Natalie had already run off, her bloodcurdling screams filling the hallway like a cloud of toxic gas.

She stopped in front of a door at the far end of the hallway. "Are you down there, Olivia?"

The distant, unfamiliar voice of a young girl answered. "Mommy, I'm here. Please, hurry."

This was immediately followed by the sound of a second, more familiar voice. "Oh, my God, please don't. Please!" Arthur Finley let out a guttural scream of agony. Then he was silent.

Natalie raced through the door. "I'm coming, Olivia!"

Before Sullivan had a chance to process the exchange, she and Greer were giving chase. When they reached the door, they saw a long staircase leading down into a vast well of darkness.

"Where are you?" The distant echo of Natalie's voice traveled up the staircase in pulsating waves, dying before it reached the surface.

Sullivan reached for her flashlight, while Greer reached for his gun.

"It might be a good time to radio in," Greer advised.

Sullivan agreed, calling in the request for backup while Greer took his first steps down the staircase.

Last year, she had been shot and nearly killed as she confronted the man who had murdered her former partner. Those waning moments of consciousness that she spent on the operating table awaiting surgery were by far the most frightening of her life.

Until now.

## Chapter Thirty-Three

Donald Tisdale's apartment was every bit the cold, empty shell that Fiona imagined it would be. There were no reminders of the life that he'd once lived, aside from a recliner that was oddly situated under a doorframe—*the site of his suicide?*—a few magazines scattered about the living room, and a mountain of mail covering the kitchen countertops.

But the reminders of his death—from the crime-scene tape, to the black fingerprint dust on the walls, to the empty plastic vials used to collect whatever it was he left behind, to the pungent stench of decay—were plentiful.

Fiona had become so transfixed by the condition of the apartment that she almost hadn't processed the fact that Olivia was nowhere to be found.

She'd called out to her several times but was met with silence each time. At first, she assumed that Olivia had simply been hiding, unconvinced of Fiona's assertion that she was alone. But after several verbal assurances of her safety were ignored, Fiona came to a conclusion that was startling and at the same time, utterly predictable: the voice that lured her in here didn't belong to Olivia.

"Where is she?" Fiona asked the empty apartment. Given the dark specter of recent events and her mounting belief that those events were not merely figments of her splintered consciousness, she was confident that the apartment would find a way to answer. When it didn't, she asked again. "I said, where is she? Are you keeping her somewhere? Did you use her to bring me here?" She grew angry at the silence. "What the hell do you want?"

A thin shaft of light suddenly illuminated the hallway.

Fiona resisted the instinct to run for the door, choosing instead to take a step toward the light. She stopped when something stirred inside the bedroom.

"Why am I here?" The question was spoken aloud, but it was aimed more at herself than whatever else she thought might be able to hear it.

"*To see.*"

The words were faint, but they were unmistakable, and they made Fiona jump. But she held her ground.

It was with a mixture of fear and curiosity that she took another step forward. "What am I supposed to see?"

She heard something heavy sliding across the bedroom floor. It came to a rest with a heavy clang.

"*Here.*"

It was the same soft voice that had lured Fiona into the apartment, the same voice that she now knew didn't belong to Olivia but to her sister Hannah.

Fiona took a step toward the bedroom, then stopped and listened, not to the apartment but to the inner voice that recognized danger long before her conscious mind could. The voice was silent. She took another step, stopped again, and listened. This time she could hear it, very faint, as Hannah's voice had been. But it was just as unmistakable.

*Keep going,* it said. *You're supposed to be here. You're supposed to see what's in that room. You're supposed to help, so help. This isn't the time to be afraid.*

She was plenty afraid as she moved toward the bedroom. The fear diminished a little bit with each step, but not enough to ease the intense pounding in her chest. Had she chosen to listen to her flight response, which had been honed by millions of years of evolution, instead of an unreliable inner voice that deceived her time and again, she would have never walked into this apartment in the first place.

But it was too late to look back now.

Once Fiona reached the bedroom, she could see that the source of light had come from inside the closet. Aside from the strange placement of a large trunk in the middle of the floor (*the heavy sliding sound?*) there was nothing to suggest that anyone else had been here.

Then Fiona saw the flicker of a shadow move across the light. Something was in the closet. She had considered calling out to whatever was in there, but she couldn't think of anything more fruitless under the circumstances than saying "*hello?*", so she abandoned the idea and kept moving forward.

When she reached the closet, she was surprised to see that it was empty except for a pile of Donald Tisdale's work uniforms strewn haphazardly in one corner. A square piece of plywood with a small handle and broken hinges rested against the back wall less than a foot away.

It wasn't until Fiona walked into the closet that she noticed the hole in the floor.

She walked up to it, half expecting something to jump

out at her. When nothing did, she blew out a tentative sigh of relief and moved in for a closer inspection.

Seeing nothing in her immediate field of vision, she got down on her hands and knees, pulled out her previously useless cell phone, and turned on the flashlight feature.

She moved the light around the dark, shallow space but saw nothing. Curiosity once again getting the best of her, she stuck her arm into the hole as far as it would go and felt around.

After some time, her hand finally found something. It was thin and plastic. The two curved tips on either side told her that it was a pair of eyeglasses. She recognized the oval-shaped spectacles the moment she pulled them out. They looked just like the pair that Olivia wore, the pair that belonged to her sister, but with two major differences: the crack in the lens and the large splatter of dried blood that dotted the frame.

"Oh, Jesus."

The realization settled in fast and hard. The glasses were Hannah's, which meant the blood most likely was hers, too. She saw evidence that the police had been inside the bedroom, and it was unlikely that they would have missed the hole in the floor. So how had they missed this? Fiona shuddered when she considered that maybe they hadn't. Maybe the glasses weren't there at all when they looked. Maybe they were meant for her to find, and only her. But why?

*To see,* Hannah's voice said in her mind.

Pushing the thought away, Fiona stuck her arm down the hole again. It wasn't long before she came upon something else, thick, heavy, and braided. When she pulled it out, she felt an immediate charge.

The rope was approximately two feet long, with one

end tied off in a loose slipknot that had the makings of a noose. An image of the recliner in Donald Tisdale's living room suddenly flashed in front of her. An image of Tisdale followed. He was standing on the chair, adjusting the rope that had been secured to a hook. After slipping his neck inside the noose, he lifted his legs.

The details were clear and present, like a traumatic memory permanently seared into her brain.

Fiona dropped the rope and stood up. She immediately felt dizzy and had to make her way to Tisdale's bed to sit. She took in a deep breath and closed her eyes, hoping that the sudden nausea would pass.

Hannah's pale, listless face was visible in the darkness. She wore the same cracked eyeglasses that Fiona found on the floor. The dried-on blood was now a fresh pool that dripped off the frame like an endless stream of crimson teardrops.

Fiona opened her eyes, but Hannah was still there; not as a startling image in her mind but as a physical presence in the room.

Crouched down in the corner next to the bed, she covered her head with her hand, but it wasn't enough to stop the open wound from spilling blood onto the baseboard.

Using what was left of her strength, Hannah began hitting the wall with a closed fist while she mouthed a word that looked like *Help*. A last, desperate attempt to save herself.

She continued pounding on the wall as she rose slowly to her feet and staggered out of the bedroom.

Fiona stood up to follow her.

When Hannah made it into the kitchen, she collapsed

to her knees again, the blood from her head pooling on the floor beneath her.

Fiona instinctively ran to help, but by the time she got to the kitchen, Hannah was gone.

*That's because Hannah was never here*, she told herself. *None of this is real.*

When the front door opened to reveal Donald Tisdale rounding the corner with a large plastic bag in his hands, it certainly felt real.

Fiona walked out behind him, following at an unnecessarily safe distance—*he isn't real, Fiona, remember?*—until he reached her apartment. After a quick knock on the door, a man who she was certain was Arthur Finley opened the door and stepped out into the hallway. Though she stood some distance away, Fiona could hear their conversation as if she was standing in the middle of it.

"Is that everything?" Arthur asked in an agitated voice.

Donald Tisdale breathed in and nodded, his frayed nerves making a vocal response difficult.

"Okay, bring it in. Hurry."

Arthur suddenly grew more agitated as Donald moved toward the apartment.

"Dammit, would you watch what you're doing? It's dripping all over the place." Arthur pulled a handkerchief out of his pocket and dabbed at the carpet before quickly pulling Donald inside and shutting the door.

*The blood stains in front of 607. Hannah was trying to make me see her the entire time.*

Without warning, the scene in Fiona's mind shifted, and she was back inside Donald Tisdale's apartment, standing with her back to the front door, the same as when she had first entered. The space looked exactly as it had before, but for one major difference: she wasn't alone this time.

Donald Tisdale stood in front of the recliner, staring up at the noose that dangled from the hook on the doorframe. He didn't look at all certain of what he was about to do, even as he stepped on the recliner to position his head inside the noose.

"*That's right. Do it.*"

At first, Fiona thought that Hannah's voice was a manifestation of her mind apart from the vision in front of her. But when Donald Tisdale jumped at the sound of it, she realized that the voice was part of the vision.

The unmistakable look of terror that came over his face all but confirmed it.

"*You don't deserve to live. Not after what you did to me.*"

A child's hand suddenly appeared on the doorframe. Hannah was watching him.

Donald started crying. "*Please, don't.*"

And torturing him.

"*I don't want to die. Not like this.*"

Hannah's hand gripped the doorframe tighter.

As if being led against his will, Donald put his hand on the noose and forcefully tightened the knot.

"*Do it, now.*"

"*No.*" The voice that answered sounded like Hannah's. "*I can't do it.*" But it wasn't Hanna's. "*This is wrong.*"

It was Olivia's.

"*You have to.*" Hannah's response was dripping with spite. "*He took me away from you, Liv. He has to pay, too, just like Donald did.*"

In the millisecond that it took to blink, Fiona was someplace else; dark, cold and unfamiliar. But it also felt present, grounded, and real.

The first image that Fiona saw in the darkness was Arthur Finley on the floor, his body immobile. His eyes were wide with fear as he stared at something that Fiona couldn't see. He didn't speak.

Suddenly, Olivia appeared above him, holding the knife that she took from Fiona's kitchen. She was shaking.

"*Please,*" Hannah's voice said in the darkness. "*I can't leave if you don't do it.*"

"*But I don't want you to leave.*"

"*It's cold here, Liv. And so dark. It feels just like dying did, but it never stops. I just keep dying and dying and dying. Do you want that for me?*"

Olivia shook her head as tears streamed down her face in furious bursts.

"*Then kill him. Let me finally be free.*"

Olivia took a deep breath, held it in, and raised the knife above her head.

"*Oh, my God, what are you doing?*" Arthur Finley tried to move but couldn't. "*Please, you don't have to do this.*"

"*Yes, I do.*"

Olivia brought the knife down in one swift motion. Arthur was screaming before the blade had even penetrated his flesh. When it did, he went silent.

Before Fiona could see what happened next, she was back inside Donald Tisdale's living room.

When she saw no sign of him, or the noose, or Hannah, she knew that she was back in present time and space. She knew that Olivia and Arthur Finley were here, too. And she had to get to them.

Fiona didn't know how long she'd been on the floor; she only knew that it was a struggle to get to her feet. Once she did, she ran straight for the door.

She stumbled as she crossed the threshold into the hall, losing her balance and falling hard to the floor. When she looked back at Tisdale's apartment, she saw a dark, formless mass hovering inside the entryway. The more Fiona stared at it, the more it began to take shape until its features mirrored the girl that she knew to be Hannah. But the thing she was looking at wasn't Hannah. It was something empty–and evil.

Fiona rose to her feet, only to fall again. When she looked back at the doorway, the thing wasn't there. When she turned to lift herself up, it was in front of her, blocking her path to the elevator.

Hannah's face, or the spectral representation of it, was expressionless, yet the anger that radiated from its pale gray eyes burned hot. Its stringy black hair was caked with smears of dried blood, while an open wound just above the left eye oozed a yellow, putrid liquid that fell to its bruised and swollen feet in a steaming pool. When it smiled–*Oh, my God, the thing smiled*, was Fiona's only thought–its cracked lips split wide open, allowing more of the yellow rot to spill down its chin.

Fiona's limbs were tight with fear. Unable to run, the only thing she could do as the thing lumbered toward her was cower away from it. She closed her eyes as the chill of its withered being slowly settled into her bones. She couldn't speak, so she mouthed the words "Please, don't" over and over until she couldn't anymore.

"Fiona?"

When she opened her eyes, the thing was no longer there.

But Iris was. "Sweetheart, are you okay?" She offered a hand to help Fiona off the floor.

"Not at all," Fiona answered in a subdued tone that wasn't at all reflective of the relief that she felt at that moment. "Where did you come from?"

"I was out running errands with Quinn and just got

home. I heard a strange noise when I stepped off the elevator. I don't make a habit of investigating strange noises in this building, but something told me to investigate this particular noise. Thank goodness I did." Iris suddenly pulled out her cell phone and began typing.

"What are you doing?"

"Sending a text message to Quinn, telling him to hurry back."

"You should be calling the police."

"The police?"

"Something really bad is happening here."

"Involving who?"

"Olivia and Arthur Finley."

"My God. What is it?"

Fiona struggled to piece the fractured images together. "Is there some kind of basement level in the building?"

"Yes. It's a large storage space that Arthur uses. Why?"

"That's where he and Olivia are. We have to get down there." Fiona started toward the elevator.

"Wait a second. Why would they—"

Fiona stopped. "I don't have time to explain it, Iris. But if we don't get down there to stop her, she's going to kill him."

Iris's face flattened with shock. "Olivia?"

Fiona shook her head, still struggling to process the thought.

"Her sister."

## Chapter Thirty-Four

"*Take out the knife, Olivia. Take it out now.*"

The words resonated in Olivia's mind like an angry thought. But it wasn't her inner voice she was hearing. It was Hannah's.

"What will happen if I do?" She was forced to say the words aloud, as Hannah left no room in her head to think them.

"*He'll bleed. And then he'll die.*"

Olivia looked at Arthur Finley, lying silently on the floor, blood seeping through fingers that he'd cupped around his wounded leg. She didn't know how deep the knife had gone, but she felt something hard against the sharp tip as she pulled it out, and she imagined bones.

She wanted to ask him if he was okay, but she was afraid of what would happen if she did. So, she played along, like the good little sister that she was. Hannah was a whopping fifteen minutes older than her, and in the all-too-brief time they'd had together, she never let Olivia forget that.

"And when he dies, will this all be over? Will you finally be able to leave?"

*"It will all be over, Liv. I won't hurt anymore. You don't want me to hurt anymore, do you?"*

The tears came the moment Olivia reached for the knife handle. "No."

Arthur Finley looked at her with wide, fearful eyes, but he was powerless to stop her. Hannah had seen to that. It was Olivia who knocked on his door. It was her voice that lured him out of his apartment and into the storage basement. But it was Hannah who made sure he didn't leave.

Olivia wasn't sure how she did it, but she seemed capable of a great many things now. And unfortunately, none of them were good.

There were times when Hannah's presence had been a source of comfort, especially during those long nights that Olivia spent in her room, waiting out the latest fight between her mother and Noah. She never saw Hannah, but she felt her spirit, and it clung to her like a warm blanket.

Those were the times that allowed Olivia to remember her sister for the good person that she was. She remembered Hannah's laugh, loud and giddy and infectious. She remembered the way she always fidgeted with her glasses, sighing every time they fell off her nose—which was a lot. She remembered the way Hannah fussed over her; always seeing to it that her kid sister's hair was just right, making sure that her clothes, worn-down as they were, always matched, and giving her advice on what to say to the kids at school so that they wouldn't dislike her quite so much.

But that Hannah was mostly gone.

When Olivia felt her presence now, she didn't feel warmth. She felt emptiness and guilt. And it was guilt that allowed Hannah to lead her here, to this cold, dank basement, to do something that no part of her wanted to do.

"*What are you waiting for? They're coming.*"

"Who?"

"*Mom and those two police officers. We have to get them next.*"

Olivia took her hand off the knife handle. "What do you want to do to Mom?"

"*This is all her fault, Olivia. She's the reason I ended up like this. And if we don't stop her, it's going to happen to you, too.*"

"But Mom didn't do anything. It was Donald Tisdale." She looked at Arthur with scornful eyes. "And him."

"*She did everything. She never loved us. She hated us. All she wanted was to be with Noah. We were just in the way.*"

"That's not true," Olivia countered, knowing in her heart that it was.

"*She wanted me to go away. And when I did, she was secretly happy. That's why she didn't look for me. That's why she never liked to talk about me and took all of my pictures down. I didn't exist to her anymore, just like Eva doesn't exist to her anymore. And if we don't stop her, she's going to find a way to make you not exist, too.*"

Hannah's voice began to stab at her brain like a million pinpricks. She grabbed her head and attempted to shake the pain away, but it wouldn't stop. "No. Please. I don't want to."

"*Do it, Olivia. For me.*"

"I can't hurt Mom, or anybody else."

"*You have to.*"

"This isn't you, Hannah. You were a good person, just like me. It didn't matter what Mom, or Noah, or anybody else did. We were good. We still are. Don't let them turn you into something else."

For the first time, Hannah's voice took on the soft resonance that Olivia had always known. *"But I am something else."*

"No, you're not. Your spirit is still the same. Nothing can change that unless you let it."

Olivia's mind was suddenly silent.

"Hannah?"

*"Don't confuse me, Olivia."*

"I'm not trying to confuse you. I'm trying to help you remember."

*"But I can't remember."*

"You have to try."

Another long silence, then: *"No. I have to leave."*

"Hannah…"

*"Help me leave."* The familiar voice that Olivia knew was gone, replaced by the one she feared.

"I can't, Hannah. I'm sorry."

*"Do it. Or I will."*

Olivia stood up and backed away from Arthur. She filled her lungs with as much air as they could handle, then let it all out with a single word. "No!"

In an instant, the pain in her head subsided. The space in her mind was clear, leaving room for her own thoughts, her own will, to take over.

She knelt beside Arthur Finley, who had been silently watching her.

"You hurt my sister, and you deserve to be punished. But I don't. I deserve to live and be happy, just like Hannah deserved to. You took that from her, but you won't take it from me."

From someplace distant, she heard her mother's voice. "Olivia? Are you down here?"

Olivia stood up, preparing to call out to her. But before she did, she looked down at Arthur. "I'm sorry I did that.

Just make sure you don't move, so it doesn't bleed worse. Someone is coming to help."

Olivia suddenly felt pain in her head, much worse than it was before. Then she heard a sound, like ripping paper.

"Too bad they won't make it in time." Olivia felt her lips forming the words, but they came from someplace outside of her. "I wanted you to die slowly and painfully like I did. But because Olivia wouldn't help me like she promised, that can't happen now. So, it has to be fast."

Olivia felt like she was on a tiny boat in the middle of the ocean, being pulled and pounded and thrown in every direction by giant, angry waves.

She was powerless to resist it. Powerless to stop it.

She couldn't see the knife handle, but she felt it in her hands as she ripped it out of Arthur Finley's leg. The last sound she heard was his screaming. It exploded in her mind like a thousand light bulbs turned on at once, then steadily grew dimmer and dimmer until it, and everything else she had recognized as existence, faded into complete nothingness.

## Chapter Thirty-Five

The sight of Arthur Finley's partially open front door only exacerbated the stirring of dread inside Fiona's chest.

She'd wanted nothing more than to come down here to see him milling about the lobby, like he usually was, waiting patiently for the inevitable distress calls that were part of his everyday existence. Seeing him would, of course, raise very real and very frightening concerns about the state of her sanity (or lack thereof), but if he were safe, it meant that Olivia was likely also safe. She would find a way to deal with the psychological consequences. If she were lucky, she would eventually find a way to laugh them off when Corona Heights, and every terrible experience she had in it, was finally behind her.

But the notion was wishful thinking at best. The outcome of her arrival here, she now understood, could not have possibly been any different.

"Should we at least go in?" Iris asked as she stuck her head inside the door. "He could still be here."

"He's not," Fiona said confidently.

Without saying anything else, she continued down the hall until she came upon another open door. This one led to something very dark.

"Is this…"

Iris nodded. After typing something else into her cell phone, she joined Fiona in the doorway. "I've only been down there once. When Sam and I first moved in, we had more stuff than would fit in our apartment, and Arthur let us store a few things. We had to add fifteen bucks to the rent every month, but it was worth it. I haven't been back down there since and had no plans to until I moved out. It's a bit creepy, even for me."

"That doesn't make me feel any better."

"It wasn't supposed to." She eased past Fiona and began making her way down the stairs. "It doesn't look like there are any lights on, so stay close. I don't want to lose track of you down here."

*Too late,* Fiona thought as she took her first step down. *I'm already lost.*

While they were in the elevator, she had tried to explain as much as she could about her experience in Donald Tisdale's apartment, as well as her experience with Olivia before that.

Iris didn't say anything, even after the story was finished, which wasn't like her at all. And Fiona couldn't escape the sense that she was somewhat irritated at the notion of being here.

Iris suddenly chuckled. It was very light, but under the circumstances, very startling.

"What's so funny?" Fiona asked in a nervous whisper.

"Nothing. It's just that things can get so easily miscon- strued sometimes. I understand that, and I'm working on expressing myself better. Trust me. It has nothing to do with you."

"What do you mean?"

"That was my long-winded way of saying that I'm not irritated. Quite the opposite, actually."

Fiona's mouth flew open with shock. "Oh, my God. How did you…"

"Not now. Did you hear that?"

The instant Fiona's foot touched the last step, she heard it.

"That had to be Arthur," Iris declared.

Fiona nodded. His scream was barely audible, like he was someplace far away. "He has to be down here, right?"

"He is." Iris stopped to listen. "And so is she."

Fiona stopped, too. When she heard the other voice, she clutched Iris's arm. "Olivia. We have to find her."

Iris grabbed Fiona's hand to prevent her from running away. "You can't just take off down here. You can barely see two feet in front of you, and there's no telling what you'll run into. We have to find some kind of light."

Another scream, this one measurably closer.

"We don't have time. She's going to kill him."

Without any regard for Iris's words or her own safety, Fiona took off running in the direction of Arthur's voice. The only thing she could see as she looked back at Iris was her stunned face illuminated by the glow of her cell phone.

"Fiona, please wait!"

"I can't. Call the police!"

It only took a few steps for Iris to fade completely out of sight.

"Somebody help me!" Arthur's voice was somehow farther away now.

Fiona stopped. "Shit."

With a wave of trepidation washing over her, she changed direction and ran toward where she now thought his voice was coming from. But she wasn't sure anymore.

She stopped, blinked several times to force her eyes to adjust to the dark, then took off running again.

She didn't get more than a few feet before she ran into something very large and very hard, hitting it shoulder first. The force from the impact sent her careening backward. She stumbled but kept her feet.

Ignoring the radiating pain in her arm, Fiona pushed forward, only to run into something else, resulting in the loud clang of metal meeting cement.

The noise reverberated in her head long after it was over, and she was forced to put her hands up to her ears to stop the auditory bleeding. When the bleeding finally ended, she brought her hands down. That was when she heard the voice.

"What did you do to my daughter?"

Before Fiona could turn around, she felt something cold and heavy graze the side of her head.

The blow was enough to stun her senses, and for a moment, she saw nothing but tiny orbs of light dancing in the darkness. When the dancing lights faded, she saw Natalie, her sharp features washed out by the pale blue of her cell phone screen.

The metal rod that she'd hit Fiona with dangled loosely in her other hand. And though it could have easily been the way the shadows fell on her face, Fiona was sure that she was smiling.

"So, what did you think you were going to do? Kidnap her? Keep her in your apartment?"

Fiona slowly backed away. "I have no idea what you're talking about."

"Like hell, you don't. Are you and Arthur Finley both in on this?" Natalie raised the object above her head. "It's not happening, you fucking witch. Do you understand? You'll never get anywhere near her again."

A swell of anger suddenly rose in Fiona's chest. "How dare you. After everything you've put that girl through. She's in constant fear. She sleeps on the goddamned floor. You use drugs right in front of her. Someone *should* take her away from you."

"Just like someone took your son away from you. I know all about it, Fiona. Don't think you can judge me because you can't. You're no better. At least I still have Olivia."

"Hopefully, not for long."

Natalie moved toward her. "Do you think you're going to make up for not having yours by taking mine? Is that really what you think?"

"My God, do you know what's happening right now? Olivia is down here somewhere, and she's in danger."

"I know she is. And I'm taking care of it right now."

Without warning, Natalie lunged at her, swinging the metal rod, barely missing Fiona's head.

With Natalie momentarily off balance, Fiona drove into her, shoulder first, knocking her backward. She flailed aimlessly before crashing into a large storage rack filled with gallon-size paint cans. The rack immediately collapsed, and the cans fell forward.

Natalie lay motionless underneath the pile. Fiona considered pulling her out but let the thought drift away. She instead turned in the direction where she'd heard footsteps.

Iris.

Not being able to see her, she called out. "Hey, I'm over here. Did you manage to—"

The footsteps weren't Iris's.

Fiona didn't even have time to gasp before a heavy blow to the face sent her crashing to the floor.

## Chapter Thirty-Six

G reer was the first to spot her. "Look, right there," he said as he grabbed Sullivan by the arm. She spun around in the direction of his flashlight, then added her own.

Olivia was crouched down in a far corner underneath a dim fluorescent bulb. Arthur Finley was sprawled out on the floor beside her, writhing in pain while he clutched the gaping wound in his leg. When Sullivan turned her flashlight on him, he looked up.

"Oh, God, please help me! Please, she's going to kill me!"

When Sullivan turned her flashlight back on Olivia, she noticed the knife in the girl's hand. She and Greer drew their weapons simultaneously.

Appearing completely unfazed by their presence, Olivia calmly stood up and faced them. She held the knife out in front of her. Arthur's blood covered the blade, thick beads of red dribbling from the tip.

"Put the knife down, Olivia," Sullivan said. "Whatever happened here doesn't have to go any further."

When Olivia took a step toward them, Sullivan and Greer pointed their weapons.

"Put it down, Olivia," Greer repeated.

She ignored his command and took another step forward, still holding the knife out in front of her. "If you kill her, she can finally be with me."

Apart from the surreal intensity of the scene, something about Olivia's voice felt strange to Sullivan. *Off-putting* and *otherworldly* were the words that immediately came to mind.

"You don't have to do this," she insisted. "We know about your sister. We know what happened to her. Let us help. Please."

Olivia stopped, regarded Sullivan with a blank, distant stare, then turned back to Arthur. "Do you really know what he did?"

"Yes, Olivia. We do."

"Then you should know why I want to kill him." She crouched down beside Arthur, the knife hanging at her side.

Sullivan aimed her gun at Olivia's arm and released the safety. "Don't do it."

"If I kill him, then you'll kill her. We'll both finally be free."

"Olivia, that's not how this is going to—"

"Stop calling me that!"

Sullivan turned a stunned eye to Greer, who was at an equal loss for words.

"What are we supposed to call you?" Sullivan asked after a long silence.

"Call her by her name." The voice came from behind.

Sullivan spun around to see Iris Matheson's startled face

in the white beam of her flashlight. She immediately held her hands up.

"What are you doing down here?" Greer asked as he lowered his light.

"You don't understand what you're dealing with, do you?" Iris asked as she pointed over Greer's shoulder.

He turned his flashlight back on the girl.

"That's not Olivia," Iris continued. "It may be her body, but that body is a vessel for something else now."

"A vessel? What the hell is that supposed to mean?" Greer asked.

"If it's not Olivia, who is it?" Sullivan countered in a measured tone that indicated her willingness to be convinced.

"My name is Hannah!"

When she spoke, a pulsating wave of cold air penetrated Sullivan's skin, sweeping through every open pore until it engulfed her entire body. The force of the current blurred her vision, and she closed her eyes to regain focus.

By the time she opened them, the girl was on top of Arthur. The tip of the knife was digging into his neck just enough to lightly puncture the skin. Sullivan tried to move toward them, but the cold air sank deeper into her marrow, compressing the joints in her arms and legs with paralyzing pain.

"You had your chance to help me, and you didn't," the girl snarled. "Don't act like you care now when it's already too late. He's going to die, and there's nothing you can do about it." She dug the knife in deeper, sending a thin trickle of blood down Arthur's neck.

"And if you try to stop me, you can die, too."

## Chapter Thirty-Seven

Fiona regained consciousness to the feeling of intense pressure on top of her chest. She tried to fight against it, but the weight was too heavy, her strength too depleted. Her head throbbed from the blow, and she attempted to move her hand up to assess the damage, but something knocked it away before she could. The sudden pain in her hand caused her heavy eyes to shoot open.

The first thing Fiona saw when she adjusted to the lack of light was the thick rubber sole of Noah's boot. Then she felt it as he pushed it deeper into her sternum, pressing her already sore back even harder against the cold cement floor.

With the air squeezed out of her lungs, she couldn't scream.

"Fortunately for you, she's not dead," Noah said as he pushed his boot down harder. When Fiona began flailing against him in a desperate search for air, he took his foot off her chest and drove it, heel first, into her stomach.

The searing pain set her vision ablaze with bursts of white-hot light. She opened her mouth to scream, but her insides felt gnarled, and she was dangerously close to vomiting. Before she could attempt another cry for help, Noah was on top of her, pressing his considerable weight down against the whole of her body, locking her hands above her head.

"Don't you dare, after what you did to her. Look." Keeping one hand wrapped against Fiona's wrists, he used the other to grab her face. "I said look," he repeated, turning her head toward the mound of paint cans covering Natalie's motionless body.

After holding her there for what felt like an eternity, Noah finally released his painful grip. "You don't get to play the victim, do you understand? You came into our apartment, uninvited, with the purpose of doing what? Huh? Did you think you were going to take Olivia and walk out of there without anyone noticing? Did you think you were going to just take her from her mother? From me? I work my ass off every day to make sure that child has a roof over her head and food in her mouth. And here you come, riding in on some shiny white horse, thinking you're going to save the goddamned day. You can't even take care of your *own* child. What makes you think you can take care of our's?"

Noah pressed down harder against her. "Do you remember our conversation in the coffee shop? I tried to be nice. But you flat out dismissed me. Do you remember what I said about what would happen the next time we met?"

Fiona shook her head as she held what little breath she had tightly in her chest.

"I predicted that you would need my help. And guess what? You do. You need my help to leave this place alive.

Don't you?" He slowly slid his hands up the side of her body, across her chest, and onto her neck, where he rested them firmly across her windpipe. "Don't you need my help, Fiona?"

Seeing no other choice but to play along, Fiona nodded.

"Then, ask for it."

When she didn't respond, Noah wrapped his hands around the diameter of her neck and squeezed.

"I said ask for it."

Fiona fought hard against the indignity of emotion that caused a cluster of tears to pool in her eyelids, but they came streaming down her face anyway. "Please, help me."

Noah brought his face down until it was mere inches from hers, looked into her eyes—seeing nothing in them that sparked even a fleeting moment of compassion—and smiled. "Absolutely not."

Suddenly, and without any change in his demeanor, Noah tightened his grip around Fiona's neck, slowly pinching off the air, until the pressure behind her eyes caused them to bulge from the sockets. A milky film clouded her vision, blurring Noah's monstrous features until they disappeared into the ether of her oxygen-starved brain. She slapped, punched, scratched, and gouged, but no amount of resistance could free her from his grip.

Then she thought about Jacob, and the marigolds that he would bring to her funeral, and the bright, sunny, sandy beach that they would never experience together, and the wrongs that she would never make right, and she fought harder, blindly wailing away at any part of Noah that her hands could strike, until she made contact with something soft, and, based on his abrupt release of her throat, excep-tionally delicate.

He fell off Fiona just enough to allow her to squirm

away. She managed to get only a few feet before he grabbed her hard by the back of the head, bringing a forceful and immediate end to her retreat.

He pulled her head back and kept it there, stretching her neck to an unbearable degree, before finally saying, "You gouge my eye, I bash your skull. Seems like a reasonable trade-off."

Noah pulled her head back a few more inches before suddenly releasing it. There was a loud cracking sound before his body fell on top of her, then to the floor, in a heavy, lifeless heap.

"Get up, Fiona."

She'd heard Quinn's voice but couldn't process the fact that he was there until she felt his hands scoop her off the floor.

She breathed air into her lungs in quick, shallow bursts until the burning in her chest and throat began to subside. Quinn held her up until her legs were strong enough to support herself.

"Are you okay?"

Fiona nodded. "Thank you." She draped her arms around his broad shoulders and clung to them as her body succumbed to the weight of the moment by releasing violent spasms of emotion.

Quinn tightened his grip of support. "What's happening down here? My mom sent all these cryptic text messages telling me to hurry over. Then she told me to come down here. Where is she?"

In an instant, all thoughts of Noah and Natalie and her own brush with death went away, as did the pain in her chest and throat. Her circuits went live with a sudden surge of adrenaline.

"She's looking for Olivia."

Quinn scanned the vast, dark space. "Where could they possibly be?"

The image was quick, flashing in and out of her mind with the bright burst of an old-time camera bulb. But it illuminated everything around her.

"This way. We have to hurry."

She grabbed Quinn's hand and led him through the darkness, confidently navigating the space like a submarine's sonar navigates the blackest depths of a murky ocean.

## Chapter Thirty-Eight

When Sullivan and Greer advanced on the girl with their weapons drawn, Iris stepped in front of them.

"What are you doing? Get out of the way."

Greer tried to move around her, but Iris blocked his path.

"Step aside, Mrs. Matheson," an irritated Sullivan added.

Iris stood her ground. "No. This isn't the way. You have to lower your guns."

"We will not," Greer said emphatically. "She's going to kill him."

Iris was equally emphatic. "If you take one step farther with those guns pointed at her, she will absolutely kill him."

"We don't have time to discuss this," Sullivan said. "And if you continue to interfere with—"

"Look at her," Iris interrupted. "She hasn't moved."

Though she still held the knife to Arthur's throat, the girl's agitated breathing had appeared to settle. She was calm now, almost curious, her glassy eyes regarding the three of them like they were oddities from a foreign civilization. But the threat she posed was still very real, and it was Sullivan's responsibility to neutralize it.

"We don't wait until someone pulls the trigger before we act, Mrs. Matheson. People die that way. We die that way."

"But no one has to die here," Iris asserted. "If she really wanted to kill Arthur, she had plenty of opportunity before now. And it would have been impossible to stop her. It's not too late, but only if we do it another way."

Sullivan looked at Greer. He shook his head in disagreement.

"What other way?" Sullivan asked reluctantly.

"You have to lower your guns first."

Sullivan considered Iris's words for a long moment before turning back to Greer and nodding. "Do it, Marcus."

"No chance. She'll move on him the second we drop them."

"Please, Detective Greer. You have to trust me." Iris put a gentle hand on his forearm. "Like Detective Sullivan said, we don't have much time."

When he looked at Sullivan and saw that she had already lowered her gun, he begrudgingly did the same.

"Now what?" a visibly nervous Sullivan asked.

Iris turned her attention to the girl. "She's been waiting for something."

"What?"

Iris ignored Greer's question and began walking toward her.

The girl moved the tip of the knife closer to Arthur's throat.

Sullivan and Greer instinctively reached for their guns.

"No," Iris said sternly. "I told you that's not necessary." When the pair lowered their guns again, Iris addressed the girl. "Where is Olivia?"

Hesitation, then: "Hiding."

"Where?"

Silence.

"It's safe now. No one is going to hurt you. Why don't you tell her to come out?"

"Because it's not safe."

"Why do you think that, Hannah?"

"Because he's still here." Her pained eyes narrowed to slits as she looked down at Arthur.

"Please help me," he said with a terrified glance at Sullivan.

Every cell in her body ached with doubt as she stopped herself from reaching for the gun.

"You don't have to do that," Iris said calmly, pointing at the knife in the girl's hand. "It won't bring you the peace you're looking for."

"I'm trapped here, and it's all because of him. All I want is to leave this terrible place, and he won't let me."

"How is he keeping you trapped here?"

"Because I'm worried that he's going to do to Olivia what he did to me, and I can't let that happen."

"Is that why Donald Tisdale is dead? Because of what he did to you?"

Silence.

"It's okay to tell us, Hannah."

"But I've already tried to tell you. All of you. No one listened."

"We're listening now."

When the girl looked at Sullivan, the tension in her face softened. "You felt me in Donald's apartment, didn't you?"

Sullivan nodded, ignoring the intense heat of her partner's glare.

"I let you find those pictures because I thought you would help me."

The hardened disbelief in Greer's eyes suddenly melted. "How did she know about—"

"I do want to help you," Sullivan answered.

"No, you don't. You only want to help *him*."

"That's not true. I want to help you, too."

"Then why don't you understand why I have to do this?"

"Because killing is wrong."

"He doesn't think so." She looked down at Arthur. "Do you?" She pushed the tip of the knife into his neck again, producing another trickle of blood.

His scream caused Greer to reach for his gun. Before he could aim it, his arm was yanked backward by a violent, unseen force, ripping the weapon from his hand.

Sullivan reached for hers in turn. She was knocked off her feet by a powerful wave of cold air that felt like a heavy hand punching her square in the chest.

When Greer attempted to come to her aid, he too was knocked to the floor, landing on the cement with a crash.

An angry female voice suddenly rose above the loud ringing in Sullivan's ears.

"Hannah, no!"

Sullivan didn't recognize the voice. She only knew that it didn't belong to Iris. As she struggled to find her bearings in the dark space, she heard the voice again.

"You don't have to do this anymore. Olivia is safe. No one is going to hurt her."

Sullivan picked up the flashlight that had fallen beside her and staggered to her feet. She pointed her light in the direction of the voice and saw that it belonged to Fiona Graves. She and a man whom Sullivan didn't know stood next to Iris, only a few feet away from Arthur and the girl.

"Killing him isn't going to help your sister," Iris said. "It's only going to send her to a dark place, just like the one you're in right now. Do you want that for her?"

The girl said nothing, but her face quivered with a fleeting hint of emotion.

"Let him go, Hannah," Fiona added. "I know what he and Donald Tisdale did to you. I'll make sure the police know, too."

The girl's eyes widened as she looked at Fiona. "You saw what happened."

Fiona nodded.

"And you also saw what I did to Donald?"

"Yes. And I know that you think doing the same thing to Arthur will help you, but it won't. He isn't the reason you're stuck here. Even if you killed him right now, you would still be in that dark, lonely, cold place, desperately trying to reach your sister. Arthur isn't the real danger."

Fiona took a few steps forward as the knife in the girl's hand slowly fell away from Arthur's neck.

"You know that, don't you?"

The girl nodded as that fleeting hint of emotion suddenly took up full residence on her pale, blighted face. "My mom. I'm scared she's going to…"

"I know you are, and I know that Olivia is, too. But I'm telling you right now that your mom won't ever have the chance to hurt her again."

"How do you know that?"

"I just know."

"She never tried to find me. They buried part of me right next...right next door to her, and she never tried to look."

"I'm sorry, Hannah," Fiona said as she choked back tears. "I'm so sorry. This shouldn't have happened to you. You were a good girl who deserved so much better. You deserved a mommy who loved you and cared for you and watched out for you like you were the most important person in the entire world. She was so wrong for not doing that because you were so very important. Do you know who else thought that?"

"Olivia."

"That's right, and she still does. She loves you so much, and she wants you to find the happiness that you always should've had."

"But what about her? She's in a dark place, just like I am. I don't want her to be there anymore."

"If you kill him, she will be."

"And what if I don't?"

"Then Olivia will finally have a chance to find that light. And so will you."

"Will you promise to protect her, Fiona? Will all of you promise?"

"We'll do the best we possibly can."

The girl surveyed the group with doubting eyes before grabbing Arthur hard by his shirt and lifting his head off the floor. "How do I know it's going to be enough?"

"You're going to have to trust us," Iris said.

"Please, trust us," Fiona reiterated.

After a long moment of contemplation, the girl released her hold on Arthur's neck and he fell backward, coughing and wheezing as he frantically gasped for air. She then stood up and turned her eyes to an area of the room behind the group. After a moment of quiet that felt like infinity, the girl finally looked back at Fiona.

"Prove it to me."

The sound of rapidly approaching footsteps suddenly gave way to the sight of a wild-eyed Natalie running at them full bore. The hammer in her right hand didn't become visible until she took a high-arching swing at Greer. He managed to duck away from the head blow, only to offer up his shoulder. His agonized scream barely rose above the crack of his shattered collarbone.

The impact did nothing to slow Natalie down, whose beeline course was now headed straight for Fiona.

She could only utter the words "You'll never—" before a single gunshot to the back extinguished the burning light of hatred in her eyes. She fell lifelessly to the floor less than five feet from a frozen Fiona.

Sullivan immediately ran to Greer. He'd managed to sit himself up while keeping a hand pressed against his collar-bone. "Broken?" she asked him.

"Into about twenty million little pieces," he answered as he grimaced through a pained smile. "It could've been worse."

"A lot worse," she concurred as she looked at Natalie.

Had Sullivan not taken her down, she was convinced that the shock of the moment would not have afforded Fiona enough time to defend herself. The act of shooting Natalie was completely justified, and Sullivan knew she could never second-guess herself. But the sight of that young woman's dead body left her feeling empty beyond description.

The sentiment lasted only for a moment.

When Sullivan looked up, the girl's stare was fixed on her. She displayed no expression or identifiable emotion, but the air around her felt warm. The immediate sense of calm that resulted was both inexplicable and all-consuming. Suddenly, there was no more doubt, no more second-guessing, no more emptiness.

"I'm sorry he got hurt," the girl said, pointing at Greer. "I know he'll be okay. We'll all be okay now."

Sullivan couldn't find the words to respond before the girl turned back to Fiona.

"I really do think everything is okay now," she said, smiling for the first time.

Fiona, still severely shaken, didn't smile back. She struggled to find her words, much like Sullivan had. But when she finally did, the question was the exact same one that Sullivan had come up with.

"Did you make that happen? Your mother running in here?"

She pointed at Arthur Finley. "Do you promise that he won't be able to hurt Olivia?"

Fiona looked to Sullivan for a response.

"I promise he won't be able to hurt anyone."

"And what about Noah?"

"He won't be able to hurt her, either. Not anymore," Fiona said.

"Then I can go. No more darkness, for Olivia or me."

"Hannah, wait. What about your mot–"

"Thank you, Fiona. I'm sorry I scared you as much as I did." Then she turned to Iris. "There are a lot of bad things here. Lots of people like me who can't leave. You can help them, and I hope you do."

Iris nodded as she wiped away the tears streaming down her cheeks.

The girl then walked up to Fiona. "Olivia is going to fall down. Make sure you catch her."

Before Fiona could respond, the girl collapsed in her arms.

Sullivan and Iris rushed to help as Fiona gently laid her on the floor. When she didn't immediately come to, Fiona began lightly tapping her cheeks. "Olivia? Olivia, wake up."

Her eyes slowly opened.

"That's it, honey. You're okay now."

"Fiona?" She spoke in the groggy voice of someone slowly awakening from a long, deep sleep.

"Yes, it's me. Iris is here, too, and the police. Everything is okay."

"Where is Hannah?"

Fiona and Iris exchanged a look.

"I think she's gone now," Iris said.

"Back to the dark place?"

"I don't think so, sweetheart."

Olivia slowly sat up and surveyed the space. She visibly recoiled at the sight of Arthur Finley.

"He's not going to hurt you," Fiona assured her.

"I know." When she looked to the left of him and saw Natalie, the resolve in her gentle face immediately faltered. "Did Hannah do that before she left?"

Her question was met with a prolonged silence that all but confirmed the answer.

"Did she hurt anyone else?"

Fiona shook her head.

"I'm glad. I know she wouldn't have wanted to."

"Sweetheart, what do you remember?" Iris asked.

Olivia searched her memory. "Being in Fiona's apartment and Hannah telling me that we needed to go find him," she said, pointing to Arthur. "I tried to tell her no, but she wouldn't listen."

"I know you did," Fiona said. "Don't worry about anything else, okay? It's all over now."

Olivia looked at her with a solemn expression. "It's not over yet, not until I know that Hannah's okay." Her eyes drifted across the dark expanse of the room, in search of something that no one else could see. "One knock if you're okay, two if you're not."

The group held its collective breath as Olivia waited for a response.

"Come on, Hannah. One knock if you're okay, two if you're not." Olivia's voice cracked as she repeated the command.

The sound that followed wasn't a knock as much as it was a cosmic collision that reverberated through every square inch of the basement before finally settling inside Sullivan's body with a gentle vibration that only her soul could feel.

The basement was suddenly bathed in bright light as the dozens of florescent bulbs hung throughout the space buzzed to life simultaneously. The familiar drone of two-way radio chatter and the heavy padding of patrol boots quickly followed.

Before the chaos that Sullivan experienced with every fresh crime scene had the chance to set in, she caught one last quiet embrace between Olivia and Fiona. When they were finished, Olivia grabbed the purple stone hanging from her neck and gave it a tight squeeze. Fiona smiled.

"It's definitely over now," Olivia said without a trace of doubt in her voice.

And Sullivan was most certainly inclined to believe her.

## Chapter Thirty-Nine

The AA meeting had been sparsely attended. The first sessions back after a long holiday weekend often were. If slip-ups were going to happen, they usually coincided with some big event, like the three days spent celebrating the official kickoff to the summer season.

Fiona hadn't spent that Memorial Day weekend celebrating. There were no parties or barbecues, no flimsy excuses for popping open a cold one—or in her case, six. She had instead spent that weekend like she had most every other day since moving out of Corona Heights: building up the courage to tell someone the story.

Sure, she had active and ongoing communication with the police and Child Welfare officials since that night, but only Detectives Sullivan and Greer understood the full extent of what had occurred, and they were understandably tight-lipped about those certain aspects of the event that wouldn't play so well in front of a judge or their peers in the department. They had careers to consider, after all, and she couldn't blame them—Detective Sullivan in particular—

for wanting to put the incident as far behind them as they could.

Fiona, unfortunately, had no such luxuries.

The details of what happened replayed themselves in her mind every time she closed her eyes. They were there when she opened them too.

Because she couldn't trust her vision anymore, she had to vet every image that she saw for its tactile substance and grounding in reality.

Thankfully, she hadn't yet seen anything that was later proven not to have been there.

Through it all, Fiona stayed clean. Three hundred and fifty-eight days without a drink. But the craving was always there. Sometimes, it manifested as a soft itch in the back of her throat. Other times, it was showed up as something loud, demanding, and persistent, taunting her with hollow promises of escape.

*Don't you want Hannah's voice to go away? Don't you want to feel sane for one night? I know you do, and there's only one way.*

Fiona knew that way all too well, and there were moments–particularly in the quiet of night–when the path to her escape was enticingly clear.

Thankfully, she had the AA meetings to rein her back in. Without the looming specter of Noah's presence to contend with, Fiona had settled comfortably into the Sunrise Serenity group.

The intimate setting of today's session almost allowed her to broach the subject of Corona Heights, but when it came time for her testimonial, she couldn't offer up much beyond a status update on her insomnia (still debilitating), and her nervousness surrounding an upcoming interview with the local publication *Westword* for its editorial proof-reader position. When each of the attendees pledged an ongoing contribution of prayers and positive thoughts, she felt a little bit better about her chances.

After the meeting concluded, Melinda Cordova, Fiona's newly minted sponsor, invited her out for a cup of coffee. This was the third such invite since Fiona had finally committed to weekly meetings, and the conversations that followed were usually uplifting and insightful. But today's coffee chat was different. It hadn't been that way by design. Fiona had no intention of bringing up Iris and Olivia and Hannah. It simply happened.

Melinda had undoubtedly been privy to some of the details, as they had been extensively reported on in the media.

According to the official reports, Hannah Shelby, who had originally been reported missing two and a half years ago, was found dead, presumably murdered, inside the apartment building where she lived. Arthur Finley had been arrested as the prime suspect in connection to her murder. There was no public mention of Donald Tisdale.

But what the public hadn't learned was that parts of Hannah had been found buried inside the walls of Fiona's apartment, with others being scattered about in different locations around the building. Her apartment was immediately deemed a crime scene, and she was forced to leave. The police department paid for her hotel room that night, and she never came back.

Melinda listened to the story, like she always did, with her full attention. There were no unnecessary diversions, and most importantly, no judgments.

After Fiona recounted the entire timeline of events, she felt weighed down by the utter insanity of it all, embarrassed to even look Melinda in the eye when she was finished.

"That certainly is one hell of a story," Melinda said as she ran a spoon through her third cup of coffee.

"Now you know why I haven't mentioned it to anyone else."

"Well, I'm humbled that you'd save it for me. I've always believed in the supernatural. I've just never had anyone confirm it in such a dramatic way."

Melinda's easy smile did nothing to ease Fiona's anxiety.

"I'd understand if you recommend that I find the nearest psych ward and immediately check myself in. Trust me, I've considered it."

"Furthest thought from my mind," Melinda replied convincingly. "I think that what you did to try and help that girl was unbelievably selfless. Most people would have turned tail and ran the moment it got even a little bit scary. You literally put your life out there for her. I can't say for certain that I would have been able to do it."

"I guess I did the only thing that I could've done under the circumstances. I couldn't bear the thought of anything else happening to her."

"Of course, not. You're a mom."

A fact that Fiona was always happy to be reminded of.

"Where is Olivia now?" Melinda asked.

"According to Detective Sullivan, she's living with her half-sister Eva and Eva's father in Cheyenne. Had he not stepped up, I'm not sure where she'd be."

"Probably lost somewhere in the foster care system."

Fiona trembled at the thought.

"She didn't have any other family here?"

"Only her mother," Fiona answered. "And you already know what happened to her. Noah will spend the rest of his pathetic life in prison if I have anything to say about it."

Fiona trembled as she thought about the inevitable day when she would see him in a courtroom. "Even if he doesn't, he wouldn't get his hands on Olivia in a million years. Iris had considered petitioning to take her if Eva's dad couldn't, but there was no way Olivia could've stayed in that building after what happened."

"The same as you."

Fiona nodded.

"Speaking of Iris, do you still keep in contact with her?"

"Not since I moved out. It was difficult talking about things even while I was still there. It was impossible to reconcile what I'd seen. It still is. But to Iris, it was all second nature. It was like she expected it to happen. I also think she knew a lot more about Hannah than she'd let on."

"That poor girl. She suffered so much."

"Yet, no one ever acknowledged her, not even Iris. It was like her disappearance, even her life, was this dirty little secret that the building wanted to keep hidden from the world. I'll never understand it."

"Do you think the subject would come up if you were ever to see Iris again?"

Fiona shrugged. "I honestly don't know. Don't get me wrong, she's a wonderful woman, and I hope that we can maintain a friendship, but she kept an awful lot from me."

"Like the fact that she's a psychic?"

Though Iris had never made a formal declaration of her abilities, and it was never discussed after the incident, Fiona had concluded that she was indeed psychic based on her communication with Hannah and the fact that she sensed Fiona's thoughts as they entered the basement, and the way she talked about Corona Heights like it was a living, breathing thing—a notion that Fiona couldn't exactly dismiss.

"All I can say for sure is that Iris Matheson is quite the interesting case."

"Apparently, she's not the only interesting one. How do you explain everything that you saw?" Melinda asked. "Do you think that you're…"

"A psychic too?"

Melinda looked at Fiona with wide eyes before both women settled into comfortable laughter.

"I didn't know beforehand that you were going to say that," Fiona assured her. "Lucky guess."

"So, no to being a psychic."

"I wish I were. I could've avoided a lot of trouble in my life."

"Touché," Melinda replied with a knowing smile. "How do you think you were able to see so much?"

Fiona had considered the question many times, but she had yet to find an answer that fully satisfied her. "Maybe there's a door that leads to the other side, wherever that is, and it opened up for me just long enough to have a peek inside."

Melinda nodded like the answer was satisfying enough. "Do you think the door is closed?"

"It better be. I need to keep Corona Heights as far in the rearview mirror as I can."

"I agree. There are far more important things to stay focused on right now."

Fiona took in a nervous breath as she thought about Jacob.

"So, how are you feeling about finally seeing him?" Melinda asked.

"To be honest, I'm scared to death."

"I completely understand. Just remember how long you've been waiting for this moment to come. And now it's here."

The moment that Melinda was referring to was Fiona's meeting with Kirk and Jacob, scheduled to take place in less than an hour.

As per their legally binding agreement, Fiona would need to check in with the court-appointed monitor first. After her briefing, she would spend a few minutes with Kirk (a nerve-wracking prospect on its own), and, if everything else went right, spend her first meaningful time with Jacob in over a year.

Melinda was right. This was the single moment that Fiona had waited for since moving here. But now that it was here, she doubted herself.

"You've been through hell and back," Melinda said. "This is the easy part. Just do what comes naturally."

"It's been a long time since I've seen him. I'm just not so sure if it comes naturally anymore."

"You're ready."

Fiona took another long breath in hopes of absorbing Melinda's confidence. "I hope you're right."

"I am." Melinda looked at her watch. "It's time for you to get going. If you want, we can pick this up next week, after you call me to report on how things went today, of course."

Fiona smiled. "As long as you don't start charging me by the hour."

"You keep talking about all this scary stuff, and I might seriously consider it."

Fiona's cell phone vibrated with a text message notification as she walked to her car. Fearful that it may have been Kirk telling her that he'd finally had second thoughts, she checked the phone immediately. Nothing could have braced her for the shock that followed.

The message was from Iris. There was an attached photo of an amulet like the one she'd previously given to Fiona (which Fiona had, in turn, given to Olivia), but this one was turquoise, with a Celtic design. The caption underneath the picture read: *"Yours, if you need it."*

As Fiona stared at the picture, a second message came through: *"Had a random thought about you just now, as I often do. Hope you're doing well. They'd better be treating you right in that new apartment building. It couldn't be worse than CH, right? Anyhoo, you take good care of yourself. When you see that beautiful boy, make sure to give him a big hug from Iris. And remember, if you need me, I'm only a thought away."*

Fiona closed the message as a massive chill radiated down her spine. The feeling wasn't all bad.

*Quite the interesting case indeed.*

---

Fiona sat on a bench outside of the City Park Pavilion, a beautiful, grand gazebo that seemed to be prominently featured in the foreground of every Denver city skyline photo that she had ever seen.

She arrived early, twenty minutes before she expected Kirk, in part to ensure that she had time to wrangle in her frayed nerves before Jacob saw her, in part because she feared that their fragile relationship couldn't withstand even one more instance of her not showing up for something when she was supposed to.

It was a perfect early summer evening. Colorful arrays of annuals were in full bloom all around her, signifying the new opportunity for growth that a change in the seasons can bring about. After years spent in the coldest, most desolate of winters, Fiona was hopeful that her season of blooming had finally arrived.

She kept her focus on the parking lot—her nervous energy waning with each deep breath that she took—until Kirk's jeep finally came into view.

She stood up as he parked, then sat back down for fear of appearing too eager. After thinking about it, she promptly stood up again.

*Dammit, I am eager, and I should be.*

Kirk emerged from the car first. He wore a seersucker Oxford shirt, khaki shorts, and boat shoes. It was his go-to outfit for cool Seattle summers, and Fiona was happy to know that part of him hadn't changed. It left her with a glimmer of hope that other things hadn't changed either.

The instant Jacob emerged from the passenger's side, Fiona burst into tears. He wore a crisp white polo shirt and gray shorts. It was a lot more than the casual outfit an eight-year-old would choose for a normal evening. This outfit was put together with care and planning. Whether by Jacob or Kirk, it didn't matter. It showed that the meeting wasn't only important to her.

The gesture was small, its significance most likely not registering with either of them. But to Fiona, it was validation. And at this point, validation was everything.

A Silver Ford Taurus pulled into the spot next to Kirk. The woman who stepped out looked very official and very stern. The department badge she wore on the lapel of her suit jacket all but confirmed her status. She had a few words for Kirk before the three of them walked toward Fiona.

Jacob was the last of the three to notice her, and when he did, he stopped.

Fiona's heart sank as she assumed that the ultimate

worst-case scenario she'd imagined for this moment had come true.

It would begin as hesitation, then second thoughts, before ending with a tearful demand that his father take him home.

But then he started walking again. As he got a few steps closer, the smile appeared. Before Fiona could give her negative thoughts the proper burial they deserved, Jacob was running toward her. She started running, too, matching the speed of his gallop step for step.

Fiona lifted him off the ground with one sweeping motion, twirling his formidable frame in the air like he weighed nothing. When she set him down, she brushed away a thick swath of hair and began covering his forehead with warm, wet, mommy kisses.

At some point in the not-too-distant future, this kind of display would prove too embarrassing for a young boy who had moved on to matters more pressing than showing affection toward his mother. Thankfully, that day hadn't come yet.

Only when she was finished did she notice that Kirk and the CPS monitor were standing beside them.

Fiona knew that she was a disheveled, emotional mess by now, and the woman's sideways glance confirmed it.

Kirk, for his part, looked content, and that was all she could hope for. Happiness, if that was ever in the cards for the two of them, would likely come much later.

He stepped to Fiona with a nod and gentle smile, which she reciprocated, then presented the woman for introductions.

"Fiona, this is Suzanne Grimes. She's here to supervise the visit."

Kirk's tone sobered when he said that last part. It was subtle, but Fiona noticed.

"Nice to meet you, Ms. Graves," Suzanne said with an overblown smile as she extended her hand.

"Nice to meet you, too." Fiona's tone was as limp as her handshake.

"Well, I'm sure you've read the packet from the court explaining my role here and the expectations for the visit. But if there's anything you need me to clarify, just let me—"

"There isn't."

Kirk looked uncomfortable. He dealt with it by turning his focus to Jacob. "Hey, bud, your mom told me that she's never been to this park before. Fortunately, you know this place like the back of your hand. Why don't you show her some of your favorite spots?"

"Yeah, I guess I can do that." He turned to Fiona with an eager smile. "There's a really neat playground right over there. You wanna go check it out?"

"I'd love to, honey. Show me the way."

When he grabbed her hand, she nearly melted into the ground.

"It's right this way."

He started to pull her away when Suzanne stopped them.

"Could you guys hold up a second? I just need to grab my pad."

Fiona, Jacob, and Kirk looked on as she fished around in her oversize work bag until she pulled out a steno pad and pen.

"Sorry I wasn't more prepared." She said this with an easy smile that she assumed everyone would reciprocate. When no one did, she put it away.

When Jacob looked at Fiona, the bright gleam in his

eyes was gone. Fiona was prepared to express her heartbreak at this development in excessively harsh terms, but
Kirk spoke up first.

"Um, Ms. Grimes? Would you mind stepping over here
for a minute? There are a few things in the packet that I
don't quite understand. My lawyer couldn't figure it out,
either. Would you mind walking me through it again?"

Suzanne looked confused. "I'd be happy to go over it
with you, Mr. Lawson. But I'm not sure if now is really the
best time."

"It's the perfect time," Kirk insisted.

Suzanne looked at Fiona, then back at Kirk. "Well, I'm
afraid I don't have one on me at the moment."

"I do. It's right here in the car. Why don't you come
with me, and I'll grab it."

"But I think Ms. Graves and your son—"

"Please, Ms. Grimes. These questions can't wait."

Suzanne appeared irritated, but she gave in. "Fine, but
only if it doesn't take too much time."

"It won't."

Kirk slowly escorted her to his car, briefly looked back
at Fiona, and waved his hand. When he mouthed the word
"Go," she quietly led Jacob by the hand.

"Come on, honey. Let's go find that playground of
yours."

Fiona followed closely behind as he sprinted toward the
large sandy pit that had every manner of playground appa-
ratus imaginable.

"Can you push me on the swings?"

"Of course."

Jacob jumped on the nearest one, gripping the chain
handles tightly. "Just so you know, I like to go really high
now."

"Oh, really? And when did that change? You used to be scared to death of these things."

"A lot's changed, Mom."

A heavy lump settled in Fiona's throat. "I know."

"But don't worry, there's plenty of time to catch you up on everything. Isn't there?"

When Fiona looked behind her, she saw Kirk and Suzanne at his car. It didn't look like his *questions* would be answered anytime soon.

"Fortunately, we have all the time in the world, honey."

"Good. Now start swinging!"

He let out an ear-piercing giggle as Fiona pushed him high into the air.

"Higher, Mommy! Higher!"

When Jacob's flight finally reached its apex, Fiona stepped away, closed her eyes, and slipped off her sandals.

The warm sand felt perfect on her toes.

The only sound she heard was Jacob's giddy laughter, the same laughter that she imagined would lead her to that sandy, sun-filled beach, and that perfect life, where everything was always as it should have been; the place that she would be able to call home.

Life may not have been perfect, and it probably never would be. But she knew one thing for sure as she felt the grainy sand in between her toes and the warm sun shining down on her face.

She was one giant step closer.

As Jacob's swing finally came to a stop, Fiona cast a glance around the empty playground.

"Looks like we've got the place to ourselves, kiddo. Where do you want to go next?"

Jacob jumped off the swing, then took in the possibilities with giddy anticipation. When his eyes finally found the long tube slide a few feet away, his smile vanished.

"We're not alone, Mommy. I think that girl wants to play with me."

Fiona took another look around the playground. "Who are you talking about, sweetheart? I don't see anyone."

"Over there, on top of the slide."

From what Fiona could see, the platform was empty.

"She's waving like she wants me to come over. Don't you see her?"

Fiona smiled nervously and looked again. "Honey, I don't see anyone. Are you sure—"

Her heart plunged into her stomach before she could finish the sentence. *Don't even think about it, Fiona. Don't you dare.*

She stiffened her chin before turning back to Jacob. It only made the quivering worse. "Maybe your poor Mom is going blind. Old age, and all. Is the girl your age?"

Jacob's longing gaze remained fixed on the slide. "I think so."

*Don't ask anything else. Let it go. Please, let it go.* "What does she look like?"

"Mommy, she's right there," Jacob insisted, pointing again to the empty platform. "The girl with dark hair and glasses. And…is that a Taylor Swift T-shirt?" He laughed like it was the funniest sight in the world. "Look, she just went down the slide." After a long moment of waiting, his smile abruptly vanished. "Wait, where did she go?"

Fiona looked once more at the empty tube, desperate to conceal the cognitive breakdown that was occurring beneath her façade of calm.

Jacob's face was suddenly awash with concern. "Maybe she got stuck. Should we go check on her?"

He made a quick move toward the slide. Fiona stopped him with a gentle hand on the shoulder.

"No, Jake," she replied in between the clipped breaths that she hoped would mask her panic. "We should let her play in peace. I'm sure she's perfectly safe."

"Are you sure?" Jacob asked, a wave of disappointment overtaking the concern in his eyes.

Fiona could no longer feel her toes on the sand and squeezed Jacob's shoulder to ground herself. *He's here, Fiona. And you're with him. That's all that matters right now.*

"I'm sure, honey."

She led Jacob to the merry-go-round and pushed as hard as her suddenly fatigued muscles would allow.

Thankfully, he never looked at the slide again.

THE MYSTERY OF CORONA HEIGHTS DEEPENS IN VOLUME II:
## THE HAUNTING OF APARTMENT 612
KEEP READING FOR A BONUS EXCERPT.

**Stay connected**
**Subscribe to E.M. Parker's**
**newsletter for more previews**
**and news on upcoming releases.**
**www.authoremparker.com/subscribe**

If you enjoyed *The Thin Wall*, please consider leaving a short, honest review on your favorite platform.

# The Haunting of Apartment 612

## CHAPTER ONE

T he thing in the pit of Norah Larson's stomach made itself known the instant she woke up this morning. She called it a *thing* because she wasn't sure what else to label it. *Butterflies, fear,* and *outright dread* were the words that immediately came to mind, but those were obvious choices and did no justice to the feeling. This was something else entirely; something dark, heavy, and primordial. Like the murky residue of a long nightmare that ended with a sudden, brutal swiftness.

Or maybe the nightmare was just beginning.

Whatever the *thing* was, there was nothing that Norah could point to that accounted for its existence.

As far as she remembered, her six hours of sleep were uneventful, with none of the bad dreams or other nighttime disturbances that had recently become such a common part of her life here. She had been up late cramming for an anatomy midterm that she was woefully underprepared for, and with the exam now less than five hours away, she couldn't outline the functions of the endocrine system any easier than she could map the stars of the solar system.

For a moment, Norah thought that this had been the source of the *thing*. But under preparing for exams was nothing new (a sad fact that she resolved to correct before her graduation this spring), and she had always been able to pull off a passing grade, even if it was by the thinnest of margins. Her blatant procrastination aside, Norah knew that she would find a way to pass this one too.

That left no viable explanation for why her world suddenly felt like it was about to come crashing down on top of her head.

Then she heard the knock on the door.

She had just begun a yoga session that she hoped would ease her mounting anxiety. It took a full minute to ease into the King Pigeon pose that required her to bend backward until the edge of her brow touched the backs of her toes. The position was advanced, taking nearly two years to master. And now that she had, it was the go-to move when-ever she needed to drown out the noise in her head. Right now, there was a lot of noise to drown out.

Norah barely had time to blink before the first series of knocks shattered her concentration.

Choosing to ignore the intrusion, she quickly regrouped, closed her eyes, and took in a deep breath, curving her spine another couple of inches until the tip of her nose settled into the mid-soles of her feet.

With her throat tightening and her brain filling with blood, Norah felt a blissful light-headedness that instantly dulled her heightened senses.

Within seconds, she was on another plane of time and space altogether. Far away from the fear of failed mid-terms. Far away from the barista job that she despised. Far away from the once inviting apartment building that was now cold, foreign, and lifeless. Far away from the *thing* in the pit of her stomach that told her to run away from it all.

Another series of knocks rattled the door before Norah could complete her mental escape. This series was much harder than the first, a clear indication that the intruder had no designs on being ignored a second time.

She slowly uncoiled her long, athletic frame, sighing with a force that she hoped was loud enough to communicate her irritation.

"Who is it?" she said as she sprang to her feet.

"Phillip Barlow."

Norah cursed under her breath before taking a step to the door. Her legs were wobbly, and she had to pause to allow her equilibrium to return. She wasn't sure if this was because she had stood too fast or because her landlord, a man who rarely acknowledged anyone unless their rent was late or their television was too loud, had decided to pay an unscheduled visit. She was leaning toward the latter.

The thought caused the *thing* in her stomach to expand until it swelled inside her chest.

Barlow was smiling when she opened the door. He looked nervous.

*Why would he be nervous?*

The *thing* suddenly spread from her chest into the base of her throat.

"Good morning." He gave Norah a once over, his eyes moving from her coral-colored toenails to her neon green yoga pants to the beads of sweat on her freckled face before adding, "I hope I didn't catch you at a bad time."

"Not at all," she lied, blowing a tangle of auburn hair from her forehead.

"That's good. I do apologize for stopping by unannounced. It's been a crazy morning and I'm afraid I didn't have time to phone ahead. Do you have a few minutes to talk?"

Norah fought hard to downplay her apprehension as she stepped into the hallway and closed the door to a crack, a subtle move that she hoped would communicate her disinterest in inviting him inside. "Sure. What can I help you with?"

"May I come in?"

Norah opened the door and begrudgingly allowed space for him to walk through. "Of course."

He smiled politely as he moved past her and into the apartment.

Phillip Barlow was a tall, stout man, but his diminutive posture made him appear much shorter. His dark curly hair was long and unkempt on the sides and thinning to a few pitiful strands up top. It lay in stark contrast to a patchy gray beard that contained a few traces of the light brown that had most likely been his hair color before the dye job. The pale skin around his eyes folded when he smiled. It was a trait shared by Norah's father. He reminded her a lot of her father, right down to the anxiety that his mere presence could inspire.

Barlow groaned as he helped himself to a seat on her futon. "Cozy space."

"It's not much, but it's home."

Aside from the futon that doubled as her bed, there was a loveseat, a coffee table that acted as her bookshelf, a dinette set that regularly hosted frozen dinners for one, and a small computer desk where she seemed to whittle away most of her time. There were a few family pictures scattered about, a picture of her ex-boyfriend that she hadn't gotten around to removing, and a Gray's Anatomy muscle diagram pinned to the main wall.

The space was far from impressive, but it served its purpose. Norah could have done without the sudden drafts of cold air, the strange noises that kept her awake at night, and the recent attention that that little girl's murder brought to the building. But beyond that, she couldn't complain. It was a place to live, and if the sports medicine job market was as kind as her professors promised, her stay here would only be temporary.

*God willing.*

"Well, it looks great," Barlow reiterated. "I do believe this is the first time I've been here since you officially moved in."

"I do believe you're right," Norah answered with a forced smile as she sat down on the love seat adjacent to him.

"As a matter of fact, I don't think I've seen you since…" Barlow cut himself off, either unwilling or unable to finish the sentence. "Are you doing okay?"

Norah drew in a sharp breath and held it.

Five months ago, the elderly tenant next door to her in Apartment 612 was found hanging from the doorway of his living room. Norah was the first person interviewed by the police. They questioned her for half an hour, probing the depths of their relationship (there wasn't one), asking if she had heard anything strange or seen anything out of the ordinary earlier that evening (she hadn't), and searching for any possible motive that would explain his death (like she had the first clue why he died).

Despite the ongoing police investigation and the horrifying events that followed, Norah had never once seen Barlow. He didn't stop by to check up on her, offered no reassurances that the building was safe, despite her growing concern that it wasn't, and made no promises that things would eventually return to normal. She probably should have felt slighted by his indifference, but she didn't. She simply responded with an indifferent attitude of her own.

But now, as he made himself comfortable in her living room, unannounced, uninvited, and suddenly concerned, Norah felt a bitterness welling up inside of her that she struggled to suppress.

"I've been fine."

"That's good to hear. And is the apartment in good order? Any leaks that need fixing or holes that need patching?"

"I have hot water and the lights work. That's good enough."

He gave a light chuckle before his eyes landed on the pile of textbooks atop her coffee table. "And how is school coming along?" He eased to the edge of the futon to pick up one of the books. "*Textbook of Sports Medicine: Basic Science and Clinical Aspects of Sports Injury and Physical Activity*. Sounds like a real brain full."

"It is."

"Where are you going to school?"

"Metro State. I graduate this spring."

"Good for you. Such an exciting time. What's your major?"

"Exercise science with a minor in sports medicine. I'd like to be a trainer, maybe catch on with a college or pro team at some point."

"That's fantastic. Best of luck."

Barlow was overselling his enthusiasm. He couldn't have cared less about Norah or her major. He was stalling, and she couldn't let it go on a second longer.

"I appreciate that, Mr. Barlow. Can I ask what brings you by?"

His expression flattened. "Right. I'm sure you have plenty to do, and I don't want to take up more of your time than I need to, so I'll get straight to it." Instead of getting straight to it, he sat back on the futon and crossed his legs. He cupped his raised foot to stop it from shaking. "I notice you don't have a television, so I'm not sure how much news you've seen lately."

"I avoid the news if I can help it. Too much negativity."

"I know what you mean. I probably watch more than I should. If something happens in the world, I feel like I'm better off being in the loop. Nine times out of ten I'm wrong. Anyway, it's good that you've been steering clear of it, especially now. Our building has been getting its share of press lately, and unfortunately, none of it's been good."

His words sent a chill up Norah's spine. "I don't need a television to know that. It's all that anyone around here can talk about."

"And that's the problem. People aren't just talking. They're spreading rumors that simply aren't true. I understand that residents are frightened and upset by what happened here. Hell, it's caused me more sleepless nights than I care to count. But to take such a tragedy as an opportunity to propagate wild conspiracy theories about the history of this building is flat out irresponsible. And now the media is starting to buy into the nonsense."

Norah was well-aware of the conspiracy theories that Barlow was referring to. By now, most everyone else in the building was too.

"Do you know that I was given an article just the other day that lists Corona Heights as the fifth most haunted location in the entire state?" he continued.

There was an awkward silence as if he were waiting for Norah to respond, so she did, sarcasm framing her words. "Wow, that's something."

"Most ridiculous thing ever if you ask me. But that story wasn't made up on a whim. Someone here is feeding that garbage to the public, and it's starting to have real life consequences. Tenants have been moving out in droves. In less than three years, we've gone from having a long waiting list to having one of the highest vacancy rates in the city. That wouldn't be an issue if people were clamoring to move in, but they aren't. I'm afraid that if the bleeding doesn't stop, the building will be sold and the good tenants like yourself will be out of a place to live. Which means I'll be out of a job."

That got Norah's attention. The only reason she hadn't joined the droves who moved out was because of the rent. It was far and away the cheapest in the city, given the building's downtown location and proximity to campus. She would have been hard-pressed to find a deal like it anywhere else and wasn't the least bit prepared to try, despite her apartment's not-so-desirable features. "Could that really happen?"

"Absolutely. The owners are already losing money, and the more this haunted house garbage takes hold, the more of a liability this place becomes. Corona Heights has too much positive history to end up as some derelict tourist attraction. The owners are counting on me to ensure that doesn't happen."

"What are you going to do?"

"Rehab the building's image, for starters. We're planning some physical updates, both to the exterior and common interior areas, as well as the apartments themselves. Fresh energy should help brighten the perception among the existing tenants, which will hopefully them less likely to scare off any prospective renters before they can give us a fair chance. The negative press is bad enough. We have no chance of staying afloat if we can't get our own residents to vouch for us."

"Do you really think that painting the walls a brighter color is going to be enough?"

Barlow looked surprised by the pointedness of Norah's question. "It's a good first step."

"What's your plan after that?"

He took in a deep breath and blew it out slowly as he edged forward on the futon. "That's why I'm here. I need your help."

"With what?"

"The new tenant."

"What new tenant?"

He took in another deep breath. This time, he didn't exhale. "The new tenant moving in next door to you."

"Someone is moving into 612?"

Barlow nodded. "Tomorrow morning."

The *thing* moved down Norah's throat and chest and settled back into her stomach, the pain nearly causing her to double over. "After what happened in there, I figured you were keeping it vacant."

"Quite the contrary. I've been trying like crazy to rent it out. Unfortunately, it's been a tough sell. I've had four people come through in the past month alone looking for an apartment. As soon as I led them to 612, they promptly lost interest. Every single one of them."

"A man died in there, Mr. Barlow. Can you really blame them?"

"I don't blame them. I blame the whack-jobs who are spreading lies about how he died."

As far as Norah knew, Donald Tisdale committed suicide. There were plenty of reports to the contrary, fueled mostly by a former tenant named Fiona Graves, the resident psychic Iris Matheson, and the building's own sketchy history. According to Iris, she and Fiona had several run-ins with the ghost of Donald Tisdale as well as the entity that was ultimately responsible for his death.

Norah had done her best not to believe those reports. But she did know that something wasn't right inside that apartment. A cold energy seemed to radiate through the door every time she walked past it. Sometimes, late at night, that cold energy seeped through the walls and straight into her dreams.

She could never put her finger on what it was, and she wasn't as quick to jump on the ghost bandwagon as everyone else. She only knew that it was something very dark and very real, and it hadn't existed before Tisdale's death.

There was a reason that apartment had been vacant all these months, and for the sake of everyone in the building, Norah hoped that it would remain vacant. Now that Barlow was telling her that it wouldn't, she knew exactly what he wanted her to do.

Even as he began speaking the words that confirmed it, she still held out hope that she was wrong.

"The tenant is new to Colorado, so I'm not sure if she's had a chance to read up on the place," Barlow said. "But if someone hasn't already put a bug in her ear, it's only a matter of time before they do. If it ever does come up, I'm asking you not to feed into the rumors. I don't expect you to lie. Something terrible did happen inside that apartment, and I was obligated to disclose that. I could tell that she was shaken, but it ultimately didn't affect her decision to move in. She's open-minded, and I'd like to keep it that way."

"What are you expecting me to say if she asks about it? The ghost stuff I mean."

"Have you ever had an experience that leads you to believe the building is haunted?"

Norah had to think about it a moment longer than she should have, and even then, she still wasn't completely confident. "Not that I'm aware of."

"Then that's what you tell her. You live next door to the supposed epicenter of Corona Heights's supernatural activity. Your skepticism will carry a lot of weight. It's important to have someone living in that apartment. It's even more important that they stay. I need your help to make sure that happens."

"But what if she really does experience something in there?"

"Like what? A strange noise?"

Norah bristled at his response. "I hear things all the time."

"This building is well over a hundred years old. It creaks, it groans, the pipes rumble, and the insulation is terrible. The only real danger that anyone faces around here is catching a cold in the winter because it gets so drafty. Trust me, she doesn't have anything to worry about, and neither do you."

It would have been nice to hear those words five months ago, but for the sake of expediting Barlow's exit, Norah was willing to accept his reassurance. "I'll do my best to convey the message."

"That would make me, and the owners, very happy."

With that, Barlow stood up and made his way to the door. Norah followed close behind, eager to show him out.

"I know it may sound like a strange request," he said as he opened the door. "And on the surface, I suppose it is. But I can't tell you how much it will mean to have things return to normal around here. Having someone in there who can directly refute this supernatural craziness will go a long way in doing that. Thank you for helping."

Norah nodded, still not entirely sure that she even wanted to help. "No problem."

Barlow returned the nod and started down the hallway.

Norah barely had time to close the door before there was another knock. She opened it to the sight of a smiling Barlow.

"Sorry to bug you again, but I forgot to mention something. The new tenant's name is Cassandra Scott. She's a young girl, about your age. Really nice. The two of you should get along wonderfully." He started down the hall again. "Like I said, we really appreciate this. If you need anything at all, please don't hesitate to ask."

The absence of air in Norah's lungs only allowed a tight smile.

When Barlow left for good, she closed the door then leaned against it for support, fearful that her already wobbly legs would give out completely.

*Cassandra Scott.*

The thing in the pit of her stomach finally had a name.

---

CONTINUE READING IN:
**THE HAUNTING OF APARTMENT 612**
CORONA HEIGHTS ANTHOLOGY VOL. II

Made in the USA
Middletown, DE
03 August 2023

36018857R00213